CW01265892

The Last Great Detective

Published by Long Midnight Publishing, 2024

ISBN: 979-8323177813

By Douglas Lindsay

The DI Buchan Series:

Buchan
Painted In Blood
The Lonely And The Dead
A Long Day's Journey Into Death
We Were Not Innocent
The Last Great Detective

The DS Hutton Series

The Vikström Papers

The Barney Thomson Series

DCI Jericho

The DI Westphall Trilogy

Pereira & Bain

Others:

Lost in Juarez
Being For The Benefit Of Mr Kite!
A Room With No Natural Light
Ballad In Blue
These Are The Stories We Tell
Alice On The Shore

THE LAST GREAT DETECTIVE

DOUGLAS LINDSAY

LMP

For Kathryn

Prologue

Not for the first time in the past couple of months, Detective Inspector Alexander Buchan asked himself what he was doing. There had been the odd time when he'd thought he might be getting somewhere, but when he looked back and closely examined those occasions, he was forced to acknowledge there wasn't one of them that hadn't been a false dawn.

Perhaps it was worse than that. There had never been anything that hadn't had its root in his own expectations. But this was police work, unsanctioned though it may have been, and facts and opportunities could not be wished into existence.

Since he'd been suspended from duty there'd been two months in Glasgow, privately working the case, and two months trailing his prey around Europe.

Four fruitless months.

'Can I get you anything else?'

The young woman looked at him, her face blank.

I like the Estonians, thought Buchan, the little contact he'd had so far. No artifice. No false good humour. Very practical.

'Another Americano, please,' said Buchan. 'And some more water.'

She nodded, lifted his empty cup, and turned away.

He watched her for a moment, and then looked back over the park that stretched away to his right. A small, oval lake, surrounded by lime trees, and beyond that, manicured gardens, and then the extended grassy area, trees all around. To the far right, an amusement park. To the left, beyond the white, square building that housed the café, the road split the park in half, and on the other side, two large buildings. Kadriorg Palace, and beyond that, the presidential palace.

It was the case, in fact, that from here one could barely see the presidential palace, and certainly there was no view of the front entrance.

There were four other occupied tables. There was another man on his own, head bowed, looking at his phone. There were two young Estonian women, one of them dominating the conversation. Then there was a table with German tourists, and another with English tourists. Everyone dressed for the chill weather, beneath the pallid sun of early April.

This is the sum total of what you've become, thought Buchan. A tourist, sitting in a tourist spot, in one of the major city-break destinations of Europe. Kadriorg Park, on the edge of Tallinn, drinking coffee, while looking across the road at the home of the president, and the old summer palace, originally commissioned by Peter the Great. Buchan would have been as well writing postcards back to the team in Glasgow.

Having a good time. Weather fine.

What else was there to say?

A movement to his left, from nowhere, and then a chair was pulled out at his table, and the man he'd been surreptitiously following for the past two months sat down. Buchan looked at him, unable to stop the surprise and consternation showing on his face. The man did not return the look, however, instead gazing through the trees, to the buildings across the road.

'You persevere,' said Jan Baltazar. 'Inspector Buchan, the last great detective on earth. What exactly is it I find you doing?'

Buchan was still staring at him, and finally Baltazar turned. There was no teasing mockery in his look, just cold consideration.

Buchan held the look, wondering just how much contempt there was in his own eyes. But who was that contempt aimed at? Hadn't he just been asking himself the same question?

What are you doing?

'That must be two months in all, now,' said Baltazar. He wasn't about to tell Buchan anything he didn't know, but this wasn't about exposition, this was Baltazar making Buchan aware that he knew everything. All his movements. Everywhere he'd stayed. Everyone he'd talked to. Everything he'd eaten. Quite possibly, every message he'd sent. 'You arrived in Poland on February third. The weather was unseasonably mild. Although, perhaps it is time we all adjusted out expectations for the seasons. Since then you have followed me to Silesia, to Prague and, of course, to southern Estonia.'

He stopped for a moment, letting silence tell the story. What exactly had Buchan achieved during those two months?

The waitress arrived, placed Buchan's coffee on the table, then filled up his water glass from a jug. She and Baltazar then communicated silently, for him to tell her that he didn't require anything, then she turned away, stopping at the next table to lift a couple of empty plates.

The two men looked grimly at each other. Despite what had unfolded south of Võru, Buchan hated this man, and he did not quail before him. Nevertheless, he'd spent the last two months with the feeling of imposter syndrome growing, and in all the time since he'd been suspended from Police Scotland, he had completely lost sight of who he was. Without the badge, without the title of detective inspector, he was just a guy traipsing around Europe, keeping an eye on someone, taking long distance photographs.

Baltazar broke the stare, and looked back in the direction of the buildings across the road. Through the bare branches of early spring trees, the salmon pink walls of the rear of the presidential palace.

'I was in there,' he said. 'You knew that of course, which is why you are here. You possibly took photographs of me entering the building, so you decide there is no point in taking photographs of me leaving the building. You have a picture of me arriving at the home of the President of Estonia.' Without looking at Buchan, Baltazar slowly, quietly, clapped his hands. 'Bravo, detective inspector. Item one on the evidence list, as the great detective builds his case against the master criminal.

'And what now? You presumed I would come back down the same road, so you sit here, waiting for me to leave.'

He glanced over his shoulder, back in the direction of Jaan Poska, the road behind them, then turned back, and stared into the trees. 'There sits your silver Hyundai, waiting for you to leap into action. The detective in his tiny, unobtrusive vehicle.' He made a banner gesture. 'Ninety-nine percent invisible. Discreet surveillance guaranteed.'

He glanced at Buchan, but Buchan's eyes were diverted. Staring at the wall of the white building, the café, directly before them.

'I have no idea what is in your head, inspector, but I have gained a certain respect for you over the last year. You seem to be a man of some quality. And of course, I now owe you a great debt.'

'You owe me nothing,' said Buchan.

'We both know that is not true. Nevertheless, here we find you facing formidable odds, and you have literally no chance of succeeding. But you know this. You know it is hopeless. You are waiting for a phone call from home to rescue you from this pointless mission. Following me around, hoping to identify wrongdoing, hoping to catch me meeting the wrong people. Hoping, against all hope, to catch me *in the act*.'

He tutted, he shook his head.

'I am about to leave and go around the corner. There is a small restaurant I like when I am here. NOP. You should try it. I will not ask you to join me, but you may choose to sit at another table while I eat. The woman I am meeting is not someone whose identity will mean anything to you. She works for a film company. Reval Entertainment. It is of no interest to you.'

Another pause. Buchan had come to the point of needing him to stop talking. To go, leaving Buchan to his thoughts of self-loathing and inadequacy.

'I can recommend the buckwheat waffles with fish roe and poached egg. And while you are there, I believe you are to be relieved of this absurd burden you have chosen for yourself. You will get a phone call.'

Now he turned to Buchan, his look penetrating and dark, drawing Buchan to look back at him.

'You are being recalled to your office. And not, as you have been expecting, to face a renewed tribunal before your superiors in Edinburgh. The cogs of internal justice grind far too slowly for that. It seems Police Scotland is shockingly understaffed these days. Struggling to attract officers, and to retain them once they are in. It is the same all over the west. And, of course, when you are desperate for people to stay in a job, it is nearly impossible to get rid of those who are troublesome in their own right. The mavericks, who think themselves above the law.'

The stare continued. Buchan's look gave nothing away, but then, it hardly needed to. He was being soundly thrashed in this game that had been going on between them since the previous summer, and they both knew it.

'I will not say I will miss you trailing around in my wake, inspector. Have a safe journey back to Scotland. I may see you there next week.' He thought about whether to add something, nodded to himself, then said, 'There is something I need. I will get it, and then perhaps it will be time to move on.'

Another moment or two, a last second for Buchan to look into the cavernous, dark eyes of the man he was coming to see as the most powerful player in the continental, and now Scottish, criminal world. And then Baltazar got to his feet, took a moment, reached into his pocket and tossed a two euro coin onto the table, and then walked from the café grounds, onto the path that circled around the lake, towards the road through the park.

There was a black car waiting for him, it having silently arrived, unnoticed by Buchan, while Baltazar had been talking.

Buchan did not move.

*

When his phone rang twenty-seven minutes later, he was still sitting in the same position.

1

Buchan hadn't called ahead. Nevertheless, he knew that word would have got around the office he was coming back, and so he expected Detective Constable Agnes Roth would know he was on his way.

When he'd left, he'd asked her if she could look after his cat, Edelman. He'd briefly given consideration to the idea of tossing Edelman out onto the street. Or leaving him in the apartment on his own, with a window open for him to come and go. He had a high degree of faith in Edelman's ability to take care of himself.

Ultimately, though, he'd decided he didn't like the idea of his apartment lying empty all this time. Not when Baltazar's agents had been known to break in. He didn't like the thought of them moving in and taking over, given carte blanche to do whatever they wished in his home. He'd asked Roth to move in for an unspecified period, and she'd been happy to do so.

Buchan, having climbed the stairwell in his apartment block by the River Clyde for the first time in two months, stood for a moment outside the front door. Small suitcase in hand, a backpack looped around one shoulder.

Despite being back home, he felt lost.

He contemplated ringing the bell, or knocking, as he entered, then decided instead to settle on opening the door, then hesitating a second or two before entering the apartment. From the door there was a view, down the short hallway, into the heart of the sitting room. He couldn't imagine Roth doing anything other than sitting in one of the large seats by the window, a book in hand, or a MacBook open in her lap.

He sighed, he felt a peculiar nervousness, he opened the door. Waited a moment or two, his head lowered, staring at the familiar wooden flooring, as the aroma of a warm, red wine casserole drifted out to meet him, then he opened the door and walked into the apartment.

He closed the door behind him, set the bags down on the floor, and looked into the depths of the sitting room. The room was low lit, there was music playing. The Oscar Peterson Trio, one of his old favourites. He hung his coat on the usual peg, noticing that both of the only two jackets he'd ever seen Roth wear were hanging up, then he walked through to the open-plan. Roth was in the kitchen, behind the fridge door.

As Buchan stopped on the other side of the kitchen counter, she closed the fridge, and stood looking at him, a bottle of white wine in hand. There were two glasses on the counter.

They stared at each other in silence for a few moments. It was the lightest Buchan had felt in two months.

'Hey,' said Roth.

'You knew I was coming?'

'To be honest, the stew's been on for a couple of days now. I was going to crack and eat it this evening, if you didn't show. Should be melt-in-the-mouth. Then Carter called up and said you'd just arrived.'

She smiled, she indicated the bottle. Another silence, not in the least awkward. He sensed it in her. Although things had been odd between them before he'd left – indeed, had they ever been anything other than odd since the first time she'd come to live with him, over a year previously – he could tell she was as pleased to see him as he was to find her home.

'You might want red with dinner, but…,' and she raised the bottle of sauvignon again.

'That'd be nice,' he said.

She didn't move.

From nowhere he felt the need to walk round the counter and take her into his arms, and felt the thrill of it through his body at just the thought.

There was a meowing at his feet, and he looked down. The moment broken. Edelman, who usually had a better sense of timing, rubbed himself against Buchan's leg, and he bent down and scratched the cat's head.

'Hey,' he said. 'You been looking after Agnes?'

Above them, on the counter, the sound of pouring wine.

2

'Mostly Warsaw and Gdańsk,' said Buchan. 'He had a long weekend in the south of the country, from there he travelled on to Prague. And when the boss called inviting me to return, I was in Tallinn.' He paused, then added, 'A few days in southern Estonia before that.'

Oscar Peterson was still playing, they were sitting at the small table, wine and dinner. Edelman had greeted Buchan's return for a minute or two, and then had retreated to his familiar spot by the window.

Outside the day was fading, darkness creeping over the city from behind, the lights now on in the buildings across the river.

'Tallinn's great, right?'

'Aye,' said Buchan. 'I was trying not to be on holiday, though.'

'Did you get anywhere?'

A pause, while Buchan allowed himself to slide into the depths of the truth of it, and then he broke the look, and applied himself to his dinner for a moment. He took a mouthful, he drank some wine, he took another mouthful, he dabbed at his lips with a napkin.

'Crap,' he muttered.

'It's OK,' she said, curiously amused by his reaction to the question, 'you don't have to give up your secrets.'

'That's the trouble,' he said, forcing himself to talk. 'I got nothing. I watched the guy for two months. I went where he went, I spoke to people he met with, I inveigled myself into places as well as I could. I used disguises, I used fake names, I used fake ID cards. I broke the law, without doubt I broke the law, in both Poland and Czechia. The only reason I didn't in Estonia, was because I hadn't got around to it yet.' He paused, he held her look across the table. Elbows on the table, hands clasped, he leant into the discussion a little further. Obviously, having not spoken to anyone at home in all this time, he needed to confess. 'And not only did I get nothing, absolutely nothing to indicate that Baltazar's business interests are anything other than legitimate, he knew. He knew everything. Every damn time I turned up somewhere, he knew. It was like they had a chip planted in my head.'

Except that one time, of course, south of Võru, when Buchan had stood right in front of him. Baltazar hadn't seen him coming then, had he?

He wasn't going to talk about that night.

'He told you that?' asked Roth. 'He recounted every one of those fake ID's to you?'

'No. It was why I wasn't getting anywhere. In fact, it was why I'd had so much access. Sometimes I'd try something entirely speculative, something I'd imagine I had no chance of achieving… and a door would open. In you come, fake Inspector Marsh of Europol, you're most welcome. It felt *too* easy at times. And that was why. They were playing with me.'

'You don't know that,' she said, looking concerned.

Buchan didn't bother countering.

'Tell me about the office,' he said, deciding it was time they moved on. 'How's it going? This is wonderful, by the way.'

'Thank you.'

He took another forkful, she took a drink of wine.

'You heard about DI Randall?'

'As I said,' he said, with a half-smile, 'I've had no contact, with anyone. Not the boss, not Sam.'

'Really? I thought you meant, like, just official channels.'

'Not any channels. Tell me about Randall.'

'She's an idiot.'

Roth said it, and immediately laughed at herself, covering her mouth, her eyes smiling at Buchan, and he smiled with her.

'I'm sorry, I shouldn't. But, oh my God. You know the Peter Principle?'

Buchan nodded.

'Well, like, she has blown that out of the water.' She laughed again. 'I mean, that woman did not stop when she reached her level of respective incompetence. She has kept on going.'

Buchan smiled along with her. There was a modicum of guilt at talking about a fellow officer behind their back, but Roth's smile was the first worthwhile thing he'd looked at in the past two months, and he was enjoying it.

And wasn't there that niggle of concern at the back of his head? Just the idea of someone being promoted into a position that far exceeded their ability. Couldn't it be because that person was someone's useful idiot? A political appointee, there to manage a specific department of the Serious Crime Unit for the furtherance of an outside agency?

'Tell me about her,' he said.

'Oh my God...' Roth shook her head. 'She's just useless. I don't know how she got in the force in the first place, never mind made detective inspector. No common sense, no particular bent towards deductive reasoning, no, you know, smarts,' and she tapped the side of her head. 'And worse, I mean, the very worst of it and her and everything about her dumb appointment, she doesn't compensate for her own deficiencies by leaning on others. I mean, that wouldn't be great, but at least if she took advice from people who actually knew what they were doing, you know? But nuh-huh, that's not her. She's the boss, and she's going to tell you what to do, even if she has absolutely no idea what that actually is. Oh my God, it's... well, sometimes it's just embarrassing.'

'I'll be working with her?' said Buchan, curious now what his place in the organisation was going to be.

'No, that's the weird thing. She's gone. Still in the building, but they put her downstairs. There's a new organised crime specific branch on the fourth floor, and she's part of that.'

'Organised crime branch?'

Roth nodded, and they shared the look across the table.

The main threat to law and order in the city, having arisen in the past year, was Baltazar and his gang from Poland. There perhaps had never been more need for an organised crime branch than now. And yet, how could they possibly trust it, not with the way Baltazar's people had infiltrated the police service?

'And what about you?' asked Buchan. 'I thought you might be gone by now.'

'I have seven days left,' said Roth.

'You're done a week on Friday?'

'Yep. Two days, got the weekend off, one more week and then,' and she made a take-off motion.

'Good,' said Buchan. 'I'm glad you're following through. What's the plan?'

'Going travelling,' she said. 'Where to is still in play. Probably Switzerland, then into Italy. We'll see.'

'Sorry,' he said.

'Why?'

'I kiboshed your plans to make the Alps in winter by asking you to look after furball.'

He glanced round at Edelman, almost to see if he'd noticed the mild pejorative.

Edelman didn't lift his head.

'Don't be daft. You know I'd already decided against heading off that soon. I gave my notice for the middle of April over a month ago, so you've timed your return to perfection for me. I just haven't been able to make any definite plans, that's all. And now I can. Something to do at the weekend.'

'OK, good,' said Buchan. 'You signed up for a master's course?'

'St Andrews in September. English Lit.'

'Nice. What happened to Leiden?'

'Oh, I don't know. Thought I'd stick around Scotland for a while. Maybe try to do a year abroad at some point.'

Buchan didn't really have an opinion on Roth studying English literature, but he was glad, nevertheless, that she was doing something. That she was getting out of the police.

'What about you?' she asked. 'Did you consider not coming back when you were called?'

They held a look across the table, Buchan's face impassive.

The answer was very straightforward. He hadn't thought about it, because he hadn't even considered the idea of not coming back. And that was because he'd been so lost, that when the call came, his biggest feeling had been one of relief, despite the fact Baltazar had been the first one to mention it to him.

He was beginning to think that perhaps his time in Police Scotland was coming to an end. The future was just around the corner, and he had no idea how it would look, and what he was going to do with it. But if it was to come, he first needed closure on this damned Baltazar business. There needed to be a winner and a loser, and if he was going to be the latter, he would go down swinging.

That had been the problem with Warsaw, and Prague, and Tallinn. He'd been plodding around Europe, completely directionless. Now he had no idea why he'd been summoned, and he seriously doubted it was just because they were short-staffed. But it didn't matter. He was back, closer to the action, and now that he was here, something was going to happen. Good or ill, it seemed as though it hardly mattered anymore.

'No,' he said simply.

She smiled, with an understanding look. She knew him.

He broke the look, he took some more dinner, he kind of shrugged.

'Here we are, anyway,' he said. 'We'll see how it plays out.'

'I'm glad you're home,' she said, the words delivered at a peculiar rush, and she looked slightly embarrassed. 'Sorry, that's…'

'Thank you. I'm glad you're here.'

They stared across the table, a moment stretching into another, and then Roth laughed and shook her head.

'I used to be so much more forthright. I don't know what happened.'

'Well, you kind of left me standing there at one point before I went away,' said Buchan, something he'd thought of saying many times, words he'd never thought would actually leave his lips.

'Sorry, it just felt…'

She took a drink of wine. Paused, then downed the glass and set it back on the table.

'Look, boss,' she said, 'this is dumb. You mind if I just…'

Her eyes were wide, and Buchan, despite himself, and who he was, was falling into them, and the two months of trailing hopelessly around Europe had left him vulnerable to the idea of experiencing anything, and he said, 'I don't mind at all.'

'I know it's maybe wrong, or it's like something out of the nineteen fifties, and you're still my boss and you're however many years older than me, but I don't care. *I don't care.* And you shouldn't either. I missed you. I'm surprised you didn't hear my heart cannon off the ceiling when you walked through the door earlier. And soon enough you won't be my boss, and the age thing'll just disappear. We can watch *Funny Face* with Audrey and Fred Astaire, and think, well, at least we're not as bad as them.'

He smiled along with her, and she laughed at the relief of finally saying it, the words spoken silently, or out loud in the presence of no one but Edelman, so many times in the past few months.

The laughter ended, slowly the smiles died away, and then they were just two people sitting at a table, staring at each other, accepting the inevitable.

Buchan held her look for a few moments, drowning

hopelessly in it, then he pushed his chair back, walked round the table as Roth got to her feet, and took her into his arms.

3

Buchan was standing at the window, waiting for Chief Inspector Liddell to get off the phone.

Despite having achieved nothing over the past few months, the travel around Europe and the complete disconnect with home meant that it felt like forever since he'd stood at this window, looking down on the river. Glasgow Bridge to his left, Clyde Street leading into the Broomielaw across the water, the constant flow of traffic. A distant siren, and the sound of a car horn, angry in the chill rush hour of seven-thirty-nine of a morning in April. The sky had cleared, the river seemed becalmed, impossible to tell if the tide was coming or going, impossible to tell which way the river flowed.

He was aware of the silence behind him, and he turned. He'd managed to completely shut off the sound of Liddell's phone call. She was staring at him, waiting for him to engage.

'Welcome home, inspector,' she said.

He nodded, then found the words, 'Thank you.'

He wasn't used to change, he didn't like life running at a hundred miles per hour, racing away in front of him. Two days ago he'd been sitting in a park in the furthest reaches of the European front. The previous night he'd opened the door and walked into a relationship with Roth. This morning, back to work, not knowing why, with the tasks that lay ahead an unknown landscape. He was dealing with it all by shutting down, feeling nothing, and staring blankly across the office at his boss, who was sitting back, regarding him warily.

'Where have you been?'

'Two month holiday, travelling in Europe.'

'Two month holiday? Was that in Poland, by any chance?'

'Passed through,' he said. 'One of many.'

He was returning to work with a mantra of trusting no one, and perhaps it felt wrong to extend that to Liddell – if he didn't trust her, then he really ought not to have come back – but he wasn't sure she would be as circumspect with information as he himself would be. The circle of people she thought trustworthy, was going to be much greater than the one Buchan was constructing around himself.

'Jesus, inspector,' she said finally, shaking her head. 'Fine, we shall be practical. You remain under investigation. The inquiry into the conduct of this office during the events that led to Detective Sergeant Houston's murder last year has been suspended since you walked out on it, but frankly, we all know there will still be pieces being moved around off the board. Whatever shit you were in as a result of that inquiry, of course increased ten-fold as a result of your actions in the autumn. As ever with this damnable organisation, these things take time. Perhaps that's fortunate, but I suspect we'd all prefer everyone just got on with it.'

'Why am I here?' he said, his impatience suddenly finding words.

'Reasonable. We're swamped. Pure and simple. I've been badgering them to let you back, pending a resumption of the inquiry, and they finally relented. Of course, I never wanted you suspended in the first place, regardless of how infuriating your actions have been.'

'Why now?'

'Because I asked.'

'You said you've been badgering them, and that you didn't want me suspended in the first place. So, why now?'

'I don't know, inspector. My complaint fell on different ears, or perhaps one morning the chief in Glasgow looked at the newspapers, and read yet another excoriating piece on the disaster that is policing in the city, the understaffing and the sick absences, and thought, we need everyone we can get, regardless. It's not like they don't know you're good at what you do. It's not like we don't *need* you.'

'I don't know what it is that's brought me back here,' said Buchan, 'but it's not that. There's a reason why it's now.'

'So, why'd you come?'

He hesitated. He'd spoken of his failure, his weakness, to Roth, but he didn't want to do it here, even though Liddell would, dispassionately, be far more aware of the ineffectiveness of his two-month European investigation. Was it just pride, or was there more distrust of his superior than he cared to admit?

'Whatever this is, it's coming to a head. I need to face it.'

He left it at that, Liddell had nothing to say.

'Tell me about the organised crime unit,' he said, making

the decision for them both that the preliminaries were over.

Liddell took a deep breath as she accepted the turn in the conversation, then she nodded to herself. Time to get on.

'You know the changed landscape. Bancroft's gang was eliminated last summer, and since then, William Lansdowne, with Baltazar's backing, has been taking over. This time last year, Lansdowne was a small-time, south side gangster. Now he controls the city.'

'Really? What about –?' began Buchan, but she cut him off.

'He's crushing them. The Taylors, the Tennents, the Russells. Sadiq and his crowd, and the Albanians in Bridgeton. Even that nascent Chinese mob trying to kick off in the west end. All of them. Either eliminated or brought under the umbrella of Lansdowne's organisation.'

'There's been nothing like last summer though?'

'No, there hasn't. When I say either-or, there in fact haven't been many eliminations. Most of the people see the lay of the land, the way the wind blows. And this wind is blowing from the east. They know it's not Lansdowne who's in control. Since Baltazar appeared on the scene, he's had dominion. Glasgow has been swept up, and now he's bringing Edinburgh under his control, and soon enough there won't be a drug dealer, a con artist, or a street corner extortionist in Scotland who isn't channelling most of their profit his way.'

'And when Scotland's done, he heads south.'

'Exactly. Not sure whether he's in position to take London, but this man's reach is extensive, and I'd put nothing past him.'

'Who's idea was the specialised unit?'

She paused before answering, though it was impossible for Buchan to tell whether it was to allow her to concoct a cover story.

'It came out of discussions.'

'Between whom?'

'It's Police Scotland, inspector, and you've only been away a few months. Nothing's changed. There are a lot of meetings. There is a lot of talking. It happened, and that's all that matters.'

'Rose is heading it up?'

'DI Savage was brought over a few weeks ago. She's still putting her team together. You should speak to her when you get the chance, but she's still juggling, and maybe it'll be a while before she has the time. Meanwhile, you need to speak to Samantha, and get caught up. The casework of SCU has not reduced in your absence.'

And suddenly, with that, the conversation was over, and silence raced in to fill the room. He stood before the desk, staring down at the chief inspector, wondering if there was anything else to be said, already accepting that any further questions he might think of would be better answered by his own team.

Liddell made a small gesture to the door. It was time for Buchan to rejoin the fray.

4

The corpse was bundled in a corner of the alleyway, somewhere in the morass of streets in the city centre. There would've been a lot of blood, but much of it had been washed away by the overnight rain. Indeed, the body had been discovered by a passer-by who'd noticed what remained of the stream of diluted blood, running from the pile of rubbish up against the wall, to the drain in the middle of the alley.

'I don't know, guess the sun caught it just right, you know?'

The first words Buchan heard, as he arrived on the scene. Detective Sergeant Samantha Kane was already there, having been called to the scene even before arriving in work that morning.

'Hey,' said Buchan, approaching from the side. She hadn't seen him coming.

'Boss!' she said.

'Sam,' he said. 'I'm back.' And then, not wanting to linger over it any further – he'd already had enough of returning – he said, 'Tell me,' indicating the alleyway.

Kane smiled at the abruptness of his arrival, took a moment to adjust, then nodded at the man standing beside her, hands in pockets, eyebrows raised, looking at Buchan with expectation.

'This is Mr McArdle. He discovered the corpse, called it in forty-five minutes ago.'

'Have you left the scene?' asked Buchan.

McArdle shook his head, then lifted his phone from his pocket.

Young man, late twenties maybe. Teeth not in great shape, thought Buchan, a pallor that spoke of drug use, though his eyes were clear.

'Called it in on this, you know. Not sure, thought I should hang around, just in case. Took this lot twenty minutes to get here. Suppose that was my fault. I said the guy was dead, wasn't like there was any rush, was there?'

'Anyone pay any attention to the alleyway? Have you

noticed anyone lingering?'

He was shaking his head before Buchan had finished talking.

'I mean, like, there's people walking by and stuff, but it's just a Thursday morning, in't it?'

The police cordon had already been set up, blocking off this side of the road. There was an ambulance and two police cars. Most people passing by on the other side of the road, and most drivers passing on the street, were taking a second to have a look, but there were no spectators. No one was invested. There was little to see, particularly now that a screen was being erected to block the view.

'OK, thanks. I'll leave you to it,' said Buchan to Kane, and then he walked by the officers erecting the screen, and approached the figure bent over the corpse, halfway along the short alleyway.

'Mary,' he said.

There was a moment, the movement of the doctor's hands stopped. She turned her head, regarded Buchan warily, then got to her feet. She was wearing blue overalls, blue gloves, her head completely covered. She pulled the hood back, and carefully brought her mask to the side, hooking the strap with her little finger.

'Well, look at that.'

'What have we got?' asked Buchan.

Dr Donoghue, the pathologist, smiled ruefully. But she knew Buchan, and she knew how this would be. Straight down to business.

'One deep stab wound to the chest, and the throat slit. I got here little more than five minutes ago, so take that into consideration. There may be much to learn, but on first viewing I'd say, the assailant approached from behind, grabbed the victim's hair at the same time as they brought the knife round and buried it in the chest. I'm guessing right through the heart, which means through the ribs, which means we're looking at strength. A strong blade, a strong killer. And then, immediately afterwards, knife drawn across the throat, the body dumped down there against the wall. The trail of blood that alerted your little junky out there, obviously says the murder took place right here. For the victim to be standing in an alleyway, completely unaware there was someone approaching from behind, suggests they were either distracted or too wasted to know any better. On first call, I'm saying distracted, as simple as someone talking to him. He might well not have envisioned any threat at all. If he had, he was more likely to have had his back against the wall, to guard against this kind of thing happening. Of course, if there were two people coming for him, and one of them was handy with a knife, then it's goodnight Vienna, and not a lot he was going to be able to do about it, back against the wall or not.'

She finished, Buchan having let her talk it out, and then he nodded.

'Thank you.'

'Remember the caveats,' she said. 'You're back, then?'

'Yes. He has ID on him?'

She smiled at how smoothly he avoided the question.

'I don't think so,' she said, humouring his wish to just get on with the investigation. 'I haven't looked yet, but I think Samantha checked already.'

Buchan nodded, then he looked past Donoghue, down at the corpse.

'Of course,' said Donoghue, and she indicated for him to take a closer look. He pulled a pair of nitrile gloves from his pocket, and bent down.

'How long?' he asked.

'Pretty wide window at this stage, but I'll say between midnight and three. It was still raining then, I think. I'll let you know when I've narrowed it down.'

Buchan nodded his thanks.

Fresh blood, a new corpse, the smell of a murder investigation in his nostrils.

The circumstances that had led to this aside, it was good to be back.

5

Forty-five minutes later, and Buchan and Kane were still at the scene of the crime, although they were getting ready to leave. They'd spoken to people living across the road from the scene, they'd spoken to the people in the apartments above the shops on either side of the alleyway. They'd put in a request to all the shops in the neighbourhood for sight of their CCTV footage.

Buchan was no more hopeful for that than he'd been for getting information from the local residents. With the murder taking place in the middle of the night, as long as the killer, or killers, had been discreet, there was no reason why anyone's sleep would have been disturbed. And Buchan knew as well as anyone, that of the countless CCTV cameras along this street, they'd be lucky to find a third of them had been active. They were a deterrent, little more than that, and only occasionally produced anything worthwhile for the police.

They watched the corpse as it was removed, taking a last look at the cold, thin face of the victim, as he was wheeled towards the ambulance, and then Buchan and Kane turned away just as Detective Constable Danny Cherry arrived.

'Boss!' he said, smiling at Buchan. 'I heard you were back. Nice to see you.'

'Thanks, Danny,' said Buchan, but he was no more disposed to conversation now than he had been previously. 'You manage to pick up anything on the victim?'

A moment, while Cherry adjusted to the fact that Buchan obviously wanted to skip even the most basic, casual conversation, then he said, 'Yep, we got him. Graham Mathieson. He had a conviction for spousal abuse seven years ago, so he's on record.'

'Prison term?' asked Kane, already knowing the answer.

'Eighteen months, suspended,' said Cherry.

'Still married?'

'Far as we can tell. His wife lives in Shawlands. Just off the Kilmarnock Road.'

'OK, thanks, Danny. No one's been out there yet?'

'Only just found this out. You want me to go?'

'The sergeant and I'll take it, thanks, Danny. Can you start gathering information on him for me? We'll head out to Shawlands, then see you back at the office.'

'Boss,' said Cherry.

A moment, as though he was expecting something else, a slightly curious glance at Kane, and then he turned away with a nod, and a, 'See you later.'

6

Sitting in traffic. Buchan needed to have a chat with his sergeant, which was why he'd asked her to join him on the potentially unpleasant task of informing the wife of her husband's death – you never could tell how it would go until you were in the moment – but conversation was not coming easily to him today.

'I see you're as warm as ever,' said Kane into the silence.

She let the words hang there, and then turned and gave Buchan a small glance. He finally smiled.

'Sorry,' he said. 'Feeling a little discombobulated, that's all.'

'Weird to be back, eh?'

'Unexpected. A little out of nowhere. Suppose all I can do is what's in front of me.' He made a vague gesture down the road. 'Informing Mrs Mathieson of her husband's death, and taking it from there.' Another pause, then he asked, 'You had much contact with DI Savage since she moved in?'

'She had a chat with each of us in her first week, but that aside, not really.'

'I need to speak to her. I'd been about to, when this call came through. We'll see how this is looking, then I'll try to get down there when we're back at the office.'

'How'd you get on in Poland?'

'Nothing. I hate to say it, or to be more precise, I hate to admit it, but I was wasting my time.'

He glanced at her to see the small grimace, the acceptance of the inevitable. She had voiced her doubts to him before he'd headed off, yet she knew him to be someone who could make things happen. It was disappointing to learn that on this occasion, at least, he'd been unable to rise to it.

'I did learn that Baltazar is likely to be in the city next week.'

'Really? Well, that's something. How'd you find that out?'

'He told me.'

He glanced at her again, got her raised eyebrows in return.

'He's after something, but he didn't say what.'

'He spoke to you? How did that come about?'

'He knew where I was, he chose his moment, he sat down. He talked, he left. How's it been here?'

She kept looking at him, curious at the abrupt change in subject, but he kept his eyes on the road ahead.

'It's been OK, to be honest, particularly since Savage's unit started operating,' she said, accepting his silence. 'We were promised your replacement for a while, and then DI Randall arrived. And… well, I shouldn't. She's downstairs now, and you can meet her, and form your own opinion. Just, well, thank God she's gone. There's still, of course, the unseen presence of Baltazar. I mean, if you didn't know the guy was there, it'd be bad enough watching Lansdowne and his people spread like a virus across the city. But knowing that behind this two-bit thug with delusions of criminal competence, there's a vast network of European gangland murderous thuggery, is quite terrifying. One of those ones where you kind of wish you didn't know what you know.'

'Yeah,' said Buchan, nodding.

Nothing else to add. It was no less worrying walking back into it, particularly having returned unarmed with any of the kind of useful information he'd been hoping to collect.

'I don't know,' he said a while later. 'We're already wary, so it's not like we need to be reminded of the need for vigilance. There's something coming, and if it's impossible to get ahead of it, we're just going to have to face it head-on when it happens. And hope there's still something we can do about it when the time comes.'

'Hmm,' said Kane, nodding along, her eyes a little vacant as they looked up the road. Hope had been in pretty short supply.

'You get back yesterday?' she asked, deciding to veer off into the less depressing ground of regular conversation, if there was any to be had.

'Not until early evening. Thought I might come into the office, but I ended up coming home through Heathrow on BA. Got delayed in London.'

He waved away the words, as though bored with the mundanity of the explanation.

'Agnes still at your place, or did she take the cat home with her?'

When he didn't answer immediately, she knew, and she

lowered her eyes, accepting there was nothing coming. None of her business.

He let the silence sit, but one of the things he and Roth had talked about at breakfast was accepting the way things were, and that there was no need for subterfuge. They'd hardly be putting an announcement in the personal column in the Times, but if anyone asked, they would just tell them how it was.

'She'll be staying,' he said.

There needn't have been too much in the words, but Kane recognised something in the tone. She glanced at him, watched his impassive face for a few moments, and then felt an acceptance that she wouldn't have felt at any point the previous year.

But why shouldn't there be something there, after all? Agnes was leaving, Buchan's place at the SCU was hardly set in stone. Who knew what the next few weeks and months would throw up? If they'd finally found each other, who was she, the sergeant in the middle, to have anything to say about it?

'Good,' she said.

7

Kane had tried to ask a question once they were all sitting in the small lounge, but Sylvie Mathieson had raised a hand to stop her talking.

There was a cup of tea on the low table in front of her, steam rising into the room. Beneath the glass top, a shelf with a proliferation of magazines. House Beautiful, and Homes & Gardens, and Good Housekeeping. The room itself did not display any sign that lessons had been learned from these publications.

Sylvie Mathieson was in shock. Face pale, she'd spoken only to invite the detectives into the house upon arrival, she'd retreated to the kitchen to make herself a cup of tea, making a mug each for Buchan and Kane without asking if it was something they wanted, and then she'd walked back through to the lounge.

Kane was sitting in the adjacent sofa, close enough that she could reach out and take the widow's hand, if that was something that might seem appropriate. Buchan remained standing by the window. He'd glanced out once, and then had not looked back. Bleak housing, cloud cover here there hadn't been in the city centre, a bright day brought to its knees by the surroundings.

Kane lifted her mug and took a drink of tea, if for no other reason than to put some life into the room. The quiet was suffocating, and she'd begun to feel like they could be frozen into some piece of contemporary art, entitled *Delivery of Bad News*, or *A Widow's Silence*.

It worked. The movement of her hands, the quiet slurp of tea from a hot mug, seemed to drag Mathieson from her solemn reverie, and finally she took a breath and looked at Kane for the first time since they'd sat down.

'Tell me,' she said. 'What you said earlier…,' and made a small gesture to indicate she hadn't taken any of it in.

'Your husband's body has been discovered in the city centre,' said Kane, her voice low and soft. Easing in the bad news, for the second time. 'He was murdered.'

'How? I mean, how'd youse know?'

'He'd been stabbed in the chest,' said Kane. An inevitable hesitation, and then she pushed through. 'His throat had been slit. Given the double use of the knife, it's inconceivable the wounds could have been self-inflicted.' Another pause, and then, 'He's been murdered.'

A shake in her fingers, Mathieson reached towards the mug. Kane winced, already looking ahead to the moment when the mug slipped from her grasp, then she seemed to recognise what would happen, and pulled back. Fingers clasped, elbows on her knees, leaning forward.

'When was the last time you saw Graham?' asked Buchan, from his position at the window.

Mathieson lifted her eyes, as if only just noticing Buchan was in the room. 'Last night. I don't know, around eight. We had a fish supper, watched that new show on Netflix. Don't know what it's called. The Chinese thing about aliens and technology 'n that. Then his phone goes, and he says he has to go out. I'm like that, really, and he's like, aye, there's a job. He was just, you know, he was just like that, you know. Beck and call.'

She looked hopelessly at Kane, as though expecting her to know what she meant.

'Whose beck and call?' asked Buchan.

She stared at him again, and then turned back to Kane, and both officers noticed the moment when she suddenly realised she had two police officers in her house, and she'd been happily travelling down the route of telling them about her husband's criminal allegiances.

'Oh,' she said. Consternation flashed across her face, and she stared at the carpet. 'Sorry, I shouldn't.'

'Graham's dead, Mrs Mathieson,' said Kane. 'If you want us to find who killed him, we're going to need to know the names of people he worked with.'

Nothing, the eyes staying rooted to the carpet.

'What kind of work did he do?' asked Kane.

A further silence, but at last there was something coming.

'He worked for the newsagent on the corner of, I don't know, Grenville Avenue is it?'

'What's the name of the newsagent?'

'It's a wee independent. Like, it's probably just called the Newsagent, something like that. I says to Graham when he joined them, I says to him, I hope you know what you're doing. He says, I need the money. He wasn't wrong. I mean, we needed the money.'

She looked up again. Her eyes were reddening. I hope we don't lose her, thought Buchan.

'What was his job?' asked Kane.

'Dogsbody,' she said quickly. 'That's why he got calls at eight o'clock on a Wednesday evening.'

'Seriously, what did he do for a newsagent at eight in the evening? It was open late, and he was behind the counter? He did stocktaking? Deliveries, pick-ups?'

Mathieson was shaking her head before Kane had stopped talking. It wasn't like Kane didn't know where this was going, but she was chasing the information, trying to get Mathieson to talk.

'It's not really a newsagents, is it?' she said, with a tone of exasperation. 'That's just a cover. Are you actually in the polis?' She looked from Kane to Buchan, and back. 'I don't know what he did, he never said. But that place… you did not hear this from me, by the way, right? You did not hear this from me.'

Kane nodded.

'Look, he'd never say. Plausible deniability, and all that, right? He gave us that much. I don't know what kind of racket they were running, but Graham wasn't selling newspapers or sweeties, that's all I know.'

'You know the names of anyone else there?'

Another head shake.

'I don't believe you.'

'Plausible deniability, like I said. I don't know anything.'

'How long had he worked there?' asked Kane.

'Six months. He says he was going to give it no more than a year.' She laughed bitterly at that, then added, 'I laughed in his face when he says that, I really did. You think that's the kind of mob who let you walk away? I mean, seriously. You know too much. No bastard's letting you just walk when you know shit.'

'You have any idea why someone might have killed him now?'

She hadn't seemed to consider that question, and she lifted her head and looked curiously at Kane.

'Why?'

'Yes.'

Her eyes drifted away again, she stared away across the

room.

'That's... I mean, that's just what happens, in't it? These people. The people who are stupid enough to work for them, like my Graham. They get killed.'

'Did Graham have any idea what was coming? When he left the house last night, was his demeanour any different?'

Again, the head shaking before the question was finished.

'Nope. Off he goes, don't wait up, but I shouldn't be too late.'

She looked up at Kane, and again her eyes moved between the two detectives.

'I always thought... you know, despite everything, the shouting, and the whatever, the crap I had to take from that man sometimes, I loved him. I really did. And I always thought, you know, if something happens, I'll know. Like,' and she laughed, an unattractive sound, a sob catching in her throat, 'I don't know if that's some stupid romantic shite or something. But I thought, I'll know. I'll feel it. A disturbance in the Force. Ha,' she added humourlessly. 'Nothing like that. He wasn't in by half-eleven, and I was out like a light. Woke up at seven this morning. Didn't even notice he hadn't come home for about five minutes.'

'Did you call the newsagents?'

'Aye. They said he left around midnight.'

'That was all?'

'Aye.'

'You didn't think of calling the police then?'

Mathieson looked at her with ill-disguised contempt, then let her eyes move to the clock. Just after nine-forty-seven.

'Sure,' she said. 'Because my husband, the petty criminal, had been missing for almost ten hours. Youse lot would have called in the SWAT team. Twenty thousand police officers instantly mobilised. A great rush to flood the city with law enforcement in a desperate bid to find him.'

'OK...'

'I mean, youse would probably have done that if Graham had used someone's wrong pronouns. But disappear? Nah, no biggie. Actual crime, someone else's problem. I'm surprised you turned up in person to do this. Thought you'd have done it by text these days. *Husband dead, call eight-eight-fuckity-eight for an appointment to make a formal identification. Calls will be charged at three hundred quid a minute.*'

'What did Graham do before he worked at the newsagent?'

She laughed again, this time the bitter smile still on her face when she looked at Buchan.

8

'We sell newspapers.'

She stared harshly at Buchan and Kane, arms folded, from the other side of the counter. The owner. The young man who'd been there, head bowed, looking at his phone when they'd arrived, was standing to the side. He'd initially feinted to film the interaction, and Kane had warned him off with a look. They both presumed, nevertheless, that he'd at the very least make sure he got the audio.

'So, what was it Graham Mathieson did for you?'

Margaret McLeod looked around the small space, crammed with shelves, the shelves crammed with crisps and drinks and confectionary, a fridge in the corner, a magazine and newspaper rack along one wall.

'This,' she said. 'He did this. Sold things to customers.'

'You called him in at eight last night?'

'So?'

'It says on your door there you close at nine.'

'I needed cover for the last hour.'

'Really?'

McLeod continued to stare grimly at Kane. Buchan was as much of a spectator as the kid with the phone.

'I've got my period. It was just like, I'm not standing here anymore. You know how it is sometimes, hen?'

The kid started to snigger, managed to cut if off.

'Graham didn't come home just after nine,' said Kane.

'It's not school, is it? It's not like he has to go home to his mum. Maybe he went to the pub. Maybe he's got a shag. Maybe he just didn't want to go home.'

'Graham locked up the shop?'

The same bleak look across the counter, but Kane and Buchan recognised the calculation, the wariness of saying something that could be contradicted.

'No. I came back in to do it.'

'You got footage from that CCTV up there?'

'I delete it every morning if there's no need for it,' she said, the words tumbling out before Kane had even got to the end of the sentence.

'And you saw Graham off at nine?'

'Let's call it five past.'

'And you've no idea where he went?'

'He didn't say.'

'You told Graham's wife he left at midnight.'

The joyless stare continued between them across the counter, with its rows of chewing gum and chocolate and crisps.

'I get mixed up,' she said, her voice a dull monotone. 'Like I said, I've got my period. Can't think straight some months.'

'Graham's dead,' said Kane, bluntly.

An almost imperceptible shadow across McLeod's face. Impossible to tell if this was news to her. The low, gasped, 'The fuck?' from the kid sounded natural at least.

'How?'

'Murdered in the city centre, sometime between the hours of midnight and three.'

McLeod swallowed, the sound loud in the quiet hum of the shop. Her stare did not waver, but Kane could see the grinding of her teeth in the movement of her jaw.

'Shit,' escaped McLeod's lips.

'You any idea who might've killed him?'

Another long stare. More calculation. More than likely, however, this time she wasn't calculating what to say. She would just have been wondering what Mathieson's death meant for her, and whatever operation they were running. The interview, for all that it had given them so far, was effectively over.

'Of course not,' she said, harshly, then she quickly followed it with, 'I need you lot to leave. I've got some calls to make.'

'Really? And who would they be to?'

'None of your business.'

'One of your employees has been murdered, the same night he was working for you. It's our business.'

'I need to get his replacement lined up, he was supposed to be here this afternoon. That's the call I need to make. Happy? Now fuck off.'

Neither Kane nor Buchan moved.

9

'This is the trouble we're running into with literally every serious crime investigation,' said Kane.

Sitting in the Facel Vega, on the way back to the station. Buchan had said it was time for him to speak to DI Savage. Kane was coming back to the office to make enquiries about the Grenville Avenue newsagents, hopeful that the local station might have information on what kind of racket was being run out of there.

'There's obviously a scam, or a scheme of some description, and as soon as you hear about something like that, now you just think, Lansdowne. And if it's Lansdowne, then it means it's Baltazar. And I mean, every time. Except, of course, crime is like every other business, every other walk of life on earth. Sure, there are the major players, but that doesn't mean there aren't a tonne of little guys squirreling away in the undergrowth, doing their own thing. Since organised crime division started up, I've been tempted to take so many things down there, but Savage is like, hold the phone. Back up. Because they are absolutely swamped. And it's a classic case, you know? The suits upstairs, someone somewhere in management, comes up with the great idea of a new department, but of course, *of course* they don't have the finance to staff it properly. And everyone else in that building is either thinking, great, we can palm this off to Savage and co., or else they're thinking, shit, we don't want to be stepping on toes, we better pass this on just in case, and suddenly Savage has every crime going in the city, and she's like, what the heck? About two weeks in the edict came down from the chief. It only goes to DI Savage if you have proof it's related to Lansdowne-Baltazar. Because, really, for all it's an organised crime section, everyone knows it's aimed specifically at this new axis of hell.'

Buchan had nodded a couple of times while she'd spoken, her words confirmation of what he'd been thinking while they'd listened to Margaret McLeod's obfuscations.

'How is she?' he asked.

'How d'you mean?'

'Rose. How's she doing? You think she's coping all right?'

Kane glanced at him, but Buchan was staring straight ahead at the road, face as impassive as ever. When she didn't immediately answer Buchan returned the glance, but Kane had looked away, her eyes having drifted off, thinking over the answer.

'Not good,' was how it finally emerged. 'I mean, I don't know her, so I don't know how this compares to what she's usually like. But she's on edge. Hard not to get the impression she's on the verge of a nervous breakdown.' She smiled to herself, shook her head. 'That's what Agnes said. You know the Almodóvar movie, *Women On The Verge Of A Nervous Breakdown*? She said, she's gone full Almodóvar. It's kind of sad. Or, if she's putting it on, or it's an exaggeration in some way or another, it's working, because really, no one wants to take her anything unless they're absolutely sure.'

'I shall tread carefully,' said Buchan, after a few moments.

'She likes Penguins,' said Kane, after another short silence.

They were approaching the SCU HQ.

'She likes penguins? You mean, the David Attenborough penguins, or…'

'The David Attenborough penguins?' said Kane, unable to keep the laugh from her voice. 'Is that an actual type of penguin?'

'You know what I mean.'

'Not really. I mean, I know they're always doing penguins on those shows, but there's a tonne of different penguins.'

'I mean, does she like the birds or the chocolate biscuits?' said Buchan, then he couldn't stop himself adding, 'and you know that's what I meant.'

Kane laughed again.

'The biscuits,' she said. 'She likes the biscuits. Meet her in the canteen, get her a cup of tea and a Penguin, and that'll be a solid start.'

'Seriously?'

'It works. She even likes those dumb jokes you get on the packets. It's like, the only light relief she has in life.'

Buchan slowed as he neared the entrance to the SCU carpark. As he slotted the car into his allotted space, the spot where the Facel remained most of the time, he said, 'I'm not buying her a chocolate biscuit,' and Kane laughed again.

10

Buchan and DI Savage were sitting in the canteen. It was quiet, and they were detached, sat in the far corner against two walls.

Buchan had a coffee and a cinnamon swirl. Savage had a cup of tea and a Penguin. She'd bought the Penguin for herself. She'd sat down, read the joke on the wrapper, the slightest of smirks had come to her lips, and Buchan was glad she hadn't gone so far as to read it out.

'Don't take this the wrong way,' she said, 'but I'm not sure I'm happy about you being back, inspector. What's the story?'

'I don't know,' he said. 'That's one of the reasons I'm speaking to you.'

'Ah. Well, go ahead, speak away.'

'I was Tallinn two days ago,' he began, then he stopped as he saw the movement of her eyebrows.

'I know who else was in Tallinn,' said Savage. 'No coincidence, I presume.'

'No. Out of nowhere, he came to talk to me. He informed me I'd be getting a call requesting my return to the office. The call came twenty minutes later.'

'Jesus…'

Savage let out a long, disgruntled, concerned sigh, and looked over her shoulder. Lifted her tea cup when she turned back to the table, blew across the top, took a sip, winced slightly at the temperature.

She would, thought Buchan, be even more disgruntled if he told her what had happened two weeks previously, but it wasn't something he was sharing with anyone.

'And you still came?'

'I wasn't achieving anything in Tallinn. Or in Warsaw, for that matter. If they've got something lined up, I thought I might as well come back and face it. Whatever it is, whenever it happens… well, I just have to hope I see it coming.'

Savage nodded, her eyes dropping, a look of dejection on her face.

'My money's not on you, I'm afraid, but good luck.'

'I know Baltazar hasn't been back here in the past few months,' said Buchan, 'but have there been other comings and goings? Does he have a lieutenant over here, or is it all in the hands of Lansdowne?'

'There is a lieutenant, yes. Her name's Kasia Adamczyk. Long blonde hair, early fifties, every time she's in public she wears large sunglasses. And you know, we're talking Glasgow here. No one's needed sunglasses since the first week in August.'

'You got a picture?' he asked.

Savage nodded, lifting her phone from her pocket. Opened photos, flicked through, brought one up, turned the phone round for Buchan to take a look.

A photo that told him nothing. A woman in a raincoat walking along a damp Glasgow street. Dark blue umbrella held above her head, large sunglasses against the glaring luminescence of a dreich February day on Argyle Street.

Buchan studied the photo for a couple of moments, and then nodded, and Savage clicked it off and slipped the phone back in her pocket.

'Are you making any progress?' he asked.

'Nope,' said Savage. 'I'm just going to straight up say it. We are not. There's so much to sort through, the trail of clues so labyrinthine. And, of course, every time something happens now, anywhere in the damned city, we get local plods crawling out the woodwork saying, here, this one might be for you. It's driving me nuts.'

'What about my lot?' asked Buchan.

'Sam's OK. She got the message pretty quick. And at least I know she's good. If she does run with something that we should get, I know she won't screw it up. Can't say the same for some of the idiots on the ground.'

She scowled as she spoke, as though feeling a certain remorse about traducing her fellow officers.

They took a moment. Savage bit into her Penguin, Buchan tore off a piece of cinnamon swirl, put it in his mouth, took a drink of coffee. When he stopped thinking about work, Roth appeared in his head, and he had to quickly banish the thought. There would be time for Roth when he got home. There would be time for Roth at some point in the future, although he couldn't possibly know at this moment what the future would look like.

'So, you don't know why I'm back now?' asked Buchan.

She shook her head.

'Anything brewing?'

'I mean, it feels like it's already brewed, you know? Baltazar moved in, swept through like a tsunami, leaving behind neatly ordered, controlled destruction. He's in total command.'

'He told me he'd be back in town next week some time. Said there was something he was after.'

'What?'

'That was all I got.'

Savage held Buchan's look, returning it with one of consternation, then a small head shake.

'Jesus.'

'How about William Lansdowne?' asked Buchan. 'You speak to him much?'

'I'm always speaking to him, and never getting anywhere. We have one picture of him and Adamczyk at lunch. Jimmy's Bistro on Ingram Street.'

'Don't know it.'

'Opened last summer. Already got a Michelin. The kind of place where you pay fifty quid for a scallop. It's like *The Menu* in there.'

'It's like the menu?'

'It was a movie.'

'I don't know it.'

'It's connected to Baltazar. There is no Jimmy. The head chef's a Pole called Piotr. Adamczyk eats in there pretty much every day. That Lansdowne met her in there once, when he would've known we were watching…?'

'They don't care.'

'Exactly. And, you know, it's fair enough. We can't police lunch.'

'Crap,' muttered Buchan, and he took another piece of the pastry.

'How'd you feel if I went to speak to Lansdowne?' he asked, on the other side of another drink of coffee.

Savage pursed her lips, looked slightly put out, and then covered her disgruntlement with the mug of tea.

'I guess,' she said, lowering the cup. 'I mean, it's not like we're getting anywhere. So, sure, on you go. But, you know, I don't know what your relationship's like with the boss these days, but she's been pretty protective of the new office, that's all. You might find her up your ass, but that's your shout.'

He had a glib comment about having the boss up his ass, but he just nodded, said, 'I'm not worried about Liddell, but I don't want to step on your toes.'

'You go right ahead, inspector, step away, for all the difference it'll make. Just, you know, on the microscopically small chance you actually get somewhere, can you pass it on?'

'Of course.'

Another look across the table, words conjured up on both sides, but there was nothing else much left to say, and they both retreated to their food and cooling beverages.

11

Buchan was back in the mortuary, feeling like he was doing the rounds of all the old, familiar places, now standing in the traditional position. Buchan on one side of the corpse, Donoghue on the other. The Beatles were playing. Something from the early years, the boys singing happily about lost love and tears and crying and betrayal. He didn't recognise this one, even if the sound was unmistakeable.

Graham Mathieson's body was cold and blue, the wounds in his throat brutal. Donoghue had split the corpse down the middle, revealing the tangle of sundered heart muscle beneath the rib cage.

'The killer really brutalised the heart,' she said, making a small gesture in its direction. 'Knife in, and then,' and she mimicked the movement, the aggressive pummelling of the knife inside the wound, 'and then withdrawal when the damage was more than done, and I mean, your man would have been dead already at this point, and then the knife across the throat.'

'Trained killer?'

'I'm not sure. What was done to the heart feels vengeful or psychopathic. Same with the unnecessary throat slice. This is not a cold, clinical hit.'

'You think the killer would've had blood on them?'

'Yep. So either they'd already planned their exit strategy, or they just didn't care if anyone saw them covered in blood.'

'Maybe they hadn't given it any thought at all,' said Buchan.

'Perhaps.'

Buchan looked at Mathieson. Eyes open, giving nothing away. A small man, slight, hard to reconcile the willowy figure with the brutality that got him charged with domestic abuse. But looks meant nothing, particularly not when it came to abusive, violent men.

'Any closer to the time?' he asked.

'One, one-thirty,' she said. 'Somewhere in there.'

'And instant death?'

'Yep. And, as we established earlier, the amount of blood at the scene implies he died where he was left.'

The song finished, another one started up. This one also upbeat, though lyrically the lads seemed to be in a slightly better place.

'How's it been the last few months?' asked Buchan, breaking a silence that had suddenly seemed deafening.

'How's it been?'

He looked up. Donoghue appeared amused by the question.

'Work, or you know, my personal life?'

Buchan knew nothing of Donoghue's personal life. Never had done.

He smiled.

'Work,' he said.

'It's been no different than usual,' she said. 'I know what everyone's saying, and I know we have this turf war, this plague sweeping virulently across the city. But standing here, it doesn't look any different. Last summer's cataclysm for the Bancroft mob aside, there's been no uptick. I don't think I'm doing this any more than I used to.'

'What about methods of murder?' asked Buchan.

'Hmm. There were a couple in the last few months. Look, you know we don't get many murders around here. The Bancroft gang was quite an exception. The vast majority of what I see here, the work of my department, is establishing whether someone died of a heart attack or an intracerebral haemorrhage. The year before Baltazar arrived, there were seven murders in the city, fifteen in total in the west of Scotland. The massacre aside, the past year has seen a small rise, but it's not so different really. It's hard from such a small sample to say anything with any certainty.'

'But you recall a couple?'

'Yes. And that's aside from the business at Thornwood church in the autumn, obviously. There was a murder early in the New Year. Knife to the back of the head. Very clinical. Brought up, sharply, beneath the skull, a long blade penetrating deep into the brain. I remarked to the sergeant at the time what a nice, clean job it had been.'

'It's good to appreciate the work of a professional,' said Buchan, drily, and Donoghue smiled in response.

'Then there was another a few weeks ago. Another knife attack. You might want to speak to Sgt Kane.'

'You're only just connecting the murders now?'

'I'm not sure there's a connection to be made. Knife attacks are still the number one cause of murder in the UK. You can't go linking them all. But, perhaps you're right. Speak to Samantha, she'll have more information than I'm giving you.'

'So, tell me about the one a couple of weeks ago.'

'Knife embedded in the side of the neck,' she said, making a stabbing gesture into her neck. 'There was a little bruising on the cheek, and the hands and arms of the victim. Oh, and a hefty bruise on the leg. Obviously there'd been a fight beforehand, so I hadn't necessarily been associating that murder with the previous knife attack. The whole set-up seemed different.'

'OK, I'll speak to Sam.'

Silence arrived once more, and together they stared down at the blue corpse.

'I should leave you to it,' said Buchan eventually.

'Yes,' said Donoghue.

He turned, started walking away.

'I'm glad you're back, inspector,' said Donoghue to his back.

He hesitated, he turned.

'Thank you.'

12

He stood in the open-plan, looking down the length of the office. It may only have been a few months, but it felt like an age since he'd been here.

The usual suspects were in place, and a moment after Buchan had stopped to look over the office, it was like everyone in the room noticed him standing there, and they all stopped what they were doing and looked up.

Enough of that, thought Buchan.

'I'm back,' he said, somewhat self-deprecatingly, and there were smiles and greetings thrown his way. He nodded, he waved, then said, 'Don't let me stop you,' he smiled awkwardly at the room, and then walked around the edge of the desks towards Roth, acknowledging Cherry as he did so.

'Danny, how're you getting on?'

'Still putting the profile together on Mathieson. Not a nice man. I'll send it shortly.'

'Ellie not around?'

'Sarge gave her a shout, wanted her to speak to a couple of people regarding last night's stabbing.'

'K, thanks, Danny.'

Then he pulled up a seat, and sat next to Roth, without drawing any closer towards her.

They'd had the brief discussion over coffee that morning, but they'd been in agreement and so little had needed to be said. They didn't have to hide anything, but for the last seven days of Roth's work at the office, they had to be completely professional. Nothing for anyone to see, nothing for anyone to comment on, no intimacies between them. When he'd said this, she'd almost laughed at his seriousness, then she'd said, 'Shit, of course not. Are you kidding me?'

'There've been a couple of murders in the last few months,' said Buchan. 'I mean, after the St Andrews church murders, and before last night. Two stabbings?'

'Yep,' said Roth.

'You got the details?'

'Let me bring them up. The more recent of the two…'

She cut herself off while she brought the file up on screen, muttering conversation fillers while she did so.

'OK, here we go. This one we passed downstairs. The victim was named Charlie Hamilton,' then she turned at the movement, realising Buchan was nodding along, and said, 'You know him?'

'Drug dealer, Crow Road.'

'Yep. It immediately wrote itself into the pantheon of Lansdowne-Baltazar crimes.'

'Charlie Hamilton was not the type to stand being overrun by the big boys.'

'That's exactly what we think happened. Most of the takeovers have been peaceful, to be honest. These guys know who's in charge, they can recognise power and authority. They also recognise how much better off they're going to be having been taken over by an international conglomerate. But that wasn't Charlie. No way he was standing for that.'

'And he paid the price.'

'Died with his boots on, at least. I haven't heard anymore since we passed it on, though, so I kind of doubt Organised Crime have got anywhere.'

'And the other one?'

'The other we kept. Nice job, right enough. Knife to the back of the skull, not some random flail, but a calculated stab.'

'The doc certainly seemed impressed. You didn't pass this downstairs?'

'We think it was his wife. Everything about it says it's his wife.'

'You haven't charged her?'

'We don't have it yet.'

'You're sure, though?'

'We were.'

She glanced over her shoulder at Cherry, who was listening in, nodding along.

'Danny's been on it more than me,' said Roth, as Buchan turned towards him.

'It was written all over it. They'd argued a lot. I mean, wow, what a couple. They'd had a stand-up row in the supermarket one time. M&S at the Fort. The food section. She ended up hurling tins of soup at him, and he was batting them away with a wine bottle. Bottle finally smashed, and he was just screaming and looking like he was coming to get her, when security arrived.'

'There's a story,' said Buchan.

'They were absolutely Michael Douglas and Kathleen Turner, *War of the Roses*.'

'That's a movie?' asked Buchan.

'Yes.'

'Hated it,' chipped in Roth from behind.

'There had been five complaints filed against them from their neighbours. Late night arguments and general disturbance. And these people lived in a detached house. Mrs Ferguson has a voice that carries.'

'Oh, boy,' said Roth, 'does she ever.'

'So, it felt like a matter of time… until, I don't know, it didn't anymore.'

'Did she have an alibi?'

'She did, but one of those that just seemed so explicitly perfect, it made you wonder. She was on the last train from Inverness to Glasgow, just passing Gleneagles at the time of the murder. And, at exactly the time that the knife was embedded in her husband's head, she just happened to get into a discussion with the steward on the train. She was making a contrived complaint. Like, she'd been on the train for over two hours, and suddenly decided it was time to point out how awful it was that there wasn't free alcohol in first class. You get that on the trains to England, you know?'

'You think she might have paid someone else to do it, while making sure she was seen elsewhere, in a train carriage far away?'

'That's what we're thinking, but we haven't been able to pin anything down. If she paid someone to do it, she was incredibly surreptitious about it.'

'You would be,' said Buchan, drily.

'Yes, but we can't find where the money's come from, if she did. That kind of job, the way it looks, if you're paying someone to do that, it ain't cheap. We got access to her files, her e-mails, phone messages, bank accounts. No strange contacts, no strange movement of money, no weird payments in or out. We are, genuinely, at a loss.'

'Except there is the alternative, that it was nothing to do with her,' said Roth, 'and the stupid thing on the train was just her being herself, at that particular time.'

'What do we know of Mr Ferguson?'

'Ministry of Defence computer systems. We still haven't got a definitive answer to what his actual job was. He was one of those who came up to the city with all those MoD jobs in the eighties, then his section was hived off, then privatised. Subsequently, the ownership of that company becomes quite murky. Far as we can tell, it's now owned by the Chinese.'

'Jesus,' muttered Buchan. 'No wonder it's murky. Have you spoken to DI Savage about it, gauged her interest?'

'Sarge did, but I think they decided there was nothing to attach it to Baltazar or any of his people. You never know, but far as we can tell, it's its own thing. And, more than likely, despite the defence business and the Chinese, if we ever do manage to find proof of anything, it'll be mariticide.'

'OK,' said Buchan. 'You got his file there?'

Roth brought the file up, and opened it on an image of Brian Ferguson. A neatly clipped, grey beard, thinning hair, shirt and tie, smiling at the camera.

'Happier times,' said Buchan, mundanely.

'Yep,' said Roth. 'And I don't know that there were too many of them.'

Buchan looked at the picture for a little longer, then pushed the chair back and got to his feet.

'Thanks,' he said, nodding at Roth and Cherry in turn, and then he stepped away, and walked to his old, familiar position by the window. His old spot in the office, where he would find himself more often than he would sitting at a desk.

Down below, the river was the same flat calm, slate grey it had been first thing that morning. In the short period of time since, there'd been the corpse of Graham Mathieson, the edginess of Rose Savage, now the tales of murder from Roth and Cherry.

Wasn't this their job, though? It was the Serious Crime Unit, after all. They didn't do shoplifting, and drunken assaults on Old Firm weekend. They did this. Murder most foul. Brutal, uncompromising, never-ending. People were always going to get murdered.

The traffic was at a standstill on Clyde Street. The light had changed, but traffic was backed up off the bridge. A cacophony of car horns and anger.

A bright sky, then a spit of rain against the window.

Glasgow, thought Buchan. It was good to be back.

13

There was a woman sitting outside the door of Lansdowne's office. Not his PA. Buchan had already spoken to, and got past, the PA. This was his security detail. Sitting in a hard chair, back straight, hands clasped in her lap. A window to her left, which Buchan supposed she might occasionally allow herself a glance out of.

'Tania,' said Buchan. 'It's been a while.'

'Detective inspector.' She nodded.

'Keeping you busy, is he?'

Her face was blank. Tania, as Kane had previously had cause to remark to Buchan, was possibly the most attractive security woman on earth.

'Do I need to search you?' she asked.

Buchan smiled.

'The question itself implies innate trust, so let's just go with that.'

She gave him an almost imperceptible nod in reply.

'You can go in,' she said.

*

Lansdowne was standing by the window of his office when Buchan arrived. He didn't turn at the opening of the door, instead his presence by the window a silent invitation for Buchan to join him.

The last couple of times Buchan had spoken to Lansdowne, it had been at his home above Cathkin. If he'd known him to have an office away from the house, it would've been a ramshackle affair, up an iron staircase, to the side of a warehouse. A view of the carpark, and a trade calendar on the wall.

Now he was on the fourteenth floor of an office block on St Vincent Street, and he was standing with his hands in his pockets, looking out on the city below, the blocks on the other side of the street no more than five storeys high.

What a view, thought Buchan, yet the city right there, close enough to breathe in.

'No one lets you open a window anymore,' said Lansdowne, as though he could read Buchan's thoughts. 'Every building now, everywhere, sealed units. Air flow, air conditioning, and regulated temperatures.' He paused, and then he added, 'Nothing is real.'

'You've gone up in the world, William,' said Buchan, and Lansdowne left it a moment and then laughed.

'Up in the world,' he repeated, nodding. 'I see what you did there. I might use that.'

Finally he turned to Buchan and studied his face. Buchan was looking at the horizon. Lansdowne nodded, as if in approval, and then turned away and sat down behind the large desk.

'Pull up a pew, inspector,' he said.

'I'm good, thanks,' said Buchan. 'I shouldn't be too long.'

'You sure? I can get you a coffee. You're going to like this, you like coffee. My boy Reggie found this roast from Ethiopia. Fruity, blueberry notes, rich chocolate undertones, syrupy body. Got it for Christmas. I says to him, first decent thing you've done in a decade, maybe there's hope for you yet.' He laughed, then let the smile fade away. 'I was pulling his leg. There's no hope for him. He's useless.'

'OK,' said Buchan, deciding he might as well play along. He was here, after all, on little more than a whim, expecting Lansdowne to tell him nothing.

'Coffee?'

Buchan nodded.

'Well, there you go, inspector,' said Lansdowne, smiling, as though Buchan had agreed to marry his daughter. Then he pressed the intercom and said, 'Two coffees, hot milk, please, Janice,' cutting the intercom off in the middle of Janice saying, 'Right away, Mr Lansdowne.'

The two men stared at each other, and then Buchan lifted a padded chair by the back, placed it a little nearer the large desk, and sat down. Lansdowne's seat was automatically set a few inches higher than whoever was going to be sitting opposite him. I will bloody bet, thought Buchan, that Baltazar never sits in this seat.

'You've lost weight,' said Lansdowne, fingering his own cheeks. 'Thinner around here. You not been eating? Or are you getting some exercise? What's the secret?'

'Haven't noticed,' said Buchan.

'Hmm. You look happier though. I mean, even though I still can't imagine you ever cracking a smile, there's something about you. If it was anyone else, I might think you'd managed to get a shag.'

He burst out laughing. Buchan, as usual, hated the idea of being seen through.

'When did you move out here?' he asked, to get the conversation heading in the right direction.

'What can I say, inspector? Business is looking up. Portfolio's expanding, the people we do business with are getting more and more internationally diverse. Scotland's the place to come, haven't you heard? You have to put on a bold front for these people. It's not like we have the whole building or anything, but the chance came to take the top couple of floors, so we took it.'

'The top couple of floors?'

'Aye.'

'That's a lot of office space.'

'Check the big brains on the detective.'

'Have you filled all that space, or did you just have to take the job lot so you could get this office?'

Lansdowne laughed, nodding along.

'Very good, inspector, still sharp as a tack. Right, enough of that razor-like insight of yours. What d'you want?'

Buchan held the look across the table. He hadn't come here with anything definite in mind, instead intending to play it by ear when he arrived. Well, he was here now.

'You know about Graham Mathieson?'

Lansdowne, predictably, gave himself a moment. He hadn't known where Buchan was going to go, after all.

'He's dead,' said Lansdowne, hiding behind the bland statement of fact. 'Shame about that. Always sad when someone dies. Though, when you look at the trajectory of his career, he was a wife-beating piece of shit, so you know, what goes around and all that, eh?'

'You know about the newsagents where he worked?'

'I do now,' said Lansdowne, 'but I'm going to disappoint you, I know, by saying that I didn't this time yesterday.'

Another pause as the two men stared at each other, then Lansdowne made a small gesture, banishing the silence.

'Enough. Look, I know what you're thinking. Things have changed in those few months you've been swanning around Europe on holiday. You need to catch up. You come back, something happens on day one, and you're immediately thinking, ah-ha, this is related to everything I've been working on. If you can call what you've been doing *work*. A small-time thug gets a knife in the heart, there's a fair chance his operation is in the process of being taken over by the big boys from the big leagues…'

The door opened, and Janice entered carrying a tray with two small cups of coffee, milk already poured, no sugar. Buchan broke the stare across the desk to acknowledge Janice, and nod a thank you for the coffee. She smiled in return, then, having placed the two cups on the desk, left the office, the tray tucked in against her side.

Lansdowne, eyes still on Buchan, reached forward and lifted his coffee, then took a loud slurp and set the cup back down. He indicated for Buchan to go ahead, and Buchan did as he was bid.

'Very good,' he said, placing the cup back in its saucer.

'Very good,' repeated Lansdowne, nodding. 'I'll take it. Now, where was I?'

'You were describing yourself as a big boy from the big leagues,' said Buchan, with an almost perfect amount of derision.

'Funny. Very funny. If you don't think that's it, why are you here?'

'Because I'm speaking to the errand boy for the big boys from the big leagues,' said Buchan, and he could see the irritation flash across Lansdowne's face. Nice to be able to get under his skin, thought Buchan. At least he still had that in his arsenal. 'Tell me about Graham Mathieson.'

'You're a piece of work, aren't you? You're on your last legs at that place, Buchan. The edifice of the SCU is crumbling. They've set up some ridiculous organised crime division, which I've taken as a bit of a compliment by the way, but God knows what it means for you and your shitty little department. Or what's left of it. I noticed they originally replaced you with a moron. You must be asking yourself what that says about you. Now you've got the nerve to come here and ask questions about some dickhead who got what he deserved?' He paused, a contemptuous stare across the desk, then he added, 'Drink your coffee, and get out, the grown-ups have got work to do.'

Lansdowne glanced at his watch. He scowled.

'Tell me about Graham Mathieson,' repeated Buchan, and Lansdowne added a snort to the scowl. 'Because if you don't know what happened, it means Baltazar's operating in this city without your knowledge. And you won't want that, will you? Because you're his strongman in Glasgow, you're running the ship in this town. If he's got someone else doing his work for him, or in fact if Kasia Adamczyk's running a shadow operation, it means maybe he's not happy with you. Maybe you're in trouble. Maybe this, this absurd fourteenth floor office with its view of a grey horizon, is based on a lie. You're not his able, strong-armed lieutenant after all, because you're next on the chopping block.'

'That's the first thing you've got right since you started talking,' said Lansdowne. 'Bloody right I'm not his lieutenant. William Lansdowne answers to no man.'

He snarled as he said it.

'Bold,' said Buchan.

'You have no idea what's gone on in this city in the last year, inspector. You're a fool playing a mug's game. Well, you'll know soon enough, I expect.'

Lansdowne took another drink of coffee, and now seemed to chew it as it passed through his mouth. Buchan thought of Baltazar saying that it might be almost time to pull out, and wondered what was going on. Lansdowne might have been throwing around cheap barbs, but he wasn't off the mark. There was a hell of a lot that Buchan knew nothing about.

'You really are a piece of work,' said Lansdowne again, this time the tone harsher. 'Seriously, what are you achieving by being here? Either, I'm telling the truth, in which case I've got nothing to tell you. Or else, I'm lying.' He paused and then barked out a laugh. 'What are you going to do then?' Another pause, he lifted his cup and drained the coffee, indicated for Buchan to drink up, and pressed a button on the small machine to his left. 'That's the trouble with you, Buchan. And, I might add, the rest of your lot. Your sergeant and all your little constables. Oh, and the lovely DI Savage. She's nice, eh? Bit of a nippy sweetie look about her, you know, but see if she let her hair down, put on a bit of lippy, and dressed like an actual woman, she might be worth a go.' The door opened, Janice returning with the tray. 'Great rack on her, by the way,' continued Lansdowne, partially making the gesture, then letting out a low whistle. Then he laughed again, and added, 'Can't let Moira hear me talking like that. She thinks it's vulgar. Thanks, Janice. And can you see the inspector to the door, please, he was just leaving.'

'Mr Lansdowne,' said Janice.

She looked expectantly at Buchan, who was staring across the desk at Lansdowne.

In the fits and starts of any investigation, the one step forward two steps back of it, this had been just another nothing.

'How did you know Mathieson took a knife to the heart?' asked Buchan.

A moment, the flash of concern across the eyes, then Lansdowne barked out a laugh, and tapped the side of his head.

'Contacts, inspector. I know people. They tell me things.'

He laughed again. Buchan stared grimly at him across the desk.

14

Late afternoon, the last gathering of the troops to wrap up the investigation for the day. Buchan had returned to work with renewed determination, but wasn't going to sweep in and have everyone working sixteen-hour days. It might come to it at some point, particularly if the Mathieson murder did turn out to be connected to the Baltazar incursion into the Scottish underworld, but there was no need at this early stage.

Buchan, Kane, Cherry, Roth, and Detective Constable Ellie Dawkins. Roth had set up the ops room, the whiteboards beginning to fill with information.

Kane had the floor, having spent a couple of hours with the police in Shawlands.

'Sounds like the newsagents is running a low-key stolen phones racket. A couple of questions on whether it might be something more than that, other things going on, but basically it's phones. Mathieson was just beginning to establish his place in the hierarchy, starting to get known in the area. They do under-the-counter phone sales out of the shop, but they also circulate at the local pubs, clubs. That was Mathieson's end. They hadn't trusted him with that straight off, as obviously, with it being a cash business, you have to be able to rely on your point-of-sale guy, but six months or so in they seemed to be comfortable with him.'

'What's the business model?' asked Buchan. 'Start to finish.'

'They have a partner in Dundee. Each end steals phones, then sends them across to the other site, so that neither of them is trying to fence product in the area from which it was stolen. The thing that really elevates this mob is that they have a phone hacking genius. The locals don't know who, but they think it's a woman. That's all they've got. I guess whoever it is, is the Kylian Mbappe, the Tom Brady, the whatever. The high-priced talent. This person ought to get most of the money, but then, on the other hand, maybe it's some autistic genius who doesn't realise, or care, she's being exploited.'

'They don't send the phones overseas?' asked Cherry.

'I guess that's the beauty of the hacking genius,' said Kane. 'They don't need to.'

'This person can hack any phone, or are there particular brands?' asked Buchan.

'iPhones a speciality, but can do across the board.'

'And the local police haven't made a move because…?'

'They don't have enough, and they don't have the resources to try and get what they need. In the words of the local sergeant, no one's getting hurt. Take care of your phone, and it won't get stolen.'

'Well, he's not wrong,' said Dawkins, with a small shrug.

'So, what do they think about Mathieson? Any chance we're way off the mark here, this is nothing to do with Baltazar, and he was caught with his hand in the cookie jar?'

'That's what they think, yes.'

'And what about Baltazar?'

'It was like they hadn't heard of him. I mean, when pushed I got a bit of an acknowledgement, but Baltazar is not in their consideration. Far as they're concerned, this is absolutely a *no honour among thieves* crime. Mathieson was stealing from his boss, he got a knife in the heart as a result. End of.'

'He said *end of*?'

'You know I wouldn't,' she said, with a smile. 'When I mentioned William Lansdowne, he pushed back even more. Enough, he said. Enough of you lot and your SCU bubble.'

There were a couple of groans around the table.

'Tell you what, though,' said Roth, leaning into the conversation, 'if this lot out of the newsagents really have a phone hacking genius in their ranks, there's not a gang on earth – including MI5 and the FSB – who wouldn't want to get hold of them. Baltazar is going to be all over this crowd.'

Kane raised her eyebrows at Buchan.

'Baltazar did tell you he was looking for something,' she said.

'He did. The thing might well be a person. Though it doesn't explain why Mathieson was murdered.'

'Perhaps as part of a threat,' said Cherry. 'Tell us the identity of your phone hacker, or we start dismantling your crew. Margaret McLeod says no, and so it begins.'

'That has a ring of plausibility,' said Kane.

'And the locals think Margaret McLeod is the lead player in

this phone op?' asked Buchan.

'Far as they know, though it could be the counterparts in Dundee are in charge.'

'What do the Shawlands police know about them?'

She smiled, and Buchan responded with a small head shake.

'They know nothing?'

'Like Jon Snow of old,' said Kane.

Buchan stared at her, realised there was another cultural reference he didn't understand, then said, 'I'll take your word for it. You can speak to Dundee in the morning?'

'Already on it. Got a nine-thirty with a Detective Constable Martin.'

'OK, thanks. And what about the rest of the set-up? Do we have any other names?' He glanced at the board. So far there was just Margaret McLeod and Graham Mathieson. To that, they could add the unknown phone hacker.

'There are three others nominally listed as working at the shop. That's three on top of the kid we saw this morning. That kid, I'm pretty sure, does just work at the shop. I've got the names of the others, and we'll speak to them in the morning. That aside, nothing. No names, no further leads.'

'Do the locals even have a file going on this operation?' said Buchan, unusual frustration creeping into his voice.

'Oh, they have a file, there just wasn't very much in it. My poker face must've slipped, because I got a fairly grumpy *don't judge me* when I was asking about it.'

'OK,' said Buchan, a tiredness in his voice all of a sudden. 'We can get on these people tomorrow. Perhaps the idea that they might be next on the chopping block will loosen a tongue or two. Anything else?'

He looked at Kane, and then around the table, and was greeted by head shakes.

'OK, thanks, people,' said Buchan. 'Call it a wrap. And, as I often say, but obviously haven't had the chance to for several months, we've all done our time today, so everyone, up, oot! And… well, thank you for keeping going. It's nice to be back, and that you're all still here.'

He smiled, he received smiles and nods in return. No one had expected him to even acknowledge his long absence, and had no words of response.

'Boss,' said Kane, and she got to her feet, the others following.

Buchan was last to get up, looking at the boards, and only beginning to ease his chair back as the room was almost cleared. Roth stopped at the door, and he finally tore himself away from the information, and looked at her.

'You OK?' she asked.

'Yep. You?'

'Yep. Chinese carry out? My treat.'

He smiled.

'Sounds nice,' he said. 'Thank you.'

She turned and walked from the room. He took one last look at the boards, and then left the room, turning the light off on the investigation for the day as he went.

15

Crispy won tons, sesame prawn toast, salted chilli king prawn, duck chow mein, chicken katsu curry with egg fried rice, a great heap of prawn crackers, the table festooned with food, the plastic containers to the side, a spoon sticking out of each, Buchan and Roth sharing everything. And a bottle of soave. 'Honestly, it's like it's grown to go with Chinese carry out,' Roth had said with a laugh, when she'd brought the bottle from the fridge.

Hoagy was playing, one of the old records, a scratchy recording that Roth had taken to listening to in Buchan's absence. Buchan himself hadn't listened to early Hoagy Carmichael in ten years.

'Was it like you hadn't been away?' asked Roth.

Buchan nodded without thinking about it. It had.

'If anything, a little better. It was so absurdly tense just before I left, with that stupid inquiry going on. And… well, there's a lot that's weird. The inquiry hasn't gone away, but it has at least gone quiet for the moment. Today, the looming presence of Baltazar aside, it felt a little more like the old days. A murder, our crew getting everything together, working out the lay of the land.'

'Meanwhile having to deal with the local station, who are inevitably too busy with spurious crap to have the time to have done anything useful,' she said, and she smiled a little guiltily.

'You're not allowed to say that out loud.'

'We're all thinking it though.' She slurped up some noodles, her tongue running along the top of her lips, then added, 'But I'm worried about you all the same, boss.'

'Why?'

'There must've been a reason you got summoned back here, and it wasn't because Graham Mathieson's dead. Even if they'd known it was coming, and we'll assume they didn't, it's not like the office wouldn't have coped in any case. Since DI Savage's unit was established, we're more on top of things than we have been since forever.'

Buchan nodded, staring contemplatively at the food,

wondering what to load onto his plate next, then he absent-mindedly picked up a won ton with his chopsticks.

'Sure, overall, I mean across Police Scotland,' said Roth, 'things are pretty ugly numbers-wise. But just not our happy little investigative section, that's all. If they were going to bring you back, I'm sure there are other places it would've made sense to put you.'

'Well, it's not like I'm coming back with my eyes closed. Let's not be complacent, and just hope we can get on top of it when it arrives.'

'Sure, boss,' she said. 'But I'll stay worried until Baltazar's behind bars, if that's OK with you.'

Buchan smiled, lifted the katsu curry dish, and put a couple of spoonfuls on his plate.

'I think it's time you stopped calling me boss,' he said. 'At least, when we're not at the office.' A pause, then he added, 'Uncomfortable though it may be. I'm sure we'll get used to it.'

She smiled, she leant her chin in her hand, studied him from two and a half feet.

'What does the former Mrs Buchan call you?'

He thought about it, his brow furrowed.

'I don't think she actually ever used my name. And I never used hers.' A little further thought, the brow still creased as though this was the first time that had occurred to him, then he shrugged it away.

'Anyone else? Someone, at some time, must've called you something! You can't always have been inspector. Like, when you were fourteen, for example.'

She was laughing, amused by the idea.

'My dad called me Squirt until I was taller than him, then he reluctantly switched to Alexander. My mum never shortened it.'

'Wow. I am not calling you Alexander, that's even more formal than inspector!'

'Well, take your pick from the million abbreviations,' he said, sharing her amusement, 'and we'll see how we get on.'

She continued to stare across the table, teasing amusement in her eyes, then lifted a won ton.

'I think I'll go with Xander,' she said.

'I'm not sure you will,' said Buchan, laughing along with her.

'Sacha?'

'Keep going.'

Buchan had just had the thought that he did not recognise himself – and that no one else, from the chief inspector to Janey, his ex-wife, would either – when his phone pinged loudly in his pocket.

He hesitated, and Roth indicated for him to take a look.

He opened the text.

Can you meet me at the Killermont Bar on Renfrew Street at nine? Text yes/no, don't call. Not safe. Savage

He studied the text, as though there were layers to interpret, then passed the phone over to Roth.

Buchan checked the time. Thirty-seven minutes. They looked at each other, the conversation playing out without either of them speaking. Obviously he was going to go, and obviously she was going to say that it was OK, and of course he should. Nevertheless…

'I don't like the instruction not to call her back,' said Roth.

'Hmm.'

'You don't have that number in your phone, obviously. Have you got a mobile for DI Savage?'

'No.'

'You think we should try to get it? Call her, make sure this is legit?'

'You think this is a set-up, and this is me walking into a trap?'

'I have no idea, but it's not like that's the most outrageous thing on earth, is it?'

'Nope. But I don't want to get in touch with her in case it's real. It's not like she said, meet me down a dark alleyway somewhere. And, of course, if they'd wanted to get me, they've known exactly where I've been for the last two months. Taking care of me in the Estonian forests would have been a lot easier than doing it on a Thursday night in Glasgow. Ditto for getting me out the house, allowing them to deal with you. You've been alone here for the past two months. It would've been very easily done.'

'But it's not about that, though, is it?' said Roth.

Buchan started eating more quickly. Checked his watch again, took another drink of wine. Lifted his phone, replied **Yes** to the text.

'What is it about?'

'You've been brought back here for a reason. What's the

reason, boss?' A moment, she waved away calling him boss. 'Perhaps this is how it starts. They've got some set-up planned, and to do it, they need you at the Killermont in Renfrew Street at nine.'

Buchan continued to eat, stopping just short of shovelling.

'You're right,' he said.

A final mouthful, he took a slug of wine, he put the glass back on the table.

'Sorry,' he said, pushing his chair back.

'Don't be. You have to go. Just, you know, eyes open, remember. Because something is happening here, and you don't know what it is.'

'Eyes open,' he repeated.

'You going to walk?'

'Yep, should only take twenty-five minutes. I'll call when I'm there to let you know whether I'm meeting Rose, or, you know… something else. My doom, for instance.'

'Funny.'

'And don't open the door to anyone.'

'I won't.'

'Right.'

They stood a couple of yards apart in the middle of the open-plan. A moment. It crossed his mind he should do something familiar, like kiss her on the cheek as he left. Or maybe even the lips. Should he kiss her lips?

'Go!' she said, to snap the moment, and Buchan nodded a little uncomfortably and walked quickly to the door.

16

A grey evening, the roads dirty and damp, rubbish-filled drains still flooded with old rainwater. A rat down by the old Marconi building, another scuttling beneath a large, moveable, blue recycling bin. As he crossed Cadogan, and headed up West Campbell Street, the number of people slumped in doorways or against walls increased. A man curled up in a dirty, brown sleeping bag. A guy with a dog, catching the eye of any passer-by he could. A woman, mostly toothless, a transparent plastic cup with one coin in it held in her hands, staring blankly into nothingness. A man slumped over on his side, eyes open, lips moving in a silent mutter, a Ukrainian flag on a small stick beside him. A guy with a guitar singing Springsteen, changing the words for his own amusement or because he'd forgotten what they were supposed to be. A man, slumped over, asleep. Buchan slowed as he passed him, wondering if he might be dead. He was a poor colour.

Buchan stopped, someone cursed as they nearly bumped into him, swerving round as they hurried along the road. A low groan, almost inaudible against the background of the city at night, from the guy on the ground. He stretched, and the needle tucked in, or just lying on the ground beneath him, became visible, and Buchan turned away, walking quickly across Bothwell and on up the hill towards the top of town.

*

He stood at the end of the bar, the wall just behind him, eyes on the door. It was gone nine. He was nursing a slow Monkey 47, surveying the crowd.

The place was busy, the crowd young enough that he stood out. The old guy at the bar, drinking neat gin on his own. Buchan beginning to think that the reason he'd been brought here wasn't to meet Rose Savage. Perhaps it wasn't to meet anyone.

'Crap,' he muttered at the thought, lifting the drink to his lips, taking another small sip.

If he wasn't here to meet anyone, then he was here so that he wasn't at home. And, given the valid points he'd made to Roth about that before he'd left, there had to be something going on that wasn't about catching either him or Roth alone.

He checked the time. Seven minutes past nine.

How long did he give it? If it really was Savage who'd written to him, and it really hadn't been safe for her to answer a call from him, then wouldn't it be possible she might've had difficulty extracting herself from whatever situation she was in? He had to give her a reasonable amount of time.

Nevertheless, he lifted his phone and called Roth.

'Nothing,' he said, when she answered.

'How long are you going to give it?'

'Twenty minutes. Probably half-past by the time I pull the plug.'

'I had a thought. Why don't you try leaving now?'

'Go on.'

'Just an experiment. If they need you out and about for a certain length of time – and I've no idea why that is, by the way – then maybe they're keeping tabs on you. You wouldn't know for sure, but you could walk out of the place, look like you're coming home, and if your phone goes again, same number, DI Savage asking you to give her a few more minutes, then it could mean you're being watched.'

A pause, he didn't immediately respond. Thinking it through. Innately, he liked the idea.

'If there's nothing, then you can just go back into the pub. If there's something… well, you can decide either way how to play it.'

'Good,' he said, simply. 'I'll call again in five.'

He hung up. He lifted the gin, downed the rest of the glass, placed it firmly on the countertop, then walked slowly through the crowd.

Out of the door, stopped for a moment to take in the chill of the April evening, the sky not yet completely dark, then he began walking down the hill, back towards the river.

His phone pinged in his pocket. He stopped. Before he'd even looked at it, he turned quickly to see if he'd been followed outside. No one there.

'Crap,' he muttered.

He checked his phone. Roth had been right.

Running late. Give me five minutes. Maybe ten. Savage

He studied the message again, then slipped the phone back into his pocket. Another look around, but there was no one in the vicinity. No one who could be watching, unless there was currently someone in a dark room in the building opposite.

He made the call on what had to be done. Roth had nailed it, and there was no way the text from Savage was legitimate, the timing a coincidence. And if there was no one out here keeping an eye on him, then it meant there was someone in the pub, who would now be waiting for him to come back in.

Buchan turned away, and walked quickly down the hill. He was aiming for the next crossroads, then he stopped as he passed a small flight of steps against the black marble of a building entrance, on the other side of the road. There was a guy on his side, eyes open, staring at nothing. A sleeping bag, a black plastic bag over the top of it. A green beanie.

Buchan hesitated for no more than a second, then crossed the road, and took a few notes from his pocket, quickly counted, said to the man on the ground, 'Fifty-five pounds. Beanie and the bin liner.'

The guy looked at him strangely.

'What?'

Buchan thrust the money a little closer, on the verge of just taking the beanie from him.

'The beanie and the bin liner.'

The guy's eyes widened. There was a little light in his face. Buchan took it as a yes. He pressed the money into his hand, then took the beanie from him, the plastic bag, and then shuffled down quickly into the doorway, back against the wall, beanie drawn over his head, the bin liner pulled over his body, up to his neck, his shoes and the ends of his trousers all that was visible of his clothing.

The beanie stank, he felt the grime of it against his scalp.

He grimaced, ground his teeth.

'This is my doorway, pal,' said the guy. The light had gone from his face. 'You can fuck off if you think you're sleeping here, by the way.'

'I'm not sleeping here,' said Buchan, his voice low. 'Now shut up.'

'I mean, give us another hundred, you can sleep here.'

'I said, shut up. I'll be gone in five minutes.'

Movement at the door of the pub. A young woman, but she

was there with a purpose, looking up and down the street. Buchan hunkered closer into the wall, the beanie already pulled down to cover his eyebrows.

She hesitated, but he knew she would come this way. It was his obvious path of retreat, back towards the river, and his apartment.

She started walking quickly. She was wearing a loose-fitting, light jacket, Lycra jogging pants, shoes for running in.

Down the road, on the other side, until she got to the crossroads. The look along the road, two cars stopped at the lights, the sound of traffic no closer than a block or two away. Quiet enough that Buchan heard her low curse.

She took her phone from her pocket, considered calling someone, then thrust it back in. Another moment, then she ran across the road, just as the lights changed. A loud horn from one of the cars, she shouted a rough, Glaswegian 'Fuck off!' in response, and then she was across the road, running down the hill.

'Dammit,' said Buchan, and he was up, pushing off the bin liner, and hurrying across the road, 'Give us the hat back, ya bastard!' thrown at him as he ran off.

Close to the wall, beanie pulled low down, he walked quickly after her, as she hesitated once again across the road. She looked round, she looked through him, the beanie seemingly all that it took to fool a quick glance, but her look would return. He didn't have long.

She had her phone in her hand again, as he caught up with her. A couple of people ahead walking in the same direction, no one, as far as he could tell, with eyes on him.

He wondered how rough he should be, knowing that if this was a man, he wouldn't balk at grabbing him, thrusting him against the wall.

These are killers you're dealing with here, said the voice in his head.

She turned as he was directly behind her, his mind still not made up, and suddenly they were standing no more than a yard apart. In between street lamps, shadows cast in the night.

Buchan whipped off the beanie, casting it down on the pavement.

'You were looking for me,' he said.

She stared harshly at him, her moment of surprise disappearing in an instant, and then he could practically see the options flashing through her head, her eyes flickering, as though a machine reading algorithms on the inside of the cornea.

'Tell me,' said Buchan.

He never saw the punch coming. Left uppercut to the jaw, brutal, a practised swing. Buchan's knees buckled. A moment of confusion, of not being able to think anything, and then he collapsed, his head banging on the pavement.

17

A phone was ringing. Buchan's phone. The sound mingled with the sound of falling rain.

He opened his eyes, and had no idea where he was. Black walls. A wet street. Dull lights. No one in the vicinity. Something clawing at his head.

The smell made him shudder, his head twitched sharply, and he felt a little more life come into him. He touched his head, his hand coming to rest on the beanie. The green beanie he'd worn earlier. He took it off, threw it across the small set of stairs. There was no one on the other side. There'd been someone there earlier, hadn't there? The man's things were still here. The sleeping bag was still here. Buchan was in the sleeping bag. The phone stopped ringing.

He'd taken the hat off, but the smell of the bag, of everything else in this squalid doorway, was still rancid.

The phone started ringing again. He breathed in, gagged a little at the stench, reached into his pocket for the phone.

Roth.

He took another moment, couldn't think of anything else, couldn't think any more clearly, and answered.

*

Forty-three minutes later. She'd picked him up. He'd told her to bring a towel for him to sit on in the car, though he hadn't said why. They'd argued about whether he should go to A&E. He'd won. He'd come home, clothes in the wash, then into the shower. The bang on the head hadn't produced any blood. There was a small swelling under his chin where the punch had landed. He felt the lump on the inside of his mouth.

They were at the kitchen table, a cup of tea each. He'd asked for a gin, she'd contemplated just giving it to him, trying not to mother him, and then had insisted a cup of tea would be better medicine in the first instance.

The air in the kitchen still smelled of dinner, though all the leftovers had by now been sealed in plastic boxes.

‘Will you be able to do an e-fit?’

‘Definitely,’ said Buchan. ‘But she was wearing a lot of make-up. A girl of our times. She removes the make-up, puts on a pair of glasses… really, she could walk in here and I’d probably not recognise her.’

‘No outstanding features, huh?’ said Roth.

‘Well she had a gallon of lip gloss, painted-on eyebrows, and gigantic fake eyelashes, but nothing that won’t already have been taken off.’

‘Basically you just got laid out by Barbie,’ said Roth, laughing a little awkwardly as she said it. Then, in response to his rueful look, she added, ‘At least it was MMA Barbie, so there was that.’

‘You’re hilarious,’ said Buchan, unable to stop the smile.

Then the smiles faded, they drank tea, they looked at each other across the kitchen table.

‘So, what d’you think’s going on?’ asked Roth.

‘I’m not sure. They just needed me at that pub for something.’

‘Maybe. Maybe it didn’t need to be that pub. It just needed to be somewhere, anywhere that wasn’t home. But since I was here, and they didn’t try to get in, it wasn’t about that. And since they sent you to a pub that you said was standing room only, presumably they’re not going to try to claim you were elsewhere, because there will be a lot of witnesses to you being at the Killermont.’

‘Hmm,’ said Buchan. ‘I’m not sure. I wonder if there was something about there being too many witnesses. If I’d been the only one in the pub, the staff would remember me. But I was just an old guy at the bar.’

‘You’re not old.’

‘I was in comparison to the crowd that frequent that place,’ said Buchan, then he added, ‘The only way I would’ve been more invisible to them was if I’d been a middle-aged woman.’

‘Nice. Anyway, there’s something else worrying that I haven’t mentioned,’ said Roth. ‘When I couldn’t get hold of you, I tried to track down DI Savage. Got her mobile, and I got her home number. Home rang out, the mobile went straight to voicemail.’

‘Crap. You take it any further?’

‘I managed to get hold of DS Cummins, her sergeant she

brought with her from the old job,' said Roth, and Buchan nodded his recognition at the name. 'He didn't know, but said he wasn't surprised. Said she's been really stressed. Husband's gone, kids at university, work pressure getting to her. She switches off when she leaves the office. The only work thing she'll answer is a text from him, and he'll only text if he knows it's something requiring urgent action. Since they instituted that out-of-hours policy, he hasn't texted her at all.'

'And he wasn't about to start this evening.'

'Exactly. Sure, sounds a little weird, he said. I'll mention it to the boss in the morning.'

'Crap.'

Buchan glanced at the time, wondering where else they could take it at this time of the evening.

'Hmm,' said Roth, reading his thoughts, 'I know, but I think we just have to leave it for now. However, before you do anything else, you should call the chief, let her know how this evening played out.' Then when Buchan glanced at the time again, she continued, 'The time's irrelevant. She won't care, just as you wouldn't care if this had happened to Danny or Samantha or Ellie. Or anyone on the entire force, for that matter. Make the call.'

He was nodding by the time she'd finished.

'Yep,' he said. 'You're right. I'll be quick. Maybe you could heat up a little of the food?'

'Boss,' said Roth.

*

Later, much later, the curtains open, the lights of the night illuminating the room, Buchan lay awake, eyes open, his thoughts lost in the shadows and shapes cast across the ceiling. Roth was asleep next to him, back turned, completely silent.

He was thinking about her, and what him being lured out of the house had meant. Obviously it wasn't about coming for her, because they'd had plenty of opportunity, and they hadn't done it. So what else could it have been?

Were they going to say she'd been somewhere she hadn't, knowing full well that Buchan would not lie on her behalf? She would have no alibi.

But then, there were cameras at the front of the building, there were cameras in the carpark beneath the building. There would be nothing to show her leaving.

At some point, in the depths of night, before the sky had begun to lighten, he finally fell asleep, shuddering awake with the alarm at six a.m.

18

Buchan and Kane in with Liddell, not yet eight o'clock.

Roth had been right to make him make the call to the chief. Kane had been unimpressed to only be told ten minutes previously.

'We need to find the bum,' said Kane. 'If you were left in some guy's place, with all his stuff, then something happened to that guy. And maybe they did what you did, gave him some money and told him to go elsewhere, but that doesn't strike me who these people are.'

'You think he's dead?' said Liddell, nodding along.

'He might be,' said Buchan. 'I think they'll have made a judgement on who he is, and whether they can rely on him. Their m.o. is paying people to be on their side. If they don't want paid, then they get crushed. Or killed. The whole operation is looking for control of the streets, and control relies on information. Some bum lying in a doorway, the kind of person everyone ignores, might be useful under certain circumstances.'

'You're going to speak to E-fit Alex about the bum and your assailant?' asked Liddell, and Buchan nodded. 'OK, good.'

She checked her watch.

'Dammit.'

She lifted her phone, dialled the number. They knew she was trying Savage's office. All she said was, 'Me again,' she nodded at the response, then hung up.

'I think I might be trying the patience of Detective Constable Malcolm down there,' she said. 'Anyway, please, get on. Let's make contact when someone gets eyes on Rose.'

'Boss,' they said, and then turned away.

19

Creating the E-fits with Alex hadn't taken long, Buchan content with what they'd arrived at. They weren't about to go out with them to the public, but they needed to go back to the Killermont with the image of the girl, and they needed to do the rounds of the streets with the picture of the bum in the green beanie.

Buchan was back at the newsagents in Shawlands, interviewing two of the other members of staff, before visiting the third at his home. Kane was following up with the police in Dundee about the phone hacking operation.

A back room. A tea point, a small table, a couple of chairs. A sink. An old calendar on the wall. Boxes of crisps piled high to the ceiling. A couple of forty-eight packs of two-litre Pepsi bottles. A dirty window, looking out on an unkempt courtyard.

The room smelled of cigarettes and desperation.

'How long have you worked here?'

The woman was looking across the table with undisguised contempt. She'd taken the time to make herself a cup of tea, then she'd lit a cigarette. Now, arms folded, smoke rising from beside her left elbow, steam from the mug on the table.

'Nine months.'

'What'd you do before?'

'Why?'

'Building a picture.'

'Why?'

'I know you don't want to be here, but can you not answer like you're five, please. Let me do my job, then you can go.'

The same look, this time accompanied by silence.

'What did you do before you worked here?' he repeated.

'Went to college for a few years. Worked in a couple of bars, 'n that.'

He gave her another moment, but that was all he was getting.

'And directly before you got this job?'

'Universal credit. Then they cunts took it off us.'

'You just work in the shop, or you undertake other tasks for

Mrs McLeod?'

'What other tasks?'

'That's what I'm asking.'

'I work in the shop. That's it. Wee Margaret asks me to do anything other than that, she can do one, you know what I mean?'

*

'Look, I know what they say. There's like some weird phone hacking thing. I mean, when I got this job, my mates were all like laughing n' that, they were like, you're minted, mate. You'll get your own iPhone 15 as one of the perks, and you'll be raking in the cash. Make sure you get commission and all that. I'm like that, literally none of that's happening, by the way. I sell sweeties and crisps.'

He laughed.

'Who does sell the phones?'

A moment, a little of the deer in the headlights, then he nodded, having thought it through to the other side of the answer.

'No one. No one's selling phones.'

'What about Graham Mathieson?'

'Wee Gray? What about him?'

'Did he sell phones?'

'How would I know?' he said with half a laugh.

'We've been told that he didn't work in the shop.'

Another hesitation, followed by, 'Who by?'

'If he didn't work in the shop, what did he do?'

'I don't know.'

'You ever see him work in the shop?'

Eyes a little wide. Not sure what to say, then a small shake of the head.

'You think maybe he was selling phones?' asked Buchan.

Sometimes Buchan's tone worked with interviewees, sometimes it bounced off, leaving them untouched. This guy was beginning to crumble.

'I've got to get back to work, man.'

'Not yet. You think Mathieson was selling phones?'

'Look, I don't know anything about that. They've got their thing, whatever it is, and I've got my thing.'

'Who else was part of the thing that Mathieson was part

of?'

'No way, man,' he said.

And with that he pushed the chair back, quickly got to his feet, and left the room, closing the door sharply behind him.

Buchan stared at the closed door. The stench of cigarettes still lingered in the air from the previous interviewee. This, thought Buchan, is the distilled essence of police work. Sitting in depressing, shitty little rooms, interviewing people that are never, in a million years, no matter how intimidated they feel, going to tell you anything useful.

'Crap,' quietly escaped his lips.

*

Buchan's coat smelled of cigarettes. He left it in the Facel, and entered the small, terraced house for the last of the three interviews in his shirt sleeves. The house was cold.

'Can't afford the heating,' said Cam Leslie. 'You want a jumper, you look freezing, by the way.'

'I'm fine, thanks.'

Sitting at the kitchen table, the scene from twenty minutes previously transferred to someone's home in Giffnock. It was, in Buchan's estimation, no less depressing. The back garden had been paved over. There was a small, dilapidated trampoline, a few barren plant pots.

Inside, unwashed dishes in the sink, the room smelled of onions.

'Tell me about Graham Mathieson,' said Buchan.

'Aye, right. Right. Well, it's pretty obvious what happened.'

'Go on.'

'You're not recording this, by the way, are you?'

Buchan lifted his hands, not that that showed anything. Then he placed his phone on the table, and let Leslie see he wasn't recording.

'You wired up, though?'

'For goodness sake,' said Buchan. 'We're not in some bloody motion picture.'

'Motion picture? Jesus, grandad.'

'Tell me about Mathieson,' said Buchan, gruffly.

'Fine.'

He shook his head, taking another moment thinking over

what he was about to do.

'I mean, you know what's going on here, right? If you didn't, you wouldn't be here. So, why you need me to actually tell you anything, man…'

'It's pretty basic, Cam. We can postulate, and come up with ideas, and think whatever the hell we want to think, but it doesn't amount to anything without witnesses and proof. So, I can't tell you what to say. No point in that, is there?'

'Aye, whatever. But like I say, this is off the record, or I'm shutting the fuck up.'

Buchan nodded, for all that that agreement was worth to Leslie.

'Look, we've got our shitty phone thing. I mean, it's small time, right? In this great, you know, the great scheme of whatever, it's peanuts. But see yon Bridget. She's like a genius, you know. Like an actual, certifiable genius. You met her?'

'No. She's the one who cracks the phones?'

'Aye. Holy shit, man, she's something. I mean, face like a bag of spanners 'n that. I don't mean, you know, I'd shag her or anything. But I've literally seen her break into an iPhone in ten minutes, man.'

'What's she doing working for Margaret McLeod?'

Leslie suddenly became animated, arms raised in an Italianate gesture, looking at Buchan like he'd spoken the most basic truth.

'Right? I mean, right? That's what I keep saying. She could work for anyone, she could work for herself. I mean, she could literally break into any computer network on, like, earth, I really believe that. It's not just phones. And yet, she works for wee Margaret, and Margaret doesn't have the imagination. It's like she's signed Messi, and she's using him to clean the boots.'

'Where do I find her?'

'Don't know,' he said. 'Like these days, since things started getting nasty around here, and Bridget became in demand, I think Margaret's probably got her locked in a basement.'

'What d'you mean, since things started getting nasty?'

'Since, you know, that dickhead Lansdowne started throwing his weight around, like he's some big shot, or something. He's the, you know, like the Man City of Glasgow crime. Ha. Propped up by foreign investment, bastard thinks he's the dog's bollocks.'

'You think Lansdowne took care of Mathieson?'

A pause, a wee smile coming to the corner of his lips, and then the nod.

'Go on.'

'Nothing else to say on the matter.'

'Jesus,' muttered Buchan. 'I'm not recording you.' He lifted his arms again. 'Not wired, no secret listening devices on my person. We need to know we're going in the ri –'

'Fine, fine. Jesus. Of course Mathieson got taken out by Lansdowne. I mean, these bastards may be jumped up and so full of themselves they're about to explode, but see with all that money they've got behind them? You have got to be kidding me, man. They're brutal. It was probably that wee prick of a son of his.'

'Reggie?'

'Naw,' said Leslie, disdainfully. 'Reggie? Big man couldn't slice a cucumber. I mean Michael. The wee fella's decided to go full Al Pacino. Move ahead of his older brother, position himself to take over, you know? Stupid wee bastard's been watching the *Godfather* again.'

'You *know* it was Michael who killed Mathieson?'

Leslie shrugged. A look that at least implied he knew a lot more than he was saying.

'They want Bridget?' asked Buchan.

'Aye. I mean, every bastard would want Bridget if they knew she existed, but most don't. Unfortunately, Lansdowne, and that Polish fucker who's got him by the balls, got to hear about Bridget.'

'And Margaret's not for telling where to find her.'

'Margaret thinks she can deal. I'm like that, no, Margaret, you cannot deal. Not with these people. They offer you terms, you take them.'

'And they killed Mathieson as a warning.'

'Far as I know, absolutely, man. Gray was a wee, wife-beating spanner. No bastard's touching that wee prick. Why waste your energy? Definitely Lansdowne's crew.'

'You have proof?'

'Ha!' A genuine laugh. He shook his head.

'Is Margaret going to accept their terms?'

'Margaret told Lansdowne to fuck off. Think she might be looking around for partners, you know, create a bit of a turf war. A last stand against the new power in the city, 'n all that. Stalingrad multiplied by the Alamo.' He smiled. 'Jesus.'

‘Will she get any takers?’

‘Of course not. You think there’s anyone left to raise a finger to that guy? Everyone’s in keeping their heads down mode. The eye of Sauron gets turned on them, they cave instantly. It’s the only way you survive. Hey, you know what this is like?’

Buchan made a small gesture for him to continue.

‘You know how the west went into Afghanistan because the Taliban are cunts, right? And I mean, I’m not saying they’re no’. Us lot try to impose law and order, stem the drug trade, all that stuff. And how does that go? Exactly. The Taliban, the bad guys, come back, and they’re bastards to women and they kill everyone they don’t like, and whatever, but they have a control the west could never get. If they want to end the drug trade, if they want the opium farmers to have a bad year…,’ and he snapped his fingers. ‘Just like that, and it’s done. Same with Lansdowne and that Polish bastard now. Right here. You lot would love to control crime in the city, to shut it down, do whatever. Not a chance. But those bastards have just swept through here. And see if they wanted there to be no crime in the city for the next six months – and, you know, obviously I don’t mean domestic violence and all that shite – but if they wanted to shut down stolen phone rackets, and cars, and drugs, and women, and everything else you can name, they could do it in an instant.’ He snapped his fingers again. ‘They have a power you lot can only dream of.’

‘I’m jealous,’ said Buchan, drily.

‘So, you should be.’

‘If only the police got to slit people’s throats as an intimidation tactic, think how much more effective we’d be.’

Another laugh.

‘So, who’s next?’ asked Buchan. ‘If Margaret’s not conceding, and Lansdowne’s going to keep coming, who’s next for the chop?’

Leslie stared across the table, then sat back, and spread his arms out.

‘And this is why you’re talking to me?’ said Buchan.

‘This is why I even let you lot discover my existence in the first place.’

‘You want protection?’

Another laugh.

‘Too right, man. Protection times a hundred. That full

witness relocation crap, you know. And I don't mean I want to go to Rothesay, some shit like yon. I'm thinking Yellowknife by the way. I'm talking the middle of absolute fucking nowhere, in a country far, far away. I'd go to Tatooine, if it was an option.'

'That would be Yellowknife, North-West Territories in Canada?'

'Are there others?'

'I'll see what I can do,' said Buchan, and Leslie laughed.

'I'm going to tell you what you can do. You're going to go back to your office, and you're going to get this cleared in the next couple of hours. I want out of here by, like, five o'clock this afternoon.'

Buchan held his gaze, then glanced outside at the trampoline.

'What about your family?'

'Andi buggered off with the bairn three year ago. Haven't seen either of them in six months. Don't care, neither will they. Get me out of here, Buchan. And I'm like, I want far away from Glasgow *today*, before I start talking. You think I trust anyone in this joint?'

'Why'd you trust me?'

'Reckon you're just about as fucked as I am.'

Buchan leant back, elbow on the table, a contemplative, and slightly performative chin rub.

'Not sure exactly what it is you're bringing to the table here, Cam.'

'What?'

'You have proof Lansdowne's people killed Mathieson? Without that, I'm not sure what you can do for us. We could bring down Margaret McLeod, maybe wrap up the Dundee end with it, but where does that get us? My primary task here is catching Mathieson's killer. My sideline is breaking the Baltazar-Lansdowne stranglehold. What have you got that can help in either of these?'

Leslie's face had darkened as Buchan had spoken, though he waited until he was finished talking.

'You'd better help me out here, boss,' he said, leaning into the table, lips peeled back from his teeth, the criminal's demeanour turning on a sixpence. 'See if anything happens to me, it's on you. My blood, your hands. I'm giving myself up here, you bastard, so you'd better take what you can get.'

'And you'll be wanting immunity from prosecution, as well

as your two-million dollar, lakefront property in northern Canada?'

Leslie pushed his chair back, head twitching.

'Piss off, Buchan. And you better be back here by five this afternoon with an armed fucking escort for me to the airport.'

Buchan stared across the table, contemplated an acerbic remark or two, and then silently got to his feet, and walked out of the kitchen.

*

Two minutes after he'd got into the car, his phone rang. Chief Inspector Liddell.

Savage had been found.

20

A small apartment overlooking the Clyde, the view almost identical to that from Buchan's open-plan sitting room.

This apartment was in the same block. One floor beneath, a couple of apartments to the left, closer to the city. Looking directly across at the BBC's Pacific Quay.

Carter from the front desk was talking to Buchan and Kane. They'd brought him up to view the body, to ask if he recognised her.

He hadn't.

'This place was sold a year and a half ago,' he said. 'So, you know how it is, how it has to be in this building. You can have long-term lets, sure, or you can live in your own place, obviously. But no short-term lets, no Airbnb, nothing like that. This place went for just over three hundred and fifty thousand. That's a lot of money for no one to live here, you know.'

'And, really, it's been empty all this time?'

'No. There've been a lot of people coming and going. Building management's spoken to them a couple of times, but this place sure as heck looks like it's been rented out short-term. But Mr Barlow, he's adamant. He has a lot of guests, that's what he says. A lot of guests. How do you argue with that?'

'Mr Barlow?' said Kane, and Carter nodded. 'You ever see Mr Barlow?'

'I've never seen him. Not sure if management have either. I mean, there are people letting themselves into the carpark, you know. I have the monitor. It's not like I know everyone that enters that way.'

'We're going to need to look at everything you've got,' said Buchan. 'Every archive that's not been destroyed from the past year. Starting, obviously, with last night.'

'I'll dig it all out.'

'And it'd be helpful if you could sit with someone as they go through it. It'd likely make it more efficient, and you can point out any anomalies in the people entering the building.'

'I'll get right on it,' he said.

'OK, thanks, John. You should go.'

Carter nodded, acknowledged Kane with a dip of his head, and then turned away, unable to stop himself from taking one last look over his shoulder in the direction of the corpse of DI Rose Savage, slumped on the sofa, her throat slit.

'Mr Barlow,' said Kane. 'You think that's a joke?'

'Why?'

'You know *Salem's Lot*? Stephen King?'

'Nope.'

'A house is taken in a small town by someone that no one ever sees.'

'By the name of Mr Barlow?'

'Yep. I mean, the guy turns out to be a vampire, and I'm not suggesting that correlation, but it's just the situation, that's all.'

'Random guy, unknown to anyone else,' said Buchan, nodding.

'Yep.'

'Crap,' said Buchan.

He was looking at Savage. He'd known she would be dead. He'd known it when she didn't turn up at the bar the previous evening. Perhaps both he and Roth had known it from the moment the text had come in, with its obvious instruction not to call back.

A set-up all the way, except it had been impossible to see what the set-up had actually been.

'What are you thinking?' asked Kane.

Buchan was lost in thought, staring vaguely in the direction of the corpse, his eyes unfocussed. He hadn't seemed to have heard, and then he finally turned towards her.

'I was wondering what good it did them getting me out of here, since they weren't going to try to molest Agnes. And I thought, there's not going to be footage of her leaving the building, so there's de facto proof of her not committing a crime elsewhere. Except... she didn't have to leave the building to do this, did she?'

Kane was looking at him, brow furrowed.

'You think they'll try to pin this on Agnes?'

'I have no reason to think that, other than... why did they want me out of here? Why send me a fake text?'

'Maybe they didn't. Maybe you're reading too much into this. The text really was from Savage, then she got caught out, and never got to leave.'

'Why was she in this building in the first place? She didn't live here. She was brought here for a reason.'

They held the look, until finally Buchan shook it off, shook off the awfulness of what might be coming.

'Come on, let's have a word with Mary, then get back to the office. We need to crack on.'

'Sir,' said Kane.

'Got anything apart from the obvious here?' asked Buchan, approaching the corpse.

Donoghue was bending down beside the body, but now she stood, straightened, stretched her neck and shoulders, and turned towards Buchan and Kane. She looked tired, and more upset than she would usually when examining a corpse.

'I don't like this,' she said.

'No,' said Buchan.

'Once they come for the police…'

'I know.'

'Particularly after Sgt Houston last summer. This is… out of control.'

Buchan didn't have anything to say to that. She wasn't wrong.

'Time of death between eight-forty-five and nine-thirty?' he said.

'That's a little on the nose for me just yet, but it's certainly going to be around there. You have reason to think that's the precise time?'

He nodded, but did not elaborate.

'OK, I'll let you know.'

'Anything obvious about the corpse? Any tells, or potential giveaways?'

'Looks like there's matter beneath the fingernails. You never can tell with that, but it's a start.'

'I think we'll have something for you,' said the scenes of crime officer, who was now standing further back, giving Buchan and Donoghue the space by the corpse.

Sgt Meyers, who headed up the SOCO team. Her voice was flat. More than likely, she'd worked far more with Savage than Buchan or anyone on his team ever had.

'We'll get it to the top of the list,' she said. 'If the DNA's on file, you'll have it by close of play.'

'Thanks, Ruth,' said Buchan.

He glanced at Kane, the conversation unspoken. He'd had the thought that this was going to be Roth getting set up, and now if that was to play out, the investigation had begun exactly as they would have expected. Savage's body discovered by a cleaner who just happened to have been booked for this morning, with DNA of the assailant beneath the fingertips of the victim.

'Anything else outstanding?' asked Buchan. 'Her eyes tell you anything?'

'Yes, good spot,' said Donoghue. 'I think she might've been sedated. I'm guessing she was invited here, under whatever pretence, given a drink, she walked straight into that and did not see it coming, and boom. I would say sparked out on the sofa. Hmm… If there's matter from her attacker beneath her fingernails, perhaps she was just largely incapacitated on the sofa, rather than completely out. I don't know. We'll see how it plays, then I'll get back to you asap.'

'K, thanks, doc,' said Buchan, and with a nod to Kane, they turned away.

21

Buchan had a cup of coffee, and was standing alone at the window, looking down on the river. The water was more agitated today, the waves haphazard, blown by the wind. Rain coming, he thought.

There was always rain coming.

He felt shattered by the morning. Lost. He'd tried to be positive on his return, determined to face head on whatever was coming, but the size of what they were up against seemed to be growing exponentially.

How much effort had it been for these people to kill DI Savage? It didn't seem like much. A smooth, clinical operation. Whatever resources were required, were there for them.

An apartment in Buchan's building, purchased the previous year? Surely they couldn't just have had that, solely for this murder? But if they'd been using this place for other things over the preceding few months, as seemed to be the case, were they now just going to abandon it? The spotlight was going to be on the ownership of it in a way it hadn't been before.

However this was to play out, it was yet another illustration of just how well funded, and how omnipresent this organisation was turning out to be.

And in return, how many man hours, and how much resource, were the police going to be able to throw at it? This, just another murder added to the list. Sure, this was the work of a cop killer, and you didn't have to ask too much of your fellow officers to work overtime in the hunt to track them down. But they already knew the Baltazar gang were cop killers. What else could you do, when you were already doing everything? What else could you do, when there was to be no more funding, no extra help, coming from government.

Do more with less, the mantra of every publicly-funded department for the past sixteen years.

The office was flat, a lifelessness having spread across the open-plan, the same torpor around the building that had haunted them following the murder of Det Sgt Houston. This is my room, thought Buchan, from his position at the window, his back turned to the rest of them. It's on me to get them going. To instil determination. To have them lifting phones, and making plans, and working things out. Sure, they were up against a giant, but sometimes all it took was the slightest thing. The slightest crack in the wall, to bring down the dam.

'Jesus,' he muttered quietly to himself, the cup travelling to his lips, the coffee drunk, the cup lowered.

There was an idea brewing in his head. A big and bold show of force. Throwing everything at them, tackling them head on. But how was he going to muster the determination in himself, before he attempted to instil it in others?

He turned and looked over at his staff. Heads down, eyes on screens. Cherry on the phone. He could feel Roth *not* looking at him. There were two people back there, the back of the long office, that he didn't even know. New in the past two months. The part of the open-plan that didn't come under his section. What could he say to them to inspire them, this old-time detective who had returned from overseas, seemingly on a pale horse, bringing death in his wake?

'Stop it,' he muttered.

The door opened, Liddell entered. She nodded at one or two of the others, then came to stand beside Buchan at the window, and together they turned away from the room and looked down on the river.

Silence for a few moments. Buchan, truth be told, didn't know what to say. She'd come to see him, and he decided to let her do the talking.

'We need a war room,' she said from nowhere, to break the silence. 'I have had...' She stopped, she took a deep breath. He sensed her fizzing with rage. Savage had only been on her staff for a few weeks, but it wouldn't have been any different if it had been one day or fifteen years. 'I have had enough of lying down to these people. I have had enough of this shit, inspector. We need to start fighting back.'

'You being held back by people up the chain?' he asked.

'The continued unseen forces at play within the service? Yes, undoubtedly. I've been told that a decision on the continuation of SCU as any kind of an entity is coming shortly. There's been a lot of fighting internally, a lot of politics. We can presume the politicians and police officers arguing against our abolition have not been bought and paid for, but who knows?

This damned country of ours… Sometimes we're little more than a banana republic. God, we'd give banana republics a bad name. We don't even have the wretched bananas. We're a deep-fried Mars Bar republic. Just as corrupt, and a lot more unhealthy.'

'They're going to have set up Agnes for Rose's murder,' said Buchan, his voice low.

Buchan had already spoken to Roth about it. She'd looked uncomfortable. 'It'll be fine,' had been forced across both of their lips at the same time. *It'll be fine.*

'Why d'you say that?'

'They got me out of the apartment. There's no one to vouch for Agnes. Someone, somewhere, is going to have managed to get hold of her DNA. A hair, a something, and that's what they're going to find on Rose.'

'But why? Why would they come for Agnes? Why not you? Me? Why go to the effort?'

She looked at Buchan, and he returned the grim stare. She held his gaze for a few moments, and then turned and looked at Roth. Roth was watching them, but looked away when Liddell's eyes fell upon her. Then Liddell turned back, glanced at Buchan again, and nodded as she looked back at the river.

'They come for her, but it's about you.'

'Yes.'

'Causing Agnes pain and distress, is going to trouble you a lot more than if they just come at you head on.'

He didn't reply this time. He hadn't thought it needed to be said. Sometimes he felt let down by others' inability to let the obvious go unspoken.

'Damn it,' said Liddell after a few moments. She glanced over her shoulder, as though counting off everyone in the section. 'The ops room is set up for Mathieson's murder?'

'Yes.'

'Right, let's get in there. I don't care what you've got, inspector, I want to hear it. We need an action plan. It's time to go to war.'

She took a step towards the door, then looked around the few desks closest to her.

'Sergeant Kane, Constables Cherry, Dawkins, Roth, ops room, now.'

Then, without looking back at Buchan, she turned away and walked quickly through the door.

Buchan followed, glancing at the others as they rose.

'The whirlwind has arrived,' he said, as he got to the door, holding it open for them to pass through ahead of him.

Displays of determination such as this, born of anger, looked and sounded bold, but he was sceptical all the same. No matter how angry any of them became, no matter what words were passed across the desk inside the small, airless room, nothing would have changed on the other side.

The only things that moved the dial were proof, evidence and witnesses, and they were all in short supply. He still had Cam Leslie, of course, and he couldn't allow himself to forget about him, but he remained sceptical, nevertheless. The only thing to be gained by shutting down Margaret McLeod at this stage, was directly helping Lansdowne.

'You never said how you got on with the Dundee end of McLeod's phone theft operation,' said Buchan to Kane, as they walked along the corridor.

'I'm remembering,' she said, tapping the side of her head. 'Apparently we need to find someone called Bridget.'

'Yeah, Cam Leslie just told me about Bridget.'

'Did he know where to find her?'

'Bridget is Big Foot multiplied by Lord Lucan.'

'Excellent,' said Kane, drily. 'At least that should be straightforward then.'

22

Buchan squinted unhappily at the ceiling.

'What's this?' he said, as though the music coming from the overhead speakers was taking on a physical form.

'Early eighties George,' said Donoghue, as she sliced into DI Savage's stomach.

Kane and Buchan were both wearing face coverings, though it did not hide Kane's distaste. She could not, nevertheless, look away. Buchan, having glanced at the ceiling, looked at the top of Donoghue's head. He'd seen the inside of enough corpses.

'Seems kind of dull,' he said.

She finished making the incision, and then turned and laid the scalpel down to her side.

'It's relaxing,' she said. 'Could do with a little less synthesizer myself, but it was the eighties. It happened.' A pause, and then she added, 'Look at *Electronic Sound.*'

'I don't know what that means,' said Buchan.

'George got hold of one of the first synthesizers. Late sixties. Released the album, *Electronic Sound*. Just noise and sounds really, no songs, but interesting all the same.'

'He was up all night thinking of the title,' said Kane, drily. Then she added, 'Can we talk about the inspector?' indicating the corpse.

Silence for a while, bar the slow, synth-laden chords of *Baby Don't Run Away*.

'We have a problem,' said Donoghue.

She didn't look up. Buchan and Kane waited.

'The matter beneath the fingernails. A couple of small hairs.' She tapped the top of her head, an indication of their origin.

'Constable Roth's,' said Buchan.

'Yes. We have her details on file after…,' and she didn't finish the sentence. It was over a year since Roth's kidnap and ordeal, but it wasn't like any of them needed it explained.

'So, from the bloods, I'm going to say that the inspector

was knocked out. Given that I can't imagine Constable Roth killed DI Savage, something I presume you agree with, I'd say this was a set-up. As we discussed back at the apartment, Rose was likely knocked out not long after she arrived. The evidence was planted, Rose was then murdered.'

They wondered if she was going to continue, but the silence lengthened, and then she raised her eyes, leaving her fingers holding open the stomach.

'She has no alibi,' said Kane. 'It would've been easy for her to get down there, commit the murder, and get back to the boss's apartment.'

'Yes.'

'And the main evidence in her favour is that we know this is bullshit. But we can't be the one's investigating it. It'll have to be an outside force, and they're going to have to take the evidence at face value.'

'Yes,' said Donoghue. 'Feelings, beliefs, won't come into it. She had opportunity, and there's evidence placing her at the scene of the crime. Given that this is there, I think we know that once the results come back from Ruth and her team, there'll be more. And, given the fake phone message that got you out of the house, given AI, given all the tools at the disposal of someone wanting to lay a trap, paint a picture, to frame someone…' She sighed, she shrugged. 'You're going to have a job on your hands.'

Buchan had a low curse on his lips, but he left it there, unuttered.

The effect of Liddell's fighting talk, inspiring him to present his bold vision for attack in the meeting, when he'd even managed to convince himself for a short time, had already worn off. The ill feeling in the pit of his stomach wasn't going anywhere, and certainly wasn't going to be banished by words and determination, the kind of thing aimed at getting a football team, two-nil down at half-time, to get stuck in for the second half.

That Liddell herself had not been convinced by his plan had not helped. He hadn't known what she was expecting.

'Come on,' he said. 'We should get back to the office.'

He sounded defeated. Kane had nothing for him.

'I'll get the report to you when I'm done,' said Donoghue, and Buchan nodded, and turned away.

23

'There's worse,' said Kane.

Sitting in the Facel, the short drive back to the office. Buchan did not respond. He expected nothing else. This was going to keep getting worse. The thought of him and Roth in bed the night before, the flippancy of it, the fun, seemed wrong when the world was burning. When Rose Savage had been dead a few yards away beneath them.

'DI Savage spoke to each of us when she started up the organised crime unit. Me, Agnes, Danny and Ellie. Each of us in turn. It didn't go well with Agnes. Clearly… I don't know much about Rose, but she obviously wasn't sympathetic about Agnes, and her absence last year. And even more unsympathetic about her having handed in her notice. She even brought the war into it.'

'Ukraine, or world war two?' asked Buchan darkly.

'The latter. You think some guy who got traumatised by the Normandy landings got to go home and sit out the rest of the fight? That's what she said. Ignoring, of course, that if someone had had Agnes's injuries after the Normandy landings, they would literally have been sent home, and more than likely would've sat out the rest of the fight.'

Early Friday afternoon, the traffic heavy, the going slow. Buchan waited.

'Agnes was torn by that. Part annoyed, part guilty. She even spoke to me about it, said that maybe Savage was right, that she shouldn't be resigning. Not now. For my part, I was just angry, as was the chief. We told Agnes she was leaving, even if we had to throw her out the door. The chief spoke to Savage, and that was that. That should've been that, at any rate.'

She paused, but Buchan could tell there was more to come.

'The war comment, the disapproval about Agnes leaving, Rose managed to get that in while just arranging a time to speak to her. And when she did speak to her… well, I guess Rose had been put back in her box by the chief, but no one had said anything to her about not bringing up the subject of you. And

Rose was keen to talk to Agnes about you.'

'She hasn't said.'

'No, I guess not. None of the rest of us were there, but Rose's people downstairs heard the shouting. Rose was not complimentary about your part in proceedings. Agnes got defensive. Rose strayed into the territory of you and Agnes as a couple.'

She glanced at Buchan, his jaw set hard.

'Did Agnes give you the download?' he asked.

'Yes.'

'Anything further?'

'Nope.'

'What did the chief do about that?'

'She was more light touch.'

'You mean, nothing?'

'Nothing. Not sure what she was going to do. She might have had to be more hands on if Agnes hadn't been leaving, but since she was, and it wasn't like she wanted to lose Rose, having just got her on staff, she let it go. I think Agnes gave a good enough account of herself, and at least by the end of it she wasn't feeling bullied into staying.'

Buchan sighed heavily, annoyance bristling through him.

'Which means that word got around about that argument,' he said. 'Word got to Lansdowne, and he's used it.'

Kane nodded, staring bleakly ahead at the queue of traffic.

Silence fell upon them.

Buchan had taken the bare bones of a plan into the war room, a little over an hour and a half previously. To put together everything they could on everyone they knew to be associated with the Lansdownes, no matter how slight, no matter how unlikely to gain a conviction, and then to make arrests. A great sweep of them. Late Saturday morning. Cherry had noted that unusually both Rangers and Celtic were playing at three o'clock that day, the Celtic fans, away to Hearts, not having too far to travel. The police could take sadistic pleasure in picking these people up as they were about to head off to a game. And if that hadn't been in their plans, there would be golf to disrupt, or there would be playing football, there would certainly be listening to radios and following it online. 'Petty, perhaps,' Buchan had said, 'but we're going to play every damn card in the deck.'

'What's the plan?' asked Kane, feeling restless.

'You don't like the idea of going big on arrests?' said Buchan. 'To see if we can get a chink in the armour, get someone to break.'

'I do, though I feel it's going to be side-tracked. Agnes is going to have to go home and wait for whoever's given this case, because it has to be out of bounds for us now. More than likely, that's Agnes done, given she's only got a week left. And we know she didn't do this, but let's not assume this plays out in her favour. Either way, it has a long way to run. So, now we go out full force to round up the Lansdowne gang, and with some of these people we know the evidence is going to be flimsy. In fact, some of them? Make that, all of them. If there was anything one hundred percent solid against any of them, they'd already have been nicked. So we make fifty speculative arrests on the back of one of our own being credibly accused of murder. That's how it'll look to anyone on the outside. And maybe we get one of those fifty to talk, maybe we can promise someone something to switch sides, but no one's going to be stupid enough to strike a deal without a lawyer present, and the Lansdowne lawyers will make sure the word gets around. Keep schtum. Rewards for those who do, and, more than likely, death for anyone who doesn't. And don't think the police can protect you from Baltazar, when they can't even protect themselves.'

Silence fell upon them once more.

The traffic edged further along, towards a grey beyond.

24

'You just missed Alan Primrose,' said Cherry, when Buchan and Kane returned to the office.

'Go on,' said Buchan.

'Owner of the apartment where DI Savage was murdered. Ultimately, you'll not be shocked to hear, it looks like it might be a dead end. He bought the place eighteen months ago, intending to Airbnb it. Then the building banned Airbnb. So, he started looking around for a long-term tenant, and then someone, and he's not entirely sure who, came along to offer him more money that he was actually asking for. Not so far off Airbnb levels of money, which for guaranteed year-round occupancy, was a pretty big win.'

'And he really didn't know who it was?'

'It was done with a legal firm in the city acting as intermediaries. We've called them, they don't want to divulge the name of their client. That someone was murdered, doesn't seem to be of concern. We might be able to force the information out of them eventually, but it's going to have to go to court.'

Buchan nodded. Hands on hips, staring at the carpet. Unable to shake the anxiety, its stranglehold on his stomach.

'Sam, you OK to coordinate with Ellie and Danny, see how the list for tomorrow's coming along?'

'Sir,' said Kane.

Roth looked curiously at Buchan, and he indicated for her to follow, then he led her through to the ops room, currently lying empty. Door open, light on, as though action involving the whiteboards and the progress of the investigation was imminent.

They entered, Roth closed the door behind her, they sat down, they stared at each other across the short distance of the table.

'They found my DNA on the inspector's corpse?' said Roth, to break the silence, seemingly more comfortable with the conversation than Buchan.

'Yes. Your hair beneath her fingertips.'

Roth stare was deadpan. They had, after all, been expecting it.

'I have to ask,' he began, and she made a small gesture to cut him off.

'No,' she said. 'I hadn't even seen the inspector in over a week, haven't spoken to her in a month.'

'How d'you think they managed to get hold of your hair?'

'Been thinking about that already. But, you know, if they had people using that apartment, they have people in the building, it wouldn't be out of the question for them to gain entry to your place. And Edelman, bless him, is not much of a guard cat.'

Buchan was nodding. He'd already thought it through, after all.

'The alternative,' said Roth, 'is someone at work managed to get one from my desk, the toilets, the back of my chair…'

Silence came to them again, but Roth was more in control of making sure it didn't take over.

'I have to go home,' she said. 'And SCU can't possibly run the investigation into DI Savage's murder. It'll need to be someone from outside the building, and I'll need to present myself for interview, and very possibly arrest, when that's been lined up. I'll leave now, you go and speak to the chief, wheels are put in motion.' She paused, she added, 'I'll go home and wait.'

'You could go home and pack,' said Buchan.

He made a small taking off gesture. Roth smiled.

'Thanks, boss, but I don't think so. I'll take what's coming. I didn't kill anyone, you know I didn't, everyone on the team knows I didn't. I'll take what they can throw at me.'

'Why didn't you tell me you'd had a fight with Savage?'

She held his look, she took her time. Her tongue pressed against her pursed lips.

'I was embarrassed. She got to me straight off. You know, she found the spot, found the button, pushed it. I'm not sure she meant to, or what she was thinking. Maybe she's lost a lot of staff, maybe she was getting fed up with people giving up the fight and walking away, and then here was me, doing just that…'

'You're not giving up the fight.'

'Whatever. She played her hand, we got past it, I didn't withdraw my resignation. Then she interviewed me. Did it in the open-plan down there. A quiet corner, she called it. She was edgy. I've no idea what was going on. I kind of thought… well this is embarrassing to say, but to be honest, I thought she was probably menopausal. Like that's the only reason a middle-aged woman would get unnecessarily annoyed.'

'Why did you get annoyed?' he asked, although Kane had already given him the answer.

'She was having a go at you. In fact, it was as though she was digging for stuff on you. The others said they got a bit of that as well, but she really went for it with me, presumably because we'd been living together all those months. And I just thought, no… I'm not taking this crap.'

She shook her head, looked away from him, then came back, head still shaking.

'I'm not going to go blowing sunshine up your arse, boss, but you're good at this, you take it as personally, as seriously, as anyone in this building, and I wasn't having her casting aspersions. Just no.' Another pause, a shrug. 'She didn't like my tone. Things got said.'

'You didn't have to come to my defence, but thank you.'

'I'd do it for anyone,' she said, with a small smile.

He nodded, he held her look for a moment, then dropped his eyes.

'D'you want me to move out?' she said. 'I mean, I appreciate the run away suggestion, and I'm not doing that. But maybe I should just go and stay with mum for now.'

'No, don't. If it gets ugly… I mean, even more ugly, then perhaps. But for now, no, please. Be there when I get home tonight. We can talk some more.'

'I may be under arrest by tonight,' she said.

'Go home. I'll speak to the boss.'

'I'll pass what I've been doing on the Lansdownes to Ellie,' said Roth.

'Thanks.'

Another long look, then he quickly got to his feet, squeezed her shoulder affectionately, and then he was gone and heading upstairs to speak to Liddell.

25

Buchan had come for Cam Leslie. They'd exchanged a brief text, they had arranged for Buchan to return to Leslie's home in Giffnock sometime after five.

Buchan wasn't sure what it was he thought he could get from him, but he'd obviously had more to say on the matter of Michael Lansdowne, William's younger son, and if Buchan could get anything at all on Michael, it would be an enormous step in the right direction.

Cam Leslie, however, was not answering the door.

Looking over his shoulder, left standing on the doorstep for over a minute, Buchan shook his head, took the lockpick from his pocket and got to work on the Yale.

It didn't take long.

Into the house, expecting the worst, that Leslie would already be dead.

Nevertheless, the house spoke of silence and emptiness rather than death, and a quick search through the small property revealed nothing more than Leslie's absence. It didn't mean, of course, that he wasn't already dead *somewhere*, but quite possibly he'd just had the call. The instruction. Talk to the police and die.

Buchan stood in the silence of the bleak kitchen for a minute, looking out on the damp, depressing courtyard with its rundown blue trampoline, and then he turned away, let himself out of the house, and got back into the Facel.

*

On a whim he stopped off at a semi-detached, Victorian house in Cambuslang. Home to Michael Lansdowne. He'd smirked to find Buchan on his doorstep. The interview was taking place in the hallway. Long and thin, high ceiling, a metal lampshade right above their heads.

'Never understood you living in a place like this,' said Buchan.

'Childhood home,' said Michael Lansdowne. T-shirt, jeans, hands in pockets. He indicated the lampshade above Buchan's head. 'Once when I was, I don't know, like fourteen or something, I had a cricket ball in my hand. Did a run-up along here, swung my arm over. Wasn't going to let the ball go, of course, just doing that thing you do when you're a kid, right. I mean, look at it. This is a long hallway.'

He indicated the lampshade again.

'Forgot about that, didn't I? Absolutely fucked my hand off that thing, thumb trapped between cricket ball and solid metal.' He laughed. 'Hurt like fuck. Nail came off over time. Had a story to tell, I suppose, but then I looked like a daft cunt.' He laughed again, then quickly added, 'What d'you want? Friday evening, I've got a night out with the lads to get ready for.'

'Where were you last night between nine and ten o'clock?'

He stared blankly at Buchan, and then relaxed his shoulders, and let the smile come to his face.

'I was at dad's. You know dad, likes to have the boys around as much as possible. Don't think he likes spending too much time alone with mum, to be fair.' Another laugh. 'Why?'

'Was Reggie there?'

'Nah. Reggie's got Katie and the kid. Wee Billy. William, named after the boy's grandfather. Nice bit of sucking up there from our Reggie, eh? Won't do him any good, though, will it? If you know what I mean.'

'You think you're in line to be the next chief of the clan, do you?' asked Buchan.

'The clan? Now why would you think that, inspector? Why would you think there's anything at all to be chief of? We're just an average family, doing our own thing. Nothing to see here.'

'I heard you were seeing yourself as Al Pacino in the *Godfather*. You've got the right name, after all.'

He smirked.

'I hadn't heard. Nice. I like that. Al Pacino. But you know what he did after *The Godfather*, though, right? *Scarface*. Maybe that's what I'll aim for.'

He laughed again.

'There was a gap between those movies,' said Buchan, deadpan. 'After *The Godfather* he made *Serpico*. Played the only honest cop in the department. You can dream, son.'

The smirk left his face.

'Really, Buchan,' he said, 'why are you here? You actually

accusing me of killing that Savage woman.'

'No one mentioned DI Savage,' said Buchan. 'How'd you know she was killed between the hours of nine and ten?'

Oh, son, thought Buchan, you are so bad at this. Didn't mean he was lying of course, but he was trying to be cool and glib, trying to control the narrative of the interview with the police officer, and he was very easy to knock from the perch.

'Are you like arresting me, or something?' he asked.

'You'd know already,' said Buchan.

'Fine. I'm busy. Like I said, got a night with the boys in town.'

Buchan looked coldly at him. He had his measure, and for all the theatrics of the nineteen-fifties Marlon Brando act, he still recognised the change in him over the past few months. He was growing into the role, just as Cam Leslie had suggested.

Buchan turned, and then stopped at the door.

'Mind the lampshade,' he said, and Michael Lansdowne grimaced in reply.

26

The murder of DI Savage was the lead item on the evening news. Every channel. Presented as the latest chapter of the war between the gangs and the police. The police depicted as helpless. Understaffed, underfunded, shorn of professionalism and ability, literally clueless.

Liddell had been watching a news report when Buchan returned to the office. There was a six-thirty press conference scheduled. Buchan had earlier offered to take it, knowing he would be refused.

'They're not wrong,' said Liddell, after an excoriating statement on the police from a distant member of DI Savage's family, then she stabbed at her keyboard, shutting down the live feed.

'Did you get him?' she said, with a not-unexpected testiness.

'Gone,' said Buchan. 'Not dead, so there's that. Well, not dead in his own home, at least.'

'Too bad,' said Liddell, who didn't have time for any of these people. 'The more they kill each other, the less there is for us to do.'

'It's not really panning out like that, is it?' said Buchan.

'How's it coming?' she asked, dismissing talk of Cam Leslie with a small gesture.

'Getting there,' said Buchan. Standing with his back to the window, the damp, grey afternoon being brought to a premature end because of the heaviness of the cloud.

'Tell me.'

'The list currently stands at thirty-seven names of Lansdowne and his people, though it's growing. We have just three names that are solid. Arrests could've been made some time ago, they haven't been because either we, or someone else somewhere in the city, wanted them left out there. Not that they're informants, but they're people we hope will lead us to something bigger.

'The rest can roughly be split into thirds. Ones where cases can be made, but under normal circumstances, it's way too close to fifty-fifty in favour of a successful conviction to make it worth anyone's time. A third where it's more twenty-eighty than fifty-fifty. And then a third who we know are associated with Lansdowne, but on whom we have nothing.'

'So what does that look like in terms of numbers for tomorrow? Can you make a big enough of a splash?'

'Currently we're definitely good to go on around twenty-two arrests. We can get more, though. Hopefully by tomorrow morning, we'll be pushing that well into the thirties.'

She was watching him warily, right index finger tapping. He waited for her scepticism, knowing it was coming.

'You like this plan?' she said after a few moments.

'You don't?'

'Not really. I feel like it could be a massive backfire. Or, at the very least, we publicly look very stupid. There've been too many entries in the L-column recently.'

'You asked for boldness,' said Buchan.

'We need to be going after Baltazar and his people, it's them who are running the show.'

'Lansdowne's people are Baltazar's people,' said Buchan. 'The Venn diagram is a single circle.'

'My understanding is they're getting ready to fight each other for control.'

'I've heard talk,' said Buchan, 'but I don't know where it's coming from. You know?'

She didn't answer.

'What about Kasia Adamczyk,' said Liddell. 'We go after her, we get her, we get to Baltazar.'

'Because we don't have it. And we're going against a massive, pan-continental operation. Lansdowne, for all his backing from the Poles, is still a player on our patch. We know him, we know his people. If we can turn even a couple of them, there's a chance we then get to Baltazar.'

Another break, arguments flung back and forth, Buchan with no feeling that he was winning.

'You said you'd speak to some people about manpower,' he said.

She took another moment, finally accepting they were still talking about this plan.

'I'm getting there,' she said. 'I have to be wary of who I'm talking to, which is slowing me down, and I don't want this getting out. I'm very tentatively putting pieces in place. Do those numbers include Lansdowne, and his sons, by the way?'

'Yes. It has to.'

Nothing for a moment, then she said, 'Well, I hope you have something that can stick.'

'What's going to happen with the Savage investigation?' asked Buchan.

She shook her head again, a look of even more annoyance crossing her face.

'You know, if this happened in Edinburgh, those bastards would investigate themselves. Sure, they might bring someone from another unit in, but no way would it leave the city. But Glasgow? We country bumpkins? Obviously we're not capable. Or, more likely, seen as not trustworthy. Edinburgh arrives tomorrow morning on its gleaming white horse. Detective Chief Inspector Gilmour.'

Buchan made a small gesture to show he didn't know the name. Liddell did the same.

'We'll deal with her when she shows. I have my one press conference wherein I shall be as bland and non-committal as possible, and then tomorrow morning, Rose's murder case at least will be off my hands. All our hands.'

And like that, it seemed, the conversation was over.

'I should…,' said Buchan, indicating the door.

'One more thing. We should talk about Agnes,' said Liddell. Her voice had softened a fraction, but still had much of its edge.

'We talked about Agnes. I told her to go home. She's gone home.'

'Whose home?'

Buchan didn't answer.

'Is your apartment now Agnes's home? In the very building where she is about to be credibly accused of committing murder?'

Buchan had not thought it through properly, because he was too close. Appearances counted for so much in the public arena, and this was a case that would be dissected in newspapers and online, and only rarely did anyone come out fighting on the side of the police. With one of them likely to be accused of murdering a fellow officer, the negative attention would be enormous.

'I don't know what you're thinking, or how you're

thinking, or exactly how things are between the two of you, but she needs to move out of there. Eight a.m. tomorrow morning DCI Gilmour will be here, and Agnes will be top of her list. The closer she is to you, the more you get brought into it, and you'll be brought into it quite enough as it is. So, please, have Agnes gone by tomorrow morning. You need to make it happen, as much for the unit as for Agnes herself. I'd appeal to your own sense of self-preservation, but I don't think that's something you actually have anymore.'

Buchan had been sold on it long before she'd finished talking, and he nodded. He wouldn't, after all, need to persuade Roth to leave. She'd already known she should.

'Yes,' he said.

'Good.'

Another look, another moment to see if there was anything else to be said, then Liddell nodded at the door, and Buchan turned and left.

27

He texted ahead, but when he arrived at the apartment just before nine, he half-expected her to be already gone. Not that he'd said anything about that in his text, but he knew she'd already have made the decision. She was managing to be less blinded by tumbling into this relationship than he'd proven to be.

The room smelled freshly of the previous night's dinner. Jacket off, feeling tired and empty, he stopped beside the kitchen counter.

The microwave was running, and there was Roth, standing by a wok, tossing egg fried rice.

'Leftover chicken katsu, with some fresh rice,' she said. 'You hungry?'

Buchan nodded. She smiled in return.

'Get the wine!' she said, with an enthusiasm he couldn't share.

He didn't move. He wasn't sure this was a conversation to be had with the microwave humming, the overhead hob fan on full, and the sizzle of the wok.

'It's fine,' she said. 'I'll get an Uber over to mum's later, you don't have to drive. We can drink and be merry. Mum's not expecting me until eleven-ish.'

He stood staring at her, marvelling at her youthful practicality.

'Get the wine!' she repeated.

*

'This is nice.'

'Thank you.'

'The chief called?' asked Buchan.

She looked at him, working out where the question had come from, then shook her head.

'She said to you that I really ought to leave here?'

Buchan nodded.

'Makes sense. No, she didn't call. I know what you said earlier, but it's daft. I mean, really, DI Savage was killed,' and she made a movement with her chopsticks in a vague direction behind Buchan, 'just down there. I shouldn't be here, this close to the crime. I could be accused of all sorts. Not good for you either, particularly since you've got a bit of a crime-fighting day ahead of you tomorrow.'

'One way of putting it,' he said.

She shrugged an acceptance of the way things had to be, then lifted her glass, made a small cheers gesture, and took her first drink.

'You all set for that?' she asked.

'Things are being put in place, but we're not pulling the trigger until very late. Don't want it to leak. Although, the boss has been making calls, so… I mean, we need to know we're going to have the manpower, but hard to do that without letting people know what's coming.'

'The chief can walk a tightrope with the best of them.'

'We'll see.'

He was going to make a comment about her lack of enthusiasm, but decided against it.

'You're going for Lansdowne?'

'Top of my list.'

She nodded, she held his stare, another of those bottomless looks between them, then she returned to her food.

'I was thinking,' she said. 'We're making this such a big damn thing. This massive, pan-European crime syndicate, against pretty much the whole of Police Scotland. A battle between armies. But what does it come down to? Because you, detective inspector, you're not just one of five hundred law enforcement officers. You were there throughout that first major engagement with Baltazar in Scotland. It was one of your team that was first murdered. You were there when he pulled that Polish diplomatic card out of nowhere, and walked onto that plane in Glasgow. And there you were, you, not anyone else from Scotland or from Poland or Europol, following him around Europe. And for all that he's laughed at you, for all that he's keen for you to feel the hopelessness of your actions… there's no way you didn't get to him. No matter how dismissive he was, he must've had to change the way he did things, the people he saw, because you were his shadow.

'This may be a great fight, and their resources might

massively outweigh ours, but when it comes down to it, it's you against him. One man against another.'

She paused again, and now leant into the table, resting her chin in the palm of her hand.

'Look at it like that, and that's levelling the playing field.'

She raised her eyebrows, then when he didn't immediately respond, she nodded in affirmation to herself, and returned to eating dinner.

'Thank you,' he said.

'One against one.'

'Right.'

He continued eating, he lifted his wine glass. How had the one-against-one dynamic changed with the way things had unfolded in Estonia?

From nowhere, the thought entered his head that this might be the last time he and Roth got to do this, and he tried to banish the notion as soon as it arrived.

Nevertheless, now that everything that had to be said about the case had been addressed, melancholy threatened to settle upon the table, and there was nothing that Junior Mance, playing on the Bluetooth, could do about it.

For a while they ate in silence, the evening creeping in on them, and then Buchan unusually, managed to find something within himself to stop the descent into an elegiacal abyss.

'You've still got a couple of hours before you're calling that Uber, right?' and she looked a little surprised at his tone, and smiled.

'Yes, I do.'

He took another drink, he smiled.

'Eat up,' he said.

*

He felt empty when she was gone. They had put a bold face on the goodbye, but the following day Buchan was going to be part of a great force about to come head-to-head with an impenetrable barrier, while Roth would face interrogation, and potential arrest, for a murder she hadn't committed. However DCI Gilmour intended to play it, Roth was at her mercy.

Standing alone in the kitchen, the aftermath of dinner already cleared away, Buchan looked around the apartment. Low lit, as ever. The lights from the other side of the river bright in the cold night. Edelman curled in a ball in one of the comfy chairs by the window.

The thought flitted through Buchan's head that he could go to the Winter Moon, but was gone in a second. It was well over two months since he'd been there, and he was sure no one would have missed him. He still had some affection for Janey, but that was becoming more and more deeply buried every time he saw Roth. And what other reason was there for heading there? He didn't need Duncan the priest's company, none of the other regulars ever spoke to him, and the principal thing that took him there – Monkey 47 – he had in the freezer.

Decision made, he raided the freezer for the gin, poured a small glass, then turned away from the kitchen and walked to the window.

He took his first sip, allowing his face to contort a little at the strength of the gin. He stared at the night. Cold out there, he thought. Cold for April. The climate change deniers will be chalking up a win, he thought.

Maybe that was another way to frame what was about to play out in the city. The climate apocalypse was coming. Perhaps the conflicts in Ukraine and Gaza would spread, and war would come to the west. A couple of years from now, this would be no more than a footnote. A local difficulty, just another bad thing that happened in a devastated world.

He shook his head at the dark direction of his own thoughts. Took a glance down at Edelman, but Edelman was not there for idle chitchat. Edelman was sleeping, unaware of the ridiculous political games of men.

'I need to shut up and get some sleep,' said Buchan to the room.

Nevertheless, he did not move. Sometime later he took another sip from the glass, his eyes unwaveringly looking out at the night.

28

Saturday morning. Still no news of Cam Leslie. Having ultimately expected nothing much of use from him in return for a life of luxury in Yellowknife – as if that had actually been on offer – Buchan was little more than curious.

Having checked in with the office, he slipped his phone into his pocket, stood across the road from Jimmy's Bistro, thinking through the next few minutes, then committed to what he was about to do, and crossed the road.

He was greeted just inside the door by a smiling young woman, white shirt buttoned to the neck, black skirt, minimal but elegant make-up, hair tied back.

'Good morning,' she said. 'You have a reservation with us today?'

Before she was finished talking, Buchan was already indicating to the table for two by the window on the right, saying, 'I'm meeting someone.'

The maître d' turned, followed his gaze, then came back with a small frown.

'OK, just let me check. I'll be right back.'

She turned away. Buchan gave her a couple of paces, and then walked silently behind her.

'Excuse me, Ms Adamczyk,' said the maître d' as she came to the table, 'but there's a man at the…'

The sentence died on her lips, as she turned to the door, and realised Buchan had followed her.

Kasia Adamczyk regarded Buchan coolly for a moment, then gave the woman a small nod.

'That is OK, Fiona. Please can you get the inspector a coffee, and a selection of small pastries.'

'That won't be –' began Buchan, before he was cut off by Adamczyk's, 'Coffee and pastries, thank you, Fiona.'

The maître d' departed, Buchan watched her for a moment, and then took his seat opposite Kasia Adamczyk at the table. She had a latte, a glass of orange juice, a glass of water, and a small bowl of bircher.

She ate her breakfast, and took a drink of coffee. She did not engage him. He looked around the restaurant. It was already busy, with the feel of the kind of place people came to do business over smoked salmon and scrambled eggs.

His eyes fell on two men, talking animatedly at the far side of the restaurant, a voice carrying through the low level melange of sound. Conversation, and the clink of cutlery and crockery, all to the background of Nina Simone. 'I mean, seriously, we have got to get Ewan MacGregor. Really, Toby, I don't give a flying fuck what he's doing now. He needs this as much as we need him.'

Buchan turned away. Fortunately Toby's voice, in response, did not carry so cleanly across the busy room.

She was staring at him.

'I usually eat alone, Inspector Buchan,' she said.

'If you prefer, we could make an appointment for a more formal conversation.'

'Your breakfast has been ordered,' she said. 'You can stay.'

She took another bite of overnight oats, her eyes now trained on Buchan.

'I would be curious to know what it is a detective inspector wishes to talk to me about more formally. Perhaps you could enlighten me.'

'I thought we could discuss your work with Jan Baltazar.'

She dabbed carefully at the corners of her mouth with a napkin, then laid down the spoon and pushed the bowl of bircher away from her by a centimetre or two.

'I do not know that name,' she said.

'I don't believe you.'

'And I do not care. What else?'

'What is your working relationship with William Lansdowne?'

'I do not have a working relationship with Mr Lansdowne.'

'What kind of relationship is it that you have then?' asked Buchan.

She took another drink of coffee.

She knows everything we know, he thought. We don't have her and Baltazar in the same room, so she can just say she doesn't know him. She knows we have her and Lansdowne lunching together, quite possibly at this very table, so she won't deny knowing him.

It was a stupid game, but he was the one who'd made the

decision to come here and play it.

A waiter arrived with a tray. A cafetière, a cup and saucer, a jug of hot milk. A plate with three mini pastries. An apricot Danish, a pain au raisin, a pain au chocolat.

He laid them on the table before Buchan, then looked at Adamczyk.

'Your second latte, ma'am?' he asked, she nodded, and he turned away.

'We are fucking,' she said, bluntly, then held Buchan's look, challenging him to ask her about that.

'I don't believe you,' he said, meeting the challenge.

'I do not care about that either.'

'How long have you and William Lansdowne had a relationship?'

'We do not have a relationship,' she said. 'We have sex. I do not especially care, but I am sure William would rather you did not pass this information on to his wife.'

He had another question in his head, in his mouth, on the tip of his tongue, then it died before it made its way out into the world. *How did you and William Lansdowne get to know each other?*

Pointless. The words remained unsaid, where they belonged.

He was here to gauge whether she already knew what was about to happen to the Lansdowne gang, but he couldn't even remotely get close to asking the question without giving her a hint of what was to come. His presence here felt valid in itself, and did not give anything away about the morning. But since he couldn't ask the question he needed to up front, he had to have some subtlety, some sophistry to hand, if he was to get anywhere.

Not for the first time, Buchan felt like a worthless hack, clumsily stumbling his way through an investigation, Clouseau without the pratfalls.

He carefully pushed down the French press, the idea of Clouseau in his head, visualising the coffee spurting out onto his face and down his shirt. He poured the milk, poured the coffee. Gave the pastries a glance, the thought of them like dust in his mouth.

'What is your business in Glasgow?' he asked.

'That is interesting,' she said. 'Is that something the police need to know? Is that something the police can demand to know? If I refuse to tell you, what then?'

'Nothing,' he said. 'I'm curious, that's all.'

'Why?'

She held his look, then cast a hand around the restaurant, without taking her eyes off his.

'Why me, of all the people here? Why not the three men in suits over there? Or the woman on her own, typing so purposefully on her phone? Or the two men in the far corner, so desperate for everyone to know they are producing a film? They will not, by the way, ever get to make that film.'

'How d'you know?'

'I know things, inspector.'

'You work in the film business?'

She lifted her coffee and drained the cup, then took a sip of water.

'My business is finance. Finance covers everything. There is nothing on earth that happens without finance. Entertainment, sports, retail, insurance, travel, war… policing.'

The last word spoken with intent. He stared grimly across the table, wondering if she was going to add anything else, but there was nothing. Just the merest bubble of coffee on her lips, a cold, knowing look in her eyes. She licked the coffee away, and then smiled at the waiter as he arrived to replace her drink.

'Thank you, Charles.'

'Ma'am. Everything all right for you?' he asked, turning to Buchan.

Buchan, his eyes still on Adamczyk, did not respond, then the waiter nodded at Adamczyk, and moved away.

'You are not eating, inspector.'

'I ate already.'

'Curious, since you chose to invite yourself to breakfast. Nevertheless, I think it only fair that we go Dutch. We shouldn't make any assumptions on a first date.'

She lifted the orange juice, finished the glass, then took a drink of coffee.

'I have work to do, inspector. I do not feel this conversation is going anywhere worthwhile. You are, after all I have heard, a little disappointing.'

He stared darkly across the table.

'Now, now, inspector, do not look so hurt. We Poles are known for our rather dim outlook on life. Comes with a history of being squeezed between imperialist powers. Eventually, I am sure, we will have generations who do not know oppression.'

'Tell me about your work financing policing,' said Buchan, his voice cold and direct.

This is what he knew and understood. Mutual contempt.

A smile, another trip of the coffee cup to her mouth, another delicate lick of the coffee remnants from her lips.

'What would you like to know, exactly? The amount of private security staff at our disposal? Or how about the name, rank and serial number of every serving officer in Police Scotland currently on our payroll? Or perhaps the list of government ministers and members of the Scottish parliament whose ear we have. Pay for, I should say. It is not just that they listen to us, after all.' A pause, and then she added, 'They also do. They are very compliant.'

'Yes,' said Buchan.

'Yes?'

'Yes, I'd like the names of all the police officers on your payroll, and I'd like the names of all the politicians you've bought.'

'Hmm,' she said, nodding, that awful smile still on the edge of her lips. 'Interesting. And yet, I am not sure that is your job, Inspector Buchan. Not anymore. Not now that the Serious Crime Unit has an organised crime division. I feel that perhaps this would be more appropriate for them. Leave now, go to work, and tell Detective Inspector Savage to give me a call.'

A two-way, grim, cold look across the table. Her jaw hardened, he saw a look in her eyes that he recognised. The one the best criminals had. The toughest. The most brutal. The ones who would fight you until the end. The ones who would not back down, even when backed into a corner and surrounded.

'My mistake,' she said. 'How forgetful of me. Who then will lead that department in Inspector Savage's absence? Yes, of course. Inspector Randall.' Another couple of beats, the look on her face unchanging, then she added, 'Scotland's finest.'

Buchan held the gaze for another moment, took a last drink of coffee, then got to his feet. He reached into his pocket, took out his wallet, extracted a ten pound note, hesitated, then replaced it, took a twenty, tossed it on the table, and then walked quickly to the exit, without looking at her again.

29

‘What did you do that for?’ asked Liddell.

‘I was curious to meet her,’ he said. ‘It was, nevertheless, mostly pointless.’

‘Will she have picked up anything of today’s plans?’ she asked, and to this Buchan replied with a deadpan look, and she nodded away the non-answer.

‘What does *mostly* pointless mean?’ she asked instead.

‘It was good at least to get the measure of her. Not unlike talking to Baltazar. Equally infuriating, certainly. And she taunted me with the amount of police officers and politicians they have on their payroll.’

‘Bitch,’ muttered Liddell, then she shook her head at herself. ‘I take it she didn’t give you names?’

Buchan didn’t bother with an answer.

‘DCI Gilmour in the building?’ he asked instead.

‘Yes. She was here for half an hour getting the lay of the land, then she went down to the fourth floor to speak to Rose’s staff.’

‘She bring people with her?’

‘A team of seven. They’ve been given a couple of rooms in Dalmarnock, and I’ve given them the conference room on three while they’re in our building. That aside, I’m going to leave them to it. Under the circumstances, I feel that’s best.’

‘Did you talk about Agnes?’

‘Yes. She’ll contact her, get her to come in. She’ll interview her first, then make a call on which way to go. A very straight bat.’

Buchan nodded. Nothing else to say on the matter. He had to butt out, let the thing play out as it would. Hope that Gilmour wasn’t one of the ones on the Baltazar payroll, and as that thought was in his head he felt the twisting of his stomach, and sought to dispatch it. They had work to do today, and they were going to have to focus.

‘You get any impression from Adamczyk if they’re aware of today’s operation?’

‘Nothing,’ he said, choosing not to admit to his own feelings of inadequacy.

‘How are we looking?’

‘We’ve got the numbers up to forty-three.’

‘Forty-three arrests?’

‘That’s correct. We’ll never be able to push that number all the way through to conviction, but we can make the arrests, hold them for twenty-four hours. At least half I’m confident we’ll be able to extend beyond that, and we can bring charges against maybe thirty to thirty-five. You never know with the others, we’ll see how it plays. How’s it going putting officer numbers together?’

‘I’ve made some calls,’ she said. ‘All low-key. Add that to the numbers we can call on in the building, and we should be covered.’

‘The right hand won’t know what the left is doing?’

‘The thumb isn’t going to know what the index finger is doing,’ said Liddell. ‘We’ve got this.’

‘Good.’

He stared at her in the dim light of the morning office, then couldn’t help his eyes drifting to the clock on the wall to the side of the door.

Nine-fourteen.

‘Twelve noon is go time?’ she said.

‘As near as dammit,’ said Buchan. ‘Danny and Ellie are putting together the list of suspects, Sam the list of officers at our disposal. If you can pass on the names of the add-ons you’ve managed to rope in, that’d be great.’

‘Mostly already done,’ said Liddell. ‘One more call, then I’ll firm up with the sergeant.’

‘Anything else?’

‘We’re good,’ she said. ‘I will register that I’m still not convinced this will work, but having made the decision, we need to be all in. Crack on, finalise the plans, then give me a shout when you’re about to press go.’

‘Boss,’ said Buchan, and he turned away, purpose in his stride to the door.

30

They'd cleared the whiteboards of all the information regarding Savage's murder, and they'd reduced everything on Graham Mathieson's death to a single board, leaving the other two free for the write-up of the list of suspects, and officers assigned to their arrest.

The boards were packed, a great clutter in Cherry's neat handwriting. He'd updated the list with all the available information, and now the four of them – Buchan, Kane, Cherry and Dawkins – were sitting at the desk, all facing the boards.

'Does this mark me out as being from the nineteen-fifties?' said Buchan, surprising the others with his lightness of tone.

'That you need it all on a board, rather than a spreadsheet?' said Kane, and Buchan nodded.

'Yes, it does, but you know, no one's shocked.'

At the far right of the second board, a list of known Lansdowne confederates they wouldn't be taking into custody, as they'd found no reason on which to hang an arrest. It was from them, and from the wives and husbands and partners, that the word would spread. The Lansdowne gang, wholesale busted one April Saturday at midday.

Buchan glanced at his watch, then at the clock above the door, as though needing confirmation. Just over forty-five minutes to go.

From nowhere, the nerves he hadn't thought would come.

The best way to tackle it, was just to get on with the damned job.

'Right, people, we need to start making calls. Green light to make midday arrests for officers on the list who already know who they're going for, and name and likely location of suspect for those officers yet to be informed of their target. No moves before eleven-fifty-five, then Thunderbirds are go.'

They each already knew who they had to call, chairs were pushed back, and they rose silently with determination, and walked from the room, Kane locking the door behind them on their way out.

31

Every week Rangers played at home, Lansdowne would play his Saturday morning round of golf with his two sons, have lunch at the clubhouse at the Bonnington course on the moor above East Kilbride, and then head into town, usually arriving at Ibrox Stadium sometime after two-thirty.

Buchan and Cherry arrived at the carpark in the Facel Vega shortly before midday, blue light flashing, and siren blaring, shattering the still of the countryside. Doors slammed, they marched quickly into the clubhouse, greeted as they entered by a man in his fifties. Golf slacks and gold sweater, a look of outrage. Buchan walked straight past him to the bar area. Flashed his ID at the steward, who greeted him with a little more respect than the golfer in the hallway.

'We're looking for William Lansdowne, Reggie Lansdowne and Michael Lansdowne.'

'They're not here,' said the steward.

There were currently only seven people in the bar, and the Lansdownes were obviously not there.

'The restaurant,' said Buchan, not having to feign his impatience.

'That was what I meant. They're not in the restaurant.'

'They're still out on the course?'

'I have no idea. The Lansdowne party cancelled their lunch reservation for today.'

Buchan stared at the steward, face impassive.

The first domino.

He felt the twisting of his gut.

'When did they cancel the reservation?' asked Cherry.

'I'd need to check that. They have a set reservation for every Saturday, but it had been removed when I reported for work this morning.'

'You know if they arrived to play golf?'

'You can check in the pro's shop.'

He made a small gesture in its direction, then questioningly raised his eyebrows. Nothing else to ask, Buchan turned away,

Cherry in his wake, and together they walked through the clubhouse, out of the side door, and turned into the pro's shop.

There were two customers, and a young man they took to be the golf pro, standing behind the counter, looking at a laptop.

'Gentlemen,' he said, as Buchan approached, ID held forward. There was an amused curiosity on the pro's face, though it might have betrayed a certain nervousness. 'That was your kerfuffle out there, then?'

'Were William Lansdowne and his sons booked onto the course this morning?'

The pro held Buchan's look for a moment, and then turned to the laptop, quickly bringing up the page for that day's tee times.

'Mr Lansdowne has the same booking for nine a.m. every Saturday. He and his sons are… they're a quick group, regularly playing through others.'

'They've finished their round already?'

'Actually, today, they never started.'

Buchan could feel the weight of it in his stomach.

His phone started to ring. To his right, the ping of Cherry receiving a text.

'They cancelled, or they didn't show up?' asked Buchan.

'They cancelled,' said the pro. 'Not a problem for us, of course, we always have players call on a Saturday morning looking for cancellations.'

'Did they give a reason?' asked Cherry.

There was something in his tone, and Buchan gave him a quick glance. He could tell from his face that Cherry already knew what was happening.

'No. It was one of Mr Lansdowne's staff who called. No reason was given. Obviously, missed tee times have become quite a plague at some courses, but we've never really suffered. We've never introduced a strict turn-up-and-play, or stay-home-and-pay policy. Never had to.'

'That was this morning?' asked Cherry.

Buchan had taken the phone from his pocket, hesitated, then he turned away with a glance to Cherry, passing the interview with the club pro over to him. He answered the phone, hearing the pro's, 'No, yesterday evening, I believe,' as he did so.

'Sam,' he said.

'Malky Seymour's gone.'

'He's just not where you'd thought he'd be, or he's made himself vanish?' asked Buchan, already knowing the answer, clinging to the hope that Lansdowne could be a one-off. However, he knew how this was going.

'The latter,' her voice deflated. 'He's gone. And I've had a couple of calls. And I'm about to ask you how it's going with Lansdowne, and I know the answer.'

'Fuck,' spat Buchan, the word coming from nowhere, and he lowered the phone from his ear, taking another couple of steps away from the counter, hands on hips. Staring at the floor.

'Dammit.'

Deep breath, long, slow exhalation, then he lifted the phone again.

'Sorry.'

'Took the word out of my mouth,' said Kane. 'I'm heading back to the office. I'll collate when I'm there, and give you a call.'

'It's fine,' said Buchan, his voice still on edge. 'We'll be back in twenty minutes. Danny'll catch me up if anything comes in.'

He hung up, he turned to Cherry, who had detached himself from the pro. The two officers stared at each other, but there was nothing to say. They both already recognised the full crushing awfulness of the situation.

They had set their stall on a show of grand force, an overwhelming, crushing blow to the Lansdowne operation, bringing it to its knees, getting as many of them as possible to turn against each other.

And Lansdowne had known all along it was coming, and that show of force had turned to farcical dust, blowing away in the mild spring breeze of the April noon day sun.

32

'What d'you think?'

Buchan, Liddell and Kane were standing on the right side of a two-way mirror, looking at the young woman sitting alone at the desk in the bare room, awaiting interview. Of the forty-three members of Lansdowne's family and known associates that they'd set out to arrest, she was the only one who'd been taken. Or, as Liddell had just observed, had allowed herself to be taken.

'It would seem that way,' said Buchan, 'though she was only added to the list this morning, so it's always possible she didn't get the memo.'

'You think they knew our exact list?' said Kane. 'That they knew at all is bad enough, but if they knew the exact list, then that's a whole other level of terrifying. That's going to have us all, us three, Danny and Ellie, looking at each other, and asking questions.'

'It seems obvious they knew the exact list,' said Liddell.

There was something vacant in her tone, as though she felt haunted by the crushing weight of defeat.

'Not necessarily,' said Kane. 'They could have known we were coming, and the instruction went out across the board. Make yourself scarce at midday on Saturday. We turn up to arrest forty-three people, to find forty-two of them gone, but it could well be the case that a hundred people made themselves scarce today. Two hundred.'

Both Buchan and Liddell were grimly nodding along by the time she'd finished.

'And if that's the case,' said Buchan, 'then there's no doubt that Sandra in there was instructed to give herself up.'

'What's the precise charge against her?' asked Liddell.

'Hate speech,' said Kane.

'Ah,' said Liddell, then she shook her head and added, 'Don't tell me, I don't want to know.'

A heavy sigh, another shake of the head, and she walked to the door.

'I fear this day is only just getting going in its awfulness. I have some calls to make. Let me know how it goes with hate crime girl in there,' and Buchan and Kane nodded, following Liddell from the room.

*

'When was the last time you spoke to William Lansdowne?' asked Buchan.

First question, two minutes since they'd sat down. He'd decided to test Sandra Cunningham with silence, and found that she'd passed without any trouble. She had a quality to her that said she could sit quietly for as long as it took. Buchan assumed she was following instruction. Let the interviewers come to you, don't go looking for questions to answer. Indeed, it was quite possible, he would later observe to Kane, that she'd been specifically selected, as trustworthy and capable of playing the right part.

'I don't know who that is.'

'You've never heard the name William Lansdowne?'

'Nope.'

Buchan opened the slender brown folder lying before him on the desk, took out an A5-sized photograph, and turned it for Cunningham to look at the picture. She did not look at the picture until he indicated for her to do so.

'You know this man?'

'Nope.'

'Have you ever seen his face, had dealings with him, or seen him anywhere in the course of your work or personal life, even though you didn't realise who it was?'

'I don't know him,' she said. 'You can put the question as many ways as you like, the answer's the same.'

Buchan lifted the picture and put it back in the folder, then took out three further photographs. Lansdowne's two sons, and Malky Seymour, one of Lansdowne's lieutenants.

'How about these three?' he said, laying the pictures in a neat row.

Cunningham looked at them, then, placing a finger on each photograph in turn, said, 'Nope. Nope. Shagged that guy at a music festival last summer.'

'Which music festival?' asked Buchan.

She held Buchan's look for a moment, cast a sly glance the

way of Kane, then turned back to Buchan, the smile on her thin, pale face.

'There was no music festival.'

'What does that mean?'

'I never went to a music festival, what d'you think?'

'So, what about this man?' said Buchan, tapping the third photograph.

'Pulling your chain, grandpa,' she said. 'Look at him, of course I never shagged that. Get real.'

'So, you've seen this guy, but you haven't slept with him, or you've never seen him before?'

She smiled again, this time with the small, knowing, accompanying head shake.

'I have never seen him before, officer,' she said. 'Why is it I'm here again? I mean, the lassie said when she was arresting me, but I was so like, what the fuck is going on, that I kind of missed it.'

'You were reported for hate speech.'

'Right, that was it. What was it I was supposed to have said again?'

Buchan stared coldly across the table. They were, of course, liable to get into a mire, and he couldn't let that happen.

'You called a young Asian man a brown, racist cunt,' said Kane.

She stared at Kane, who was holding her look across the table.

'He was.'

'Sorry?'

'He was racist. He called me a white bitch. What's me being white got to do with it? He was racist. He started it. He was the dickhead who brought race to the party. And you saying his skin colour isn't brown? Because I've got to tell you, hen, the guy is brown, that's just the way it is. And this is Glasgow, after all. Cunt's not even a swear word. I call my mother a cunt.'

'So, you're happy to admit that on the twenty-first of December last year, while involved in an altercation on Buchanan Street, you called Asif Malik a brown, racist cunt?'

She laughed.

'Sure, hen, on you go, whatever. What're you going to do? Lock us up for six months?'

'The maximum penalty's seven years.'

'For calling someone a cunt? In Glasgow? There'll be no

one left.'

'For hate speech, which you've just admitted to.'

Cunningham smiled. She glanced at the recording button, which Kane had pressed when they'd sat down, then looked to her right at the mirror running the length of the wall.

'Anyone behind there?' she asked. 'Like, is that where the Netflix crew are? Is this, you know, like the first season of behind the scenes with Glasgow Police Department. You can call it, *Arrest to Survive*.' She laughed, then shook her head. 'That doesn't work, does it. I only just realised, they say *Drive to Survive* 'cos it rhymes. God, I can be stupid sometimes. So, what'll this shite be called?'

'You've admitted to a crime that could lead to seven years in prison,' said Kane. She expected Buchan would be uncomfortable coming to this part. The transparent game-playing. The pointlessness of it, the obviousness, the sheer stupidity and hopelessness, guaranteed to get nowhere. 'So, let's talk about William Lansdowne and see what we can do.'

Cunningham smiled, then turned the smile to Buchan, then to the mirror, then she came back to Kane, stretching her neck and shoulders.

'Give me what you've got,' she said. 'What are you authorised to offer me, if I'm willing to spill the beans on Mr Lansdowne? I mean, I probably won't take it, but you never know, if it's good enough.'

'Before anyone goes making any offers,' said Buchan, 'you need to start by admitting you know Mr Lansdowne, how you know him, what dealings you have with him, and who else within Lansdowne's operation you're familiar with.'

'Fair, I suppose,' said Cunningham. 'OK, let's lay all our cards on the table, shall we?'

She leaned forward, hands clasped, forearms flat on the table, staring intently at Buchan. She was wearing a cheap, sweet-smelling scent, her breath had the distant aroma of mint.

'I've never seen Mr Lansdowne. Sure, I've heard of the old bastard, but I don't know him. I've done some work for some people, because really, have you seen it out there? Have you seen how fucked Scotland is? I mean, imagine how utterly and colossally fucked your country can get when it has a shit government, and then think about Scotland. We've got two shit governments. One down there. And one of our own. We are literally double-fucked. There's nothing out there. There's no decent work, health service is on its knees, you lot are too busy investigating pretendy crimes to be bothered your arse about anything actually happening on the streets. Which would explain, by the way, why when my wee brother got a brick put through his face, the polis never even bothered coming to talk to him about it, while he was waiting *twenty-seven* hours in A&E. Then some guy offers you work, offers you the chance to actually make some money, and it's not doing anyone any harm. So, you know what, you do it. Why wouldn't you? Who wouldn't take the work?

'So, aye, I do some things for Mr Lansdowne, even though I've never met him.'

'What do you do for Mr Lansdowne?'

She held Buchan's look, then leaned a little bit closer into the table, the smile returning to her face.

'This, for example.'

'What does that mean?'

'There were rumours flying around. Then Big Alec says to me – and by the way, Big Alec's not actually called Big Alec – Big Alec says, the boss reckons you're going to get nicked. You could do a runner, but we're going to need you to stand your ground. Stay home, be there when the feds arrive. No fuss, off you go, like a good little soldier. It's a load of shite, says Big Alec, they've got nothing that'll stick against you, but the boss just wants you to pass on a message.' She paused, she looked at Kane, and then back to Buchan, and then the pause turned out just to be silence, and she sat back, her hands clasped on the desk.

'Go on,' said Buchan.

'What?'

'Pass on the message.'

'Oh, right, of course.' She laughed, then she let the fake laugh drift away and once again leaned into the table. 'This is who we are. This is how it goes. You humiliate yourself with every turn.' She hesitated, she looked to the side as though struggling to remember the rest of it, her manner quite obvious and affected, then she nodded, looked back at Buchan, and said, 'When you're ready to have a serious conversation, there are deals to be made with you and your team. When you get home tonight, you'll find an envelope with fifty thousand in cash waiting for you beneath your door. We'll know if you elect to keep it.' Another pause, and then, 'Just think of the holiday that you and your little, pink-haired crack whore could have together. If only she hadn't just been arrested for murder. We can probably do something about that 'n all. If you want to talk.'

She sat back. Buchan was too angry to notice, but Kane recognised the self-preservation in the move. It might have been good for her cause for Buchan to lash out at her across the desk, but Cunningham recognised how angry he'd become, and couldn't stop herself making the instinctive tactical retreat.

Buchan held her look for another couple of moments, then pushed his chair back, said, 'Interview suspended at fifteen-thirty-eight,' clicked the recording system off, and said, 'Come on, sergeant,' to Kane, with none of his despairing rage in the tone.

33

Buchan, Kane, Liddell in the canteen. Cups of tea, a sandwich each. He had sent Cherry and Dawkins home. It was the weekend, after all, and what were any of them doing now? They had objected, they had said there were still things they could be doing, but he'd made the point that none of them knew what would happen the next day, and how long they might have to work, and they would definitely be back and on duty by Monday. Take the break, he'd said, the sergeant and I won't be far behind.

'She didn't say when this fictional Alec character told her to expect arrest, did she?' asked Liddell, after a long silence, that had seen them eat and drink, wallowing in their defeat.

'No,' said Buchan. 'I thought of asking, then chose not to. She'd only have been honest if it had suited them, not us, and we wouldn't have known if she was being honest in any case.'

He took another bite of BLT. The sandwich was, at least, unexpectedly fresh.

'And she told you Agnes had been arrested?'

'Yes. But we don't know that's the case yet, do we?'

Liddell shook her head.

'I haven't heard anything. DCI Gilmour's interviewing her at Dalmarnock. So, either Miss Cunningham knows something we don't, or else she was just using arrest as a general term for being under suspicion. Either way, she knows far more than we'd like her to, but then, that is no surprise.'

Liddell held them both with a purposeful gaze, and added, 'We are being given a royal, two-fisted, arse handing.'

She lifted her tea, took a drink, set the cup back down on the table.

Buchan leant forward. Hands together, chin resting in his hands. Terrible posture. From somewhere, though, an ounce of determination. It was the talk of Agnes, perhaps. Because, however this played out for him, and for anyone else, he couldn't have Agnes getting targeted because he'd allowed her to get close to him.

'Whatever happened today,' he said, not moving his chin from his hands, 'whatever it was that meant they could toy with us like that, it doesn't start with Baltazar, and it doesn't start with Lansdowne. It starts with whoever passed on the information. How many people did you call?' he asked, lifting his head to Liddell.

'Five,' she said, 'but the number doesn't matter. I said something different to all five, and Lansdowne was never mentioned. I'm not sure how any one of those people would've been able to deduce what was going on from my calls.'

'Not unless all five of them are on the payroll,' said Kane, and Liddell immediately shook her head, and waved it away.

'No, I just can't... we just can't go there. The people I called, I trust as much as I trust both of you. One bad apple, possibly. I guess it must be the case somewhere. But not the entire barrel.'

'Isn't that the point of one bad apple?' said Buchan, and Liddell squinted ruefully at him.

'We kept the door of the ops room locked once the information was on those boards, so no one else could've entered and taken note of it,' said Kane.

'You trust Constables Cherry and Dawkins?' asked Liddell, and Buchan was shaking his head before she got to the end of the short sentence.

'This is where we are, isn't it? This is what they want? We're looking over our shoulders, trusting no one, everyone in the team looking for the traitor. This is how we fall apart. This is how we lose.'

Kane looked away. Liddell couldn't help another small snort of dissent.

'*This* is how we lose, inspector? I have news for you.'

'Aye, all right,' said Buchan.

Silence returned.

This was not a conversation to have with any of them, thought Buchan. He needed to work it out for himself. Roth would not be there this evening, and he could go home, and talk it over with Edelman if he had to. The cat was usually good at paying attention when he knew he had to listen.

A movement at the door, and then DCI Gilmour entered. She stopped, she looked around the café, and then walked towards the table.

'You mind if I sit?'

'Of course,' said Liddell, indicating the seat next to Buchan.

'DI Buchan, DS Kane,' said Liddell. 'DCI Gilmour.'

They nodded at each other.

'Would you like us to leave?' asked Buchan.

'That won't be necessary,' said Gilmour. 'I'm just here to pay you the courtesy of an update, before you hear it elsewhere. Detective Constable Roth has been arrested and charged with the murder of Detective Inspector Rose Savage. She'll appear in Glasgow High Court on Monday morning, held on remand until then.'

'What did she say?' said Buchan, his voice unavoidably harsh.

'I'm sorry, inspector?'

'What did she say in interview?'

'I'm obviously not going to discuss that here. And certainly not with you.' The curt dismissal, then she looked back at Liddell, her body language indicating she was already about to leave. 'I've called a six o'clock press conference. I think you can expect the shit to hit the fan, but there's nothing to be done about that now. What's done is done, and given the information at my disposal, we had no option. As far as I can tell, Constable Roth is guilty of murder.'

None of them had anything to say.

'Inspector Buchan, I'll need to interview you formally, as you obviously spent the bulk of Thursday evening with the constable.'

'Of course,' said Buchan. 'I'm available when you need me.'

'Nine a.m. tomorrow morning, my ops room in Dalmarnock.'

Buchan nodded.

'And I would appreciate you not trying to speak to the constable in the meantime.'

She looked coldly at Buchan, Buchan gave her nothing in return. That blank, soulless look of his that others would so often take as contempt.

She gave them another couple of seconds, then nodded at Liddell, gave Kane a small acknowledgement, and then walked quickly from the canteen.

They sat in silence, now heavier than the silences that had peppered the twenty minutes since they'd arrived.

A low, heartfelt, ‘Fuck,’ eventually escaped Liddell’s lips. She did not look at the others.

‘As if the poor girl hasn’t been through enough in the last year and a bit,’ said Kane, finally finding some words.

Under other circumstances, there might have been a joke to be made about her falling in love with Buchan being part of that, but no one was making jokes.

Buchan looked at his watch. Suddenly the building was beginning to make him feel claustrophobic. He had to get out. He had to go for a walk along the river. He had to think. Because whatever was happening, the three of them sitting here with sandwiches and cups of tea wasn’t getting them any nearer making a breakthrough.

Liddell’s phone rang, and she brought it from her coat pocket, looked at the caller, and answered.

‘Liddell.’

She said nothing else, listening to the call while staring directly at Buchan. He kept his eyes on her, but there was nothing in her look, and the voice on the other end was too quiet for him to hear much more than a vague crackle.

Finally a couple of nods, then Liddell said, ‘I’ll deal with it,’ ended the call, and slipped the phone back in her pocket.

She took another drink of tea, set the cup back down, and then lifted the sandwich.

‘I’ve got work to do,’ she said. ‘Calls to make.’

‘What’s up?’ asked Buchan.

‘The Mail on Sunday are looking for a quote. They’ve heard that the full power of Serious Crime Unit was thrown behind a city-wide operation this morning, all hands on deck, costing somewhere in the region of half a million pounds, and don’t ask who it was who pulled that number out of their backside, and all we managed to do was arrest one person for hate speech. And we know what the Mail thinks about the hate speech law.’

Buchan stared grimly across the table at her, and she stared equally grimly back.

‘Where did you get the idea?’ she said.

‘Sorry?’

‘I asked you for ideas,’ she said, ‘and you came up with this. Where did it come from?’

‘Theodin and Aragorn riding out on the morning of the fifth day,’ said Kane, her voice distant and almost whimsical, as if taken utterly by the defeats of the day.

'You think someone put that idea in my head, inspector?' said Buchan, ignoring Kane. 'It was hardly, I don't know, hardly brilliant, original thinking in any case.'

'It just feels like the whole thing was a set-up. This is all a set-up. Agnes's arrest, us making a grand plan and then getting the rug whipped from beneath our feet, made to look fools in the process. And, big surprise, the Mail on Sunday get to hear all about it.'

He held her gaze, his face descending into anger, although she had not sounded at all convinced, as though her words were random thoughts rather than an accusation.

'Whatever, inspector,' she said testily, and then she rose quickly, did not give either of them another glance, and strode from the canteen.

*

'So, how do we make the next plan?' asked Kane.

He looked at her now for the first time since they'd come to stand at the window of the open-plan, and she knew from his face that he'd already thought it through. A moment, he turned away again, his face set hard, his determination apparent.

'I trust you, I trust the boss, I trust all of the others,' he said. 'I'm guessing you're going to say the same. And yet, the leak is coming from somewhere. We've had the place swept, but maybe there's a device we didn't detect. Maybe our phones are hacked. Maybe I had some microscopic microphone inserted beneath my hairline when I was unconscious on Thursday evening. Maybe all sorts of ridiculous tech nonsense we might think more likely to be in *Mission Impossible*. But it's not like these people don't have the resources for that kind of thing.'

'Ultimately we can't trust anyone, even when our head and heart both say that we should.'

'Exactly.'

'So, we work alone?' said Kane.

Buchan continued to look darkly down on the day, the traffic busy on Clyde Street, the river agitated.

'Yes. You and I, we need to do our own thing. The team, as a team, we can work on… well, God, I don't know anymore. We'll need to speak to Liddell first thing in the morning, and see what's left. We might just be back to whatever crap we had before all this kicked off.'

'Don't forget your nine a.m.'

'I'll try not to. But meanwhile, you and I, we need to work out a plan for ourselves, and act on it. Just go ahead, do what you think is necessary. I'll leave it up to you how much you want to risk.'

'Don't you do anything dumb, boss,' said Kane. 'I feel like you're a little off the chain. You were before you went away, and a few months off hasn't really changed anything.'

'I'll do what I have to do,' said Buchan. 'As for you, do what you're comfortable doing. Talk to me when needs be. If we step on each other's toes, then that just has to be one of the consequences. Only when we reach some sort of fulcrum, something that might be a turning point, do we share. And even then, we only do so with the utmost care.'

He glanced to his side. Kane was nodding.

'Yes,' she said. 'That's good.'

Together they looked down on the river. From the left, a long barge, low in the water, was slowly heading upriver.

'Like the breaking of the Fellowship,' said Kane, after a while.

A moment, then Buchan couldn't help the smile.

'You're going full Middle Earth, sergeant.'

Kane smiled in response.

'Theodin and Aragorn riding out on the fifth day,' said Buchan, head shaking, voice low, and Kane laughed.

'So, I watched those movies last weekend. You should watch them again. Wonderful escape, in these dark times.'

The laughter, the quiet smile, died away. Outside the afternoon drifted towards early evening.

'When Lansdowne hangs from a gibbet for the sport of his own crows…' said Buchan grimly.

Kane gave him a quick glance, nodding approvingly.

34

Buchan stood at the door of the Winter Moon, and looked around the old place. It felt like a lifetime since he'd been here.

Of course, it hadn't changed, although it was a Saturday evening and the bar was busier than usual. Nevertheless, the players were all in position. Janey behind the bar. Duncan the Pakistani priest at the counter, a bottle of Heineken in his left hand, a pencil in his right, bent over a killer sudoku puzzle. Herschel and the other guy were at their usual table, talking animatedly this evening. Leanne, the Butcher's wife, was in the far corner, reading a book. Sinatra was singing *It Had To Be You*.

He lifted his head slightly, drawn by the music. Not Sinatra, just someone who sounded like him. Bobby Darin. He shook his head, settled on Harry Connick.

Janey, having served a customer who was turning away with a trayful of drinks, noticed Buchan's arrival, and looked at him across the bar. She smiled. Duncan noticed the movement, and turned his head. Buchan finally closed the door behind him, accepted that the great peregrination of the last couple of months had ultimately led him back to exactly the same life he'd left behind, walked to the counter, and sat on his usual bar stool.

'Hey,' he said, taking in both Janey and Duncan.

'Inspector,' said Duncan.

Janey held his look for a while, then turned to the freezer, took out the bottle of Monkey 47, placed the glass in front of Buchan and poured him a double.

'On the house,' she said.

Buchan held her gaze for a moment, then lifted the glass, toasted her and Duncan, and took a sip.

Sharp and brutal and ice cold as ever, the gin biting the back of his tongue, warm and intense on his throat.

'You back at work?' asked Janey.

'Started on Thursday.'

'How's the eh… you know, the thing?' asked Duncan.

'The investigation into my misconduct?' said Buchan, his

eyebrows raised, amused at Duncan's slight awkwardness, and Duncan nodded. 'Not sure. Still there, waiting for me, like a shark lurking in the depths. How's it been?' he tagged on at the end, turning to Janey.

Janey laughed, indicating the bar.

'Picking up, I guess. It's not that anyone has any more money, I think they've all just decided to spend it on alcohol rather than food or heating, in a desperate attempt to drown out reality.'

Buchan nodded. She was being facetious, but there was going to be something in what she said. And it was this setting, too. The Winter Moon. Like stepping back in time. For some, to a moment when they were much younger; for others, a world they knew from old movies. The crooners and the jazz pianists, the black and white photographs on the wall, the feeling of being in a different world, in another era.

'Agnes was here a few times,' said Janey.

Buchan looked a little surprised, though the expression did not last on his face.

'She didn't say,' he said.

'Maybe she thought we'd have news of your travels. D'you have a good time?'

Buchan wasn't sure whether Janey would actually know he'd been working.

'Not really,' he said, simply. 'Good to be home.'

'You didn't bring Agnes with you tonight? The two of you not going steady, then?'

There was an attempt at lightness in the question, a joke in it, a mild teasing, but Buchan nevertheless picked up on the subtext. A neediness, perhaps? Jealousy? Maybe the remnants of it, he thought, but Janey wouldn't really care.

'She's been arrested for the murder of DI Savage on Thursday evening.'

The gin bottle, which Janey had still been holding in her cold hand, slipped, but only had an inch or two to go before it clunked onto the counter.

'What?' she said. 'That's… insane.'

Buchan nodded. He took another drink. He allowed himself a glance at Duncan, who was shaking his head, looking at Buchan with incredulity.

'What's going on at that place?' asked Janey.

'I don't know.'

‘That’s awful. How’s she doing?’

‘I don’t know,’ said Buchan. ‘There’s… I won’t say how it played out, but Agnes and I were together at my place. I went out for a while. During this period, DI Savage was murdered. Consequently, now that Agnes is in custody, they don’t want me speaking to her. And… they’re right. I need to stay out of it.’

‘Really?’ said Duncan, and Janey nodded along, having just been beaten to the expression of surprise.

‘Really,’ said Buchan, his voice hardening, then he took another drink.

‘If the police have arrested her, and you’re not getting involved, who’s on her side?’ said Janey. ‘Who’s looking out for the poor girl?’

Buchan wasn’t going to answer. Despite the collective weight of all the horrors that had been happening in the past few days, despite the seeming inevitability of their defeat, he refused to believe that Agnes would ever end up in court.

The whole thing with Agnes was aimed at him, of that he was sure, and Agnes had been right when she’d said that this boiled down to a case of him against Baltazar. One man against another, using whatever they could. Agnes was a pawn.

This was where Buchan was at. Not only was he finding it impossible to make a move, he wasn’t entirely sure who or where his pawns even were.

Perhaps all his pieces had already been taken off the board.

‘I can’t talk about it,’ he finally allowed himself to say, feeling the weight of accusation from Janey and Duncan, and then he saw that Janey understood, and he felt the loosening of her shoulders, the slight retreat from the conversation.

‘However it plays out,’ said Janey, ‘try not to do anything stupid.’

Buchan held her gaze, and then couldn’t help the slight laugh, the shake of the head.

‘Sure,’ he said. ‘I’ll see what I can do.’

The look lingered a little longer, than he turned to his left, as he lifted the glass and drained it.

‘How’s business, father?’ he said.

‘Slowing down, sadly,’ said Duncan. ‘That’s three chapels have closed in Glasgow in the past six months now. Sunday mornings ain’t what they used to be.’

A nod, a sad reflection on the gradual diminishing of the old societal norms, and then Buchan turned back to Janey.

‘Top you up?’ she said.

‘One more for the road,’ said Buchan. ‘Better get back to Edelman, he’ll be feeling lonely.’

He knew, however, that what he was really going back for, was an envelope of fifty thousand pounds pushed beneath his door.

Janey poured the drink, he nodded, he lifted the glass, paused, and then downed the shot in one.

*

And there it was, as foretold by Sandra Cunningham. A well-packed brown envelope lying on the floor of the hallway.

Buchan closed the door behind him, and stared down at it. He’d been wondering what he would do as he walked here, and had yet to make up his mind. Maybe he could put it in Edelman’s litter tray.

We’ll know if you decide to take it.

How would they know? If he put the cash in a drawer for use later on, when all this madness was over, how would they know? How would they know if he left it until Monday morning, and then went to the branch of the Royal Bank on Gordon Street that he occasionally used? Was it because they had him followed everywhere, or because they had eyes on his bank account? If the latter, why not just deposit the money? Nothing in a police officer’s life was quite as suspicious as tens of thousands of pounds appearing in their account.

So what was the point in the cash?

He looked up, wondering if there was a microscopic camera somewhere. Perhaps there were such cameras all over the apartment.

How small could cameras go these days, he wondered. He had no idea.

‘Dammit,’ he muttered, as he stepped over the envelope, hung his coat on a peg by the door, beside Agnes’s black jacket, and then through into the open plan.

Everything was in its place. No lights on, the curtains open, the room illuminated by the last of the day out west, and the lights on the buildings across the river.

A meow from the chairs by the window, and then Edelman eased himself slowly down off the seat, and walked across the room towards him.

Buchan let him approach, then kneeled down and stroked his ears.

'You're stuck with me this evening, I'm afraid,' he said.

Edelman seemed unconcerned. Buchan scratched his back, and then got to his feet. Round the counter, turned on the under hood lights, opened the freezer, and surveyed the selection of ready meals for one. He hadn't looked in here since he'd returned, and he noted the contents of the freezer were more or less the same as when he went away.

He took out a chicken supreme, removed the cardboard cover, pierced the film lid, and tossed it into the microwave.

'How about you, you hungry?' he said.

Edelman was licking his leg. He didn't answer.

'And what are we going to do about that thing at the front door? An envelope full of cash.'

He looked at the cat. Any answer that was going to be forthcoming was really going to have to come from within, and it wasn't happening. He'd thought already of getting Carter up from the front of the building, and getting him to take it away. An independent witness to the fact he was refusing the offer. But then, that would be involving Carter in the drama, and he didn't want to do that, even in such a low-key way.

'I know what you're thinking,' he said to Edelman. 'If there's a traitor at the office, someone I've trusted all along who's going to be revealed at the death as the fly in the ointment, this is all shaping up for it to be Agnes. It would be perfect. The miserable detective finally seems to have found someone to bring a little bit of light into his life, and then, bang, there we go. I get shafted. It turns out Agnes is the one who's in the pay of Baltazar. Agnes has been betraying me all along.'

He rubbed Edelman's ear. Edelman didn't really seem to be paying any attention.

'That's just not how this goes,' said Buchan. 'And in any case, it's been done already. Vesper Lynd, *Casino Royale*. It's not going to happen again, not even in real life.'

Edelman pressed his head more closely against Buchan's hand, in a gesture of agreement.

'No idea who it is, though,' he said. 'But you know, I just have to stick to what I said to the sergeant. From now on, I do everything on my own. You can help if you like.'

Edelman stretched his back, his claws clicking against the wooden floor.

35

Buchan knocked on the door at eight-o-one. Sunday morning, the day dawning bright and fresh. From here to Dalmarnock would only take about fifteen minutes, given the paucity of traffic on the roads. He didn't want to be late for his interview with DCI Gilmour.

The door opened on the third knock. A man in his mid-forties, dressed in pink and yellow Lycra.

'What?' he said.

His demeanour did not fit the vibrancy of his clothes.

'Detective Inspector Buchan. I was wondering if I could speak to Mrs McLeod.'

'What d'you want to do that for?'

'You're Mr McLeod?' he asked.

'Like that's any of your business?'

Buchan answered with familiar silence. Albeit, it wasn't familiar to Colin McLeod.

'Whatever,' he said. 'Stand there, I'll see if she's free.'

He slammed the door shut.

Buchan did not move.

*

'Whose side are you on?'

Colin McLeod had left on his bike, to meet up with a cabal of fifteen other middle-aged men, an iridescent packet of Spangles, intent on blocking the roads on a Sunday morning. Margaret McLeod had been in the kitchen, in her pyjamas, making breakfast. She had not got dressed, she had not stopped making breakfast. Buchan had noted the coffee machine, and accepted her offer, while refusing a bacon and egg roll.

The kitchen was an untidy bourach of expensive equipment, and spoke of enough money to indulge in kitchen accessories, but not enough money for a kitchen upgrade to allow better use of space.

Buchan always found himself agitated by this kind of

clutter. He'd been here five minutes, and already wanted to leave.

She asked the question, then bit into the roll. Rich, yellow yolk spewed out. She lowered the roll, chewing ostentatiously, wiping the side of her mouth with the corner of her hand.

Buchan settled the coffee mug down.

'There are no sides,' he said.

'Oh, I think we both know there are. This is the way of things, inspector.' Another bite, which she then talked through as she chewed. 'On the one hand you've got this leviathan, and then you've got the little guy getting crushed by the leviathan. You're really going to choose the side of the monster?'

'I'm against you both.'

She laughed, and took another bite. There was a further egg splurge, some of the drip missing the plate, and landing on the table, with an accompanying mutter of, 'Shite.'

'You can't be,' she said, wiping the spilled yolk with a finger, licking her finger. 'Your trouble is you haven't accepted your place in this yet. You haven't accepted how things are going to be. The either/or of the situation. You are not eradicating all organised crime in Glasgow this month. Just not happening. Of course it's not. So that's not your choice. Your choice is, you get rid of the monster and return Glasgow to where it was last year, just with a slightly different line-up, or you lose to the monster, along with everyone else, and the monster has dominion.'

She smiled. There was a small piece of bread at the side of her mouth. She took a slurp of tea, the bread remained undisturbed.

'Tell me about Bridget,' said Buchan.

'Bridget? Ha. Interesting. What d'you know about Bridget?'

Buchan didn't answer. She stared at him curiously, the roll suspended between mouth and plate, then she used it to think out loud, pointing it at Buchan.

'Wait, it was Cam, right? Eejit.' She laughed, showing Buchan the masticated contents of her mouth, then took another bite of roll. 'Arsehole's probably dead by now.'

'You don't know what's happened to him?'

'Nope. Thought maybe he'd done a runner, like the pussy that he is.'

'I don't think it's that.'

'No? How come?'

'Tell me about Bridget,' said Buchan, surprised she hadn't just denied the name outright. Indeed, in immediately concentrating on how Buchan had learned the name, she'd confirmed Bridget's existence.

'I'm not telling you about Bridget.'

'How d'you manage to keep her to yourself? Someone with that skillset must be in demand.'

Now they came to the interviewee's natural reticence. There was no way she was just going to give up information on the phone hacker. Buchan had decided he would just have to play the moment when it came, see which way he could bend it.

'You need to talk,' said Buchan. 'Because you're right, of course. Do I want to shut down your shitty little phone theft op? Of course I do. But if it doesn't happen, it's not that big a deal, is it? But I one hundred percent need to shut down Baltazar. So, if that means we work together, then let's see if there's anything we can agree on.'

'Well, ain't that big of you, chief. But here's the thing, what's Bridget got to do with it anyway? She's not on the board here. I mean, I might have things to tell you, things that could help you out, but I have absolutely no idea what you think you can give me that's equal to me giving up Bridget. Bridget goes, so does my operation. I'd have nothing.'

'Why aren't you training replacements?'

Another laugh. She took some more roll.

'You serious? Bridget's literally the only one who has a clue, and she's not training anyone. Not so good with people, our Bridget. Tends to a get a little conversationally hamstrung. It's, I don't know, quite endearing sometimes.'

'What age is Bridget?'

'Ha, there we go again. Is that some expert prodding from you, there? You think I'm suddenly going to slip up. She's twenty-one, five-foot-five, and lives in Cowdenbeath as a blonde, long-haired man named Roger.'

She laughed a little more.

'I want to use her,' said Buchan.

'I'm sorry, what? You want to use her?'

'Yes. Presumably Bridget is the reason you're being targeted. Low-key operations like yours are ten-a-penny around here, so why is it Baltazar's coming at you? Bridget, and Bridget alone. Mathieson's dead. Cam Leslie vanished, and, let's be realistic, also liable to be dead. There aren't many of you left, and soon enough when Baltazar's thugs knock on another door, it'll be yours. Just remember these are the people who took out the entire Bancroft gang in one evening, and they're better organised now than they were back then. So, you might want to consider your position.'

'And you think Bridget's going to be safe with you lot? Youse lot are crawling with Baltazar's people.'

'You know who?' he asked, and she laughed loudly, a small amount of food spitting onto the table.

'What are you like? You give yourself away, Buchan. You're clueless. Flailing around. What's that line the guy says to James Bond? You're a kite dancing in a hurricane. That's you, Buchan. Like I said, absolutely clueless.'

'So, let's say I'm on your side,' said Buchan, ignoring the jibe. 'How does that look from your perspective? What are you giving me to allow me to work with you?'

She took another bite of roll, the food almost finished, a couple of chews, then popped the rest of it in her mouth, immediately taking a glug of tea. Then she wiped her mouth with the sleeve of her pyjamas, something she managed to do, thought Buchan, with more elegance than was deserved of the action.

'This is the problem, you see,' she said. 'Normally I'd want protection. Normally I'd want immunity from prosecution, some shit like that. But you can't promise me *anything*. You're a dead man walking at that place. What if you say, sure, we'll have coppers at your front door until this is all over. Really? How do I know those coppers aren't bent? How do I know some other bunch of coppers won't put a bullet in the back of the heads of the ones out there? You have no authority to promise me anything.'

'Maybe not,' said Buchan. 'So, all you can rely on is me getting the job done. If Baltazar gets vanquished, doesn't matter what I've promised you, does it? You benefit either way. So, sure, let's be on the same side. You give me information, I get things done, we both win. That's how this goes.'

She rubbed the base of her chin, then made another pass at the corners of her mouth with the edge of her hand. Continued to stare at him as she lifted the mug of tea, this time managing to take a drink without it being a loud slurp.

'Interesting,' she said. 'Let me give that some thought.'

‘You know the name Brian Ferguson?’ asked Buchan, out of the blue, and for the first time since he’d sat down, he realised he’d managed to get somewhere. The shadow across her face, the slight distancing of the eyes, followed by the inevitable head shake.

‘You don’t know that name?’

‘Never heard of it.’

Another drink of tea, this time with the return of the ostentatious slurp.

‘I don’t believe you.’

‘Really? Why?’

‘I just said the name Brian Ferguson out of nowhere, you were taken by surprise, you hadn’t prepared, and boom, there it was. In your eyes, and all over your face, clear as day. You know exactly who Brian Ferguson was. Which is interesting.’

‘Is it, now? If you say so.’

‘So, what is a small-time phone theft operator doing lying about the death of an MoD tech guy? I mean, you could just have said, sure I’ve heard of him, the guy got murdered, it was on the news. But you lied.’

She took another drink, drained the mug, then set it back on the table, shaking her head.

‘Whatever. Now that you say it, fine, that guy. Since Baltazar took over, every second cunt’s getting murdered. No one’s remembering all the names.’

That’ll do, thought Buchan. It wasn’t much, but it was something to go on. She certainly wasn’t going to voluntarily give him anything useful.

He checked the time, thought through how any further conversation was likely to go, and then pushed the chair back and got to his feet. Took a last drink of coffee, although he’d allowed it to cool too much, then set it back down on the table.

He reached into his pocket, took out a card, and passed it across.

‘If you think of anything that might be mutually advantageous for us to know, give me a call.’

‘Mutually advantageous,’ said McLeod. ‘Right.’

And with a nod, Buchan turned away and walked quickly from the house.

36

Buchan was standing at the window of the small room on the third floor of the Police Scotland HQ in Dalmarnock.

It didn't take much, sometimes, he thought. In this instance, a look that had passed fleetingly across Margaret McLeod's face, that was all. Nothing more. A snap of the fingers and it had gone. But it had meant something, and that, whatever it was, felt like the first worthwhile thing he'd stumbled across since he'd started the investigation.

Brian Ferguson had been in tech. Obviously, in some capacity or other, Bridget the phone hacker was in tech. This was what any detective was looking for. The unexpected crossover, and this one made sense.

Now he needed to go and speak to Ferguson's wife, who remained, as far as he was aware, the police's main suspect. He imagined he'd make up his own mind fairly quickly on her likelihood of guilt, but it wasn't about who'd killed him. It was about whether Ferguson had had any connection to Bridget.

Nevertheless, he understood he needed to remain onside with his own service for as long as possible. And so, here he was, standing at another office window, looking down on the River Clyde, this time a couple of miles upstream from his usual spot, the river narrower, and up above the weir, where the tide did not reach.

The door opened, a moment, closed again. Buchan didn't turn. Gilmour came and stood beside him, looking down at the water. She had a cup of coffee in hand.

'No one offered?' she said, indicating the cup.

'Just had one, thanks,' said Buchan.

They stood in silence. There was nothing to see. The river was quiet at this point. No one on the path running alongside, no one on a boat or a kayak. Beyond the river, spring trees and a familiar, grey industrial estate.

'What's the plan with Constable Roth?' asked Buchan, breaking the silence. The words had just appeared, despite his determination before entering that he hadn't been going to say anything.

'Court in the morning. I expect her to plead not guilty. I'm meeting the procurator later today to discuss. Given that she's accused of killing a fellow officer, to be honest I have absolutely no idea how that will play out, bail-wise. If she is released, I think it would be a very good idea if she didn't come to stay with you again, particularly given the location of DI Savage's murder.'

Buchan didn't reply.

'You're working today?' asked Gilmour, and Buchan nodded. 'Is it related to Jan Baltazar, or anything around the murder of DI Savage?'

She was looking at him. Buchan didn't return the glance, his dead-eyed stare aimed at the river.

'No,' he said.

'OK. Obviously you don't have to tell me what it is –'

'My department still has the murder of Graham Mathieson from Wednesday evening on our books,' he said. 'Far as I know. We're focussing on that for the moment.'

'Graham Mathieson,' said Gilmour, as though she needed reminded of it, and then she nodded. 'OK, well, I expect you want to get back to that, and I certainly have a hundred things to do today, so why don't we just get on with this. I've read your statement already, so I know the situation by and large, but if I could just set myself straight on a few things.'

Buchan nodded, and then turned away from the window, walked around the desk and sat down, as Gilmour took her position opposite.

She sorted through a few papers, she lifted a pen. She clicked it in and out a few times. Then she placed her phone on the desk and said, 'You're OK if I record this?' and Buchan said, 'Go ahead,' and she started the recording and noted the date and time.

'How long have you and Constable Roth been having an affair?' asked Gilmour, looking straight at Buchan.

Expressionless, he held her gaze, wondering if that had been a serious question. The bluntness of it, the intent in the attack. Then he realised that that was exactly what his first question would likely have been in this circumstance.

'We began a relationship on Wednesday evening.'

'Last Wednesday? The day you returned from the continent?'

'That's correct.'

'And the following day, Constable Roth committed murder. That's quite a journey she went on there.'

37

He was still unhappy as he parked the Facel Vega on the wide street in Bearsden. He had spoken to Gilmour for an hour and a quarter in the end, and at no point had he manged to get a handle on her. Who she was, her motivation, what angle she was taking. He hadn't been trying to lie to her, of course, he hadn't been playing a game of any sort. He'd been in a position to be entirely honest about everything. Yet he'd come away discomfited, feeling she'd got the measure of him in a way that people didn't usually manage to.

He looked up at the large, detached house, got out of the car, locked the door and walked quickly up the garden path. He had to put the interview with Gilmour out of his mind. There was only one way for him to help Roth. He had to crack this case. And not just Graham Mathieson, or the two-month old murder of Brian Ferguson. The whole damned Baltazar ring had to be brought down, Lansdowne with him, and if it wasn't, then Buchan was going to have to be taken down trying.

He rang the bell, then took a step back, hands in pockets, and turned to look around the neighbourhood.

Large, detached, Victorian houses. Granite mostly. Each one a slightly different style, but all cut from the same cloth. Bay windows at the front, driveways and lawns, well-established trees to the front and side.

The door opened in the neighbouring house, and he glanced along, a few yards to his right, Buchan able to see little more than head height across a five-foot hedge.

A woman emerged, carrying a baby in a car seat. She looked curiously at Buchan, then turned to the door, baby in one hand, backpack looped around a shoulder, another bag looped over her arm, and locked the door behind her.

'Excuse me,' said Buchan, and she turned, annoyed. The face of someone wanting everyone else to know they're not in a position to talk. 'You know if Mrs Ferguson is at home?'

She shook her head, looking aggrieved at having been asked the question, then, as she was turning away, Buchan produced his ID card, and said, 'Detective Inspector Buchan, Serious Crime Unit. You have any idea where she might be? You know if she's travelling?'

The woman stared across the hedge, hanging on to the look of irritation.

'I think she goes to church on Sunday.'

Buchan automatically checked the time. Ten-forty-three. He still had time to grab her before the service started, as long as it was close by.

'You know which one?' he asked, just as the woman was turning away.

She paused, and although her head was now turned, Buchan could feel the disdain radiating from her.

'The Old Parish. It's, you know, two blocks away. I think she walks.'

She made an impatient gesture, and it was only then that Buchan realised the church bell was ringing. Then she was walking away, her feet crunching over gravel, to her car.

Buchan watched the back of her head for a moment, then brought out his phone, checked the location of the church, thought about it for a moment and the regular difficulty of parking at any church given that the old parish churches had obviously never built with parking in mind, and walked quickly from the house, heading to his right to take the first left.

It was a three-minute walk at a clip, no more. Along a side road, where the houses were slightly more modern, but still large, then back onto another wide boulevard, with houses as large as the ones he'd just come from. Above the trees, set back from the road, he could see the church steeple straight ahead, the bell now clear in the still morning. A couple of cars on the road, but little other sign of people.

He arrived at the gates of the church at the same time as a woman with a walker, another woman at her side with a stick. He awkwardly returned their smiles, they allowed him to go ahead, and he walked up the church path, past gravestones and bare oak trees, towards the nineteenth-century building, a church like any other.

There were three people standing in the vestibule, the morning's welcoming committee, and Buchan wondered if this small collective would make up about half the congregation, the smiles dying on the faces as he produced his ID and said, 'DI Buchan. Is Mrs Lana Ferguson here this morning?'

He was immediately greeted by silence, which he recognised as two of the people, the two women, deferring to the man to answer, and the man disapproving of the arrival of the police.

'Really?' he said finally. 'Has the woman not been through enough?'

'I'm not here to put her through anything, I'd just like a quick word.'

'Good grief. How many more words can the police have to say to her?'

Buchan stared grimly at him. The man looked at his watch, wanting to tell Buchan there was no time before the service started, but it wasn't yet ten-to-eleven, and he scowled, turned away and walked to the door to the nave, then stood and indicated down the right hand side.

'Lana is there. We would all be grateful if you weren't too long about it. And please do not make a scene.'

There were three women sitting on the right hand side, and although Buchan was tempted to ask which one was Lana Ferguson, just to irritate the man further, it was already apparent, as there was only one of the women in the right age demographic.

Buchan walked down the aisle, turning his back on the church elder without a word. The organ was playing, the music not religious, and Buchan struggled to pick out the tune as he walked. Something from the fifties, the setting and the instrument throwing him off, making him unable to place it.

ID still in hand, he came alongside Lana Ferguson, sitting at the end of the pew.

'DI Buchan,' he said, continuing with, 'Sorry to trouble you here,' as she looked at him with the kind of disdain with which every officer was well acquainted. 'Wondered if I could have a quick word.'

'Well, I'm not going anywhere. You've got ten minutes, or else you can wait until after the service. And I'm on the tea rota today, so I won't be free until after one.'

She shuffled along the pew a few feet.

Buchan sat down, card in his pocket, and then had a quick look around. There was no one within three rows, not that it particularly mattered. He leant forward, forearms resting on the back of the next pew. About to speak, she cut him off with a small laugh.

'He pullsh a knife, you pull a gun. Sorry, did I steal your line?'

He glanced to his side, the mockery on her face. She looked tired. Mid-forties, bags under her slightly bloodshot eyes. She drinks, he thought, though he could not smell it on her.

'Who d'you think killed your husband?' he asked.

The mockery vanished from her face, replaced by curiosity.

'That was unexpected.'

'Why?'

'In about eight hundred hours of questioning, you people only asked me that once. Even then, I could tell it was a throwaway. You know, it was sarcastic. And yet here we have a new player in the drama, and it's your first question. Like that's the main reason you're here. Straight down to business.'

'It is the reason I'm here,' he said. 'When you were asked that previously, you laughed at the question and told the officer she didn't give a shit what you thought, so why would you bother answering.'

'Well, she didn't give a shit. All she was interested in was me incriminating myself, or me finally submitting to her detective genius, and scribbling down a confession. But I didn't kill my husband, she obviously had no proof that I did, because there is no proof to be had, and that was all there was to it.'

'So, who do you think killed your husband?'

Another look, this time with a little more consideration. Like she was assessing Buchan the person, rather than the question.

'OK,' she said, 'you're serious. Well, I'm not sure. He was talking about something at work that sounded dumb and illegal, and once you start getting into shit like that, then who knows? Well, I mean, *I* don't know. I don't know that kind of criminal underworld crap. Neither, should I say, did Brian.'

Buchan asked the obvious question with raised eyebrows, and she nodded an acceptance that that itself had been less than half a thing.

'There was someone at work who was raking in cash on the side,' she began, her voice low. 'A lot of cash. When Brian started talking about it… look, we didn't have the best of marriages, all right? You'll know about that, your colleagues were happy to rake through every damned coal they could find. I tended not to pay too much attention.

'He starts talking about this thing, this woman with a side

hustle, a side-line in trainers, you know the kind of thing. You have a contact at the Nike store. When there's some new, limited edition running shoe, you get a call, you get in there as soon as they go on display, they always sell out in like ten minutes, and then they've instantly got a fifty percent, or even more, mark-up price on the resale. You take your split with the kid in the Nike shop, everyone's a winner. It's not new, it's not that big a deal. And I was just looking at him like, *shoes*? You're talking about shoes? Finally, we're having some big fight one day, and he says, course it's not *fucking* shoes. And I was like, what are you talking about? And he says, in a stage whisper, like the Chinese are listening, he says, phone hacking, it's phone hacking, what did you think? And,' and she stopped for a moment, a heavy sigh, head shaking. 'I just thought, oh, *fuck* off, Brian. You have trouble remembering your own Disney password, you're not hacking in to anything.'

She was done, although Buchan did not immediately ask anything further on the off-chance there was more to come. Eventually he had to press with a small gesture, and, 'What else?'

'There was nothing else. I wasn't interested. I admit, there wasn't much about Brian that interested me, and I was contemptuous of pretty much everything about him. He was a selfish idiot. And he couldn't shut up, like he was always trying to impress me with some new bullshit or another. I was always thinking, *fuck* me, Brian, read the room.'

Every time she used the word fuck, her tone dropped, the word emitted in near-silence.

'There was no further information on the phone hacking?'

'I didn't care, I really didn't.'

'What about the woman at the office who was making money from it?'

'What about her?'

'You didn't get a name?'

'Ha.'

'You didn't get a name?'

'I didn't get a name.'

'Does the name Bridget mean anything to you?'

'Bridget? Nope.'

'You know the names of anyone else in Brian's office? How many people worked in his section?'

'I don't know exactly. Like I say, I had absolutely no *fucks* to give about his work. Look, I presume you're new to the investigation, but it's all been gone over before. You'll find names and whatever on file, I'm sure.'

'You mentioned the phone hacking thing previously to the police?'

'Like I said, they didn't care.'

'Who did you speak to?'

Eyes raised while she thought about it. Buchan took a moment to look around the congregation. The church, though still quiet, now noticeably busier than it had been when he'd arrived, and he looked quickly at his watch.

'Randall,' she said. 'That was her name. Detective Inspector Randall. Something wrong about her. You know her?'

'And you told DI Randall there was someone at Brian's work who was a phone hacker?'

'Not in so many words. I did the same thing I've just done with you. Started talking about the trainers. She barely let me say anything, and I was pretty quick to thinking, *fuck* you. If you don't want to know what's going on, no skin off my nose. She was so sure, they all were, that they were going to find some amazing piece of evidence against me. And yet, some of us knew there was nothing to find.'

Around them the voices in conversation began to lower, and Buchan turned, as there was movement at the front of the church. The door to the rear opened, and a man in grey emerged carrying a large Bible, the minister in long black robes walking behind.

'Thanks for your help,' said Buchan, abruptly, and with a last glance, he was up out of the seat, and walking quickly back up the aisle, Lana Ferguson watching his back as he went.

38

He would've called the office for information at any other time. He really ought, he thought, to just call the office now. But that wasn't the spirit of the working pattern that he and Kane had agreed upon, and it applied to every aspect of it. It wasn't just about keeping things from the ops room, or not discussing specific details and plans. It meant both of them doing all of their own digging, all of their own research and paperwork.

DC Cherry was in the open-plan, looking for guidance, and curious to know what Buchan was working on. Stay on the Mathieson death, he told him, and he did not give an answer on the other matter.

He found the file on the Brian Ferguson investigation. He felt there were obvious questions to ask Cherry to clear things up, and to establish the veracity of what he'd been told by Lana Ferguson, but he couldn't afford to voice out loud that he was chasing down the Ferguson case, hoping it would lead to the in-demand phone hacker.

Of course, there had been no reason, two months previously, for anyone to be specifically interested in a phone hacker. The knowledge of the existence of Bridget and her potential part in the drama, was only a couple of days old. Nevertheless, it had been remiss of the team to not pursue other avenues of enquiry beyond the apparent obviousness of the wife's guilt.

Perhaps talk of Randall's ineffectiveness had not been exaggerated. That he had yet to speak to her, or even come across her in the office, was not lost to him. Nevertheless, he wasn't going to go looking for her now.

He left the office twenty minutes after he arrived, a clear path in front of him for the afternoon.

No sign of Kane, he wondered what she was doing, but he stopped himself lifting the phone. Their paths would cross, he thought, soon enough.

*

A large back garden, then a low wall, with open moor beyond. A bright early afternoon, he found Brian Ferguson's boss, Cameron Johnstone, at home, sitting at a garden table, with a bowl of olives, a glass of rosé, and the Sunday Times, for all the world like it was the middle of summer. He wore a gilet, as concession to the fact it was early April, with the temperature struggling to hit fifteen degrees.

'Oh, that,' said Johnstone, after Buchan had asked about Ferguson.

Buchan hadn't sat down. He didn't want to. He didn't want to get comfortable. Maybe this wasn't much, and maybe this was still a few steps removed from where he needed to be, but there was something about this, about being here, that felt like progress.

'Thought you were here about me calling that indolent little dickhead Harvie a scrotal bag of ineptitude last week. I mean, that's all you polis are nowadays, isn't it? No time to investigate burglaries, or assaults. You might, and that's a pretty big caveat, you might investigate a murder, but you're mainly here to do your master's bidding. The private army of the Scottish government.'

'I'm literally here investigating murder,' said Buchan, annoyed that he was allowing himself to be drawn into the argument. It was not, after all, like he disagreed with Johnstone's causticism at Police Scotland's government-mandated priorities.

Johnstone took a drink of wine, took a glance over his shoulder, and then shrugged.

'Fine, whatever. Only two months too late for Brian. What was it you wanted?'

'How many people worked in the section with him?'

'Nine,' said Johnstone. 'Not including me. Well, nine including Brian, and surprise, surprise, the decision's been taken not to replace Brian. Look at that, the company shaved fifty-seven grand off the wage bill in one fell swoop. That was easy, wasn't it? Too bad the rest of us have to pick up the slack, but they magnanimously declared their complete confidence in our ability to handle it. Like we were supposed to be flattered.'

'How's it been?' asked Buchan conversationally.

'We've been getting by. Trouble is, that's what we do, isn't it? Staff everywhere, in every line of work. They have pride in their own thing, so they keep chasing, they keep working, with more and more to do in the face of all this crap that gets dumped on them from above.'

'D'you think there was any possibility Brian was killed because of something at work?' asked Buchan, changing tack.

Johnstone leant back in his seat, looking curiously at him. Right hand tapping on page seventeen of the newspaper.

'Interesting,' he said.

'Is it?' asked Buchan. 'You think it's possible?'

'Well, I don't know. I mean, I literally cannot believe the police haven't been able to nail that awful wife of his.'

'You know about her?'

He laughed.

'We knew all about Lana. We'd all seen it in action. Wow, the tongue that woman has on her, and I don't mean that in a good way. She is vicious.'

'So, nothing at work?' asked Buchan.

'I don't think so. I mean, hereabouts, we're literally running the computer systems for army personnel. Army records, postings, promotions, discharges, etcetera. And we're not even on the army side of things, you know, we're purely aiming to make sure the system ticks over. We're there if there's a crash, and we're there if there are attempts to hack, that kind of thing. As IT jobs go in the big bad world of computing, we're very low down the ladder. No offence to the people in my section, but we're Albion Rovers in a world of Real Madrids, you know what I'm saying?'

'Anyone doing anything on the side?' asked Buchan.

'You mean, officially more than one job, or actual moonlighting? You know, like unofficial, off-the-books shit?'

'Either,' said Buchan.

Johnstone held his gaze, the easy stream of chitchat finally coming to an end, Buchan recognising that there was something to be said here, and he was weighing whether to talk about it.

'Nothing,' he said eventually.

'Tell me.'

Johnstone laughed.

'Tell you what? Like I just said, there's nothing.'

'I don't believe you,' said Buchan. 'Tell me about your staff. Who's got something on the side?'

Another laugh.

'I'm just not throwing anyone under the bus here,

compadre. Just not doing it.'

'D'you have anyone there with the name Bridget?'

Johnstone's brow furrowed, he did at least give it some thought, he shook his head.

'Nah.'

'No names that could be bastardized into Bridget?'

'Like what? Bridgerton?'

'You've not thought about this before obviously, so think about it now,' said Buchan. 'Have you heard the name used before? Could there be someone in the next section perhaps, someone else in the building that maybe has dealings with your office?'

Johnstone started to shake his head, and Buchan held up a hand and said, 'Think about it, please.'

He got a bit of an eye roll in response, then Johnstone looked away and stared across the low wall, out over the moor.

Buchan loved being by the river, but it would be nice, right enough, to sit out here, with this much space, this much emptiness before you. To watch the weather come in from the west. And incredibly, there were no wind turbines in view.

A moment, Johnstone turned back to Buchan, and this time looked a little disappointed he was unable to help him, and shook his head.

'Sorry, nothing.'

'You have any outstandingly skilled people on your staff?'

There was the question. Like speaking to Margaret McLeod a couple of hours previously, he recognised it right away. The moment when Johnstone knew why Buchan was here. Because obviously, yes, there was an outstanding member of staff.

'What does that mean? Outstanding?'

'Come on. Exceptionally skilled in the work of your office. You said you sort system crashes, you guard against hacking. Computer companies employ hackers, either to try to hack their own security, or to run their own security because they know the kinds of tricks and devices a hacker would use.'

Perhaps Johnstone hadn't known who it was he was actually trying to protect in his reticence, but in an instant it had become obvious to him, and Buchan made a *just tell me* gesture, as though they'd been here having this conversation for an hour.

'What?'

'Let's just get to it,' said Buchan. 'Brian told his wife he wanted to work with someone at the office who had a small side-line in hacking.'

'Oh, no…'

'Just tell me the name, and I'll be out of your hair.'

'No. None of my staff have that kind of side-line. And Brian? What was he going to do? Brian was a computer illiterate, who'd stumbled into the department.'

'Who's the hacker?'

'There is no hacker.'

'So, if you don't tell me, what happens now is that I go away, I get a court order to allow me to see the personal files from your section, and I find out who has the skills relevant to my search. And then I get to speak to them. Because that's all I want to do, and it's going to happen anyway. Though, of course, it could be that I need to protect them. And the sooner that happens, the better for everyone.'

'Why?'

'Because someone's out there looking for them. I know who this hacker works for, and one of their colleagues just died, two days ago, protecting their identity.' He paused. He definitely had Johnstone's attention now. 'Murdered. Knife in the heart, knife across the throat.'

'I heard about that.'

'I bet you did. The killer wanted to know who the victim's operation are using as a phone hacker. Now maybe it's some total stranger to all of us. Someone whose name hasn't even cropped up yet. But what if it's not? What if it's this person in your section? Either way, your dibs on her are about to end. She's either getting nicked by us – which I've got to say is much the better option – or she's getting,' and he finished the sentence with a hand run across his throat.

Johnstone was sold. He might not have been about to instantly spill the beans, but Buchan had cracked the nut, and the name was coming.

'Shit,' muttered Johnstone, and he turned away again, his look aimed in the direction of the vast open space, his eyes seeing nothing.

39

Buchan was back in the city centre. He was aiming to go to a studio apartment just off the Gallowgate, but had stopped off at the Stand Alone, the Jigsaw Man's café, for something to eat first.

'His name's Tom Parkin,' Johnstone had said.

'Where does Bridget come in?'

'I've never heard that name. Either you've got completely the wrong person, or Tom's using a nom de plume for whatever it is you think he's doing. I'll be happy if you've got the wrong man. Maybe you could just leave him alone, if that's the case.'

'There's no trans issue here?' Buchan had asked.

'Trans?'

Buchan had stared at him.

'Oh, right, trans. I mean, seriously?' was all Johnstone had had to say to that.

Buchan had requested that Johnstone didn't immediately pick up the phone and warn the kid he was coming. Nothing to stop him of course, but Buchan knew he'd managed to persuade him Parkin's best chance of survival was the police getting to him first.

He bit into his chicken and roast tomato panini. If Johnstone had made that call, the kid would already be gone. If he hadn't, there was no reason why the kid would be on any more of an alert now, than he had been this morning.

Of course, there was always the possibility that Margaret McLeod – assuming the young man working for Johnstone was the same person using the name Bridget – had warned him to make himself scarce, as there were people far more dangerous than Buchan looking for him.

He took a drink of coffee, his mind in neutral. Downtime. Twenty minutes not thinking about the case.

Like Dr Donoghue's lab, the Jigsaw Man's café regularly played the Beatles. Today, something from *Help!* or *Rubber Soul*. In Buchan's head, they blended into each other. The Jigsaw Man himself was in his usual spot, sitting at the back of the café. Today, he wasn't paying so much attention to the jigsaw. Sitting back, toying with a mug of coffee, and a glass of water. Buchan had caught his eye, and they'd nodded.

He wondered how Agnes was doing. Second day in custody. She had a stoicism he admired, but he knew her well enough now to recognise her vulnerability. She would not, at least, be scared, and hopefully they'd allow her mother to visit today, even if none of her colleagues were able to get anywhere near her.

What next for when she got out? He couldn't countenance the idea that she wouldn't. That she would be convicted. He had too much belief in himself, or perhaps too much belief in the system not allowing itself to be overrun. Either way, he was convinced it would work out fine, one way or another.

And then what? Forgetting the politics and the great gang war overtaking the streets. What about the two of them, just two people like so many others, in the middle of a much wider drama sweeping through all their lives?

Was he to come out the other side of this with a partner? For the first time in forever, someone permanently sharing his life. It had been so long since he'd had another's feelings to take into consideration.

He drank coffee, he waved away the thought. Think short term, it was easier. Agnes was looking to go to the Alps. They could go together. Stay in one of those eye-wateringly expensive Swiss hotels around the Jungfrau and the Eiger. Walk in the mountains during the day, drink wine and make love in the evening.

'Jesus, Buchan,' he said to himself.

There was a movement by the table, then the chair opposite was pulled out. The Jigsaw Man.

'Mind if I join you?' he asked.

He had his mug of coffee in hand.

'Sure,' said Buchan, unable nevertheless to stop the, 'I need to be heading off soon, though,' that automatically came into his head.

'No worries,' said the Jigsaw Man.

He sat down, he seemed to be evaluating Buchan, his manner entirely good-natured.

'I saw Agnes was arrested for murder,' he said. 'That seems unlikely.'

'It is.'

'You're working on that?'

Buchan smiled, a curious smile, not entirely sure why the Jigsaw Man had come to talk, though reading nothing nefarious in it.

'I'm afraid not,' he said.

'Too close, and therefore not allowed?'

'Correct. Sadly, plenty of other murders going around.'

The Jigsaw Man nodded.

'You look tired,' he said. 'Worried. I mean, of course you're worried. Agnes'll be fine, though. These things have a way of working themselves out.'

'Right always wins in the end?'

The Jigsaw Man smiled.

'As Carl Jung says, we should not pretend to understand the world only by the intellect. We apprehend it just as much by feeling.'

Buchan smiled again, a more natural smile this time.

'I'm not sure that helps.'

The two men looked at each other across the table, then lifted their cups and took a drink. Buchan, out of nowhere, remembered that life wasn't just about him and his own dramas.

'What's up?' he asked.

'You wondering why I've come to talk to you?'

'You had a look about you over there. A restlessness.'

'Agnes said exactly the same thing to me last week. Restless, yes, that's it. I don't know, I've been sitting here for a while now, you know. People come and go. Life. Rain sweeps across the city, and the river keeps on flowing.'

'You thinking there must be more than this?'

'Not sure that's it. Because is there more than this? Maybe not. But I think I need a change. Maybe I'll move on for a while, that's all.'

He turned and looked out of the window, lifting his coffee and taking a drink as he did so.

'I'll see. Hey, I should let you get on.'

'You ever hear the name Jan Baltazar?' asked Buchan.

The Jigsaw Man looked a little curiously at him, though he stopped short of immediately shaking his head.

'Or have you ever had anyone in the city try to muscle in on your business? Like a protection racket?'

'We don't get that here. I hear things, though, so I know what you mean. Seems to be getting ugly out there, and I don't just mean the rats. But not us.'

'Why?'

The Jigsaw Man nodded an acceptance of the question, then looked around the café. Quiet again. It was usually quiet.

'I guess we're kind of under the radar. People, I don't know, seems like sometimes they walk right past the door and don't even realise we're a café. Like, not everyone can see us, you know?'

Buchan felt as though he was stepping once again on unfamiliar ground. It was comfortable talking to the Jigsaw Man, but it felt like a discussion that belonged in another world. Like talking to Roth. If it was anyone else, Buchan would likely have asked what he'd heard, and how he knew it was ugly out there. But that wasn't who the Jigsaw Man was, and whatever path Buchan was to take to untangle the mess of this investigation, it did not run through his café.

The Jigsaw Man rose, pushing his chair back. 'I'll see you again in a day or two. Bring Agnes with you next time.'

He smiled, Buchan did his best to return it, and then the Jigsaw Man turned away.

40

A studio apartment.

The words spoke of a particular type of place for a young, single man living in the city. Twenty square metres, a sofa bed, the flatscreen on the wall, a tiny, narrow desk, a sink, a kitchen worktop with space for a microwave, but no hob; a door to a tiny toilet/shower area. No storage, lots of clutter. A smell of damp. Wooden windows that needed replaced, or PVC windows that had been done thirty years previously, and needed replaced.

The kid would spend his days huddled at the desk, on his laptop, phones plugged into his computer, trying to make the hack. Maybe he'd written his own program, allowing him to run through the phones, breaking into them, stealing information or wiping them as he saw fit, at a rate of several a day.

Buchan had been wrong.

The studio apartment was in a converted loft, with new Velux windows in both sides of the roof, and a large round window at the gable end. Lots of light, lots of space, a high ceiling. Kitchen at the far end. A dining area, with a table that could seat six. A double bed, then a lounge at the opposite end from the kitchen, the enormous television on a low cabinet, large speakers on either side. A feeling of expensive quality about the furniture and fittings. The bathroom, through the door next to the bed, would presumably be equally lavish.

'I've saved up.'

'You've saved up?' said Buchan.

'Aye.'

'How much did this place cost?'

'I don't have to tell you that,' said Tom Parkin.

'I'll be able to find out easily enough,' said Buchan, 'so why don't you just tell me. The quicker you tell me stuff, the quicker I let you get back to whatever it is you're doing with your Sunday.'

They were sitting at the table. No drinks. Nothing offered. Parkin was too young to think of the courtesy of it, not even to consider it and decide Buchan wasn't worth it. Nor had he considered, thought Buchan, that a mug of coffee can be a good thing to hide behind.

'Four-seventy-five,' he said.

'Seems a lot for someone who's more or less a civil servant.'

'Like I said, I saved.'

'What age are you, Tom? Twenty-three? Four?'

'Twenty-two.'

Buchan let that piece of information sit there for a moment, but it was obviously him who was going to have to pick it up.

'How long have you worked for Upsilon Systems?'

Parkin knew where this was heading, and was answering in instalments.

'Two and a half years,' he said eventually.

'And in that time you saved up enough to get the deposit and a mortgage on this place? Seems impressive.'

'Thanks.'

'And unlikely.'

Parkin made a small gesture, accompanied by a shrug.

'Well, I'm here, aren't I?'

'Where did the money come from?'

'I said.'

'You're lying, though. I know roughly how much you're getting paid, and there's no way you could afford this place on that. It would've been easy enough for you to say your parents gave you the money, but then, that's obviously a lie that would crumble the minute I talk to them. They could lie for you, of course, but I presume you've made that calculation while we sit here. They won't lie for you. Which is fair. No one should lie to the police, even for their own kid. Never works out well in the end.'

A cold stare, nothing yet coming in reply.

'Or, of course, there's the other thing where you just don't lie very well. You're kind of avoiding the truth at the moment, but the outright lie, that's more difficult for you.' Buchan made a gesture at the side of his head. 'Whatever's going on in there, it won't allow complete fabrication. So, let's get down to the truth, shall we? Did you know Graham Mathieson?'

A blank stare, and then the head shake. Not trusting himself to speak now, thought Buchan. He was feeling trapped.

'Did you hear about the murder in the town centre on Wednesday night?'

Buchan looked out of the window at the far end, thought about the orientation, and then pointed in the other direction.

'Not far from here. Maybe a ten-minute walk. Maybe less.'

'I don't listen to the news,' said Parkin. 'I was aware… there were sirens and shit on Thursday morning, but I didn't care. I didn't know what it was about.'

'Graham Mathieson's body was found in an alleyway. Stabbed in the heart, throat slit. A quick death.'

Parkin blinked, nothing more. The conversation still going nowhere.

'Mathieson worked for Margaret McLeod, processing and selling stolen phones.'

The giveaway look in the eyes, nothing to be done about it. Not when you weren't using to hiding yourself from others. The loud swallow, the face determinedly frozen, expressionless and cold.

'Whoever killed Mathieson did it as a warning to Margaret McLeod.'

'What?'

'Sorry?'

'What warning? What were they warning Mrs McLeod about?'

Buchan let the giveaway – referring to the woman respectfully as Mrs McLeod – pass uncommented on.

'There are far more terrifying people in this city than Margaret McLeod. More dangerous. More powerful. She has something they want. She has someone who can hack into an iPhone, like it was nothing. This person is in demand. But it's not a nice, cosy, commercial world out there. They're not going to come along and offer a contract. They're not going to put up a transfer fee, like they were Bayern Munich. They're not going to *negotiate*. They're going to crush, and overwhelm, and obliterate, because that's what they do.'

He left it at that for a few moments. Parkin was scared. Buchan didn't want to jump into it too prematurely, but he already knew he had him.

'So when they killed Graham Mathieson, they were saying to Margaret McLeod, tell us who it is in your operation who's hacking the phones, because that's quite a talent. Sure, they already know it's someone named Bridget, but I think we all know that no one in this drama is actually called Bridget.' Another flinch. 'Mrs McLeod says no. These people don't understand no. They say, tell us who it is, or people start dying. No, says Mrs McLeod. And so, we circle back to Graham Mathieson. Poor bastard, died minding his own business. He just happened to work for Mrs McLeod, and he just happened to be easy pickings when he left the pub on Wednesday evening.'

A short pause. Letting it sink in.

'Now,' he continued, 'Mrs McLeod doesn't have too many employees, so pretty quickly she's going to have to make a decision. Stick to her principles, protect the phone hacker, and die. Or, the other thing. Where she accepts her fate, and gives the hacker up. Now, these people, they're not going to kill the phone hacker. That'd be stupid, and of all the things they are, stupid isn't one of them. But that's where the good news ends. They're brutal, unforgiving, threatening, and more than happy to follow through on those threats. Last summer they wiped out an entire gang in the south side in one evening. Fourteen people.'

A tell-tale pulsing of Parkin's jaw. Breathing speeded up. Eyes wider than he would've allowed them to be had he realised. Fingers rubbing a sweating palm.

'What's it going to be?' asked Buchan.

'I don't understand.'

'What?'

'How are you here? If this lot are so, I don't know, amazing or omnipotent, or whatever, how come they haven't found me already? And if you're so amazing you managed to do it, how come you're scared of that lot?'

Smart, thought Buchan. He would never use the word scared when talking about himself, but the kid had recognised his trepidation all the same.

'I'm not amazing,' said Buchan, 'I'm just a police officer. I spoke to Mr Johnstone. I doubt any of my fellow officers had tackled him on the issue of having a computer genius in his midst. Why the opposition haven't, when it was presumably them who killed Brian Ferguson? I don't know that.'

'It was Brian's wife. She killed him,' said Parkin, though he didn't sound convinced.

'Too much of a coincidence,' said Buchan.

'Really?'

'Yes, really. Someone killed him because they thought there was someone useful in that section. So, either they never found you, or they did, and... you're already working for them.'

'What? No, I'm not!'

'Well, I'm pretty sure they're going to find you now, so you might want to consider your options.'

Parkin looked unimpressed, shaking his head, finally managing, 'Fine, whatever. What are my options?'

'I'm going to say your options are, a) come with me, or b) die,' said Buchan.

A strange noise blurted from the back of Parkin's throat, like he'd been stomach-punched. His head was still going, side-to-side, in denial.

'You just said, these people, you said they weren't going to hurt me.'

'People have a habit of getting caught in the crossfire. Collateral damage. Or could just be one of those, if we can't have him, no one can.' He made a gun gesture and pointed it at Parkin's head.

'So, what? You arresting me? You taking me into custody?'

'Nope. I need you to do something for me.'

Another worried look, Parkin's head still not completely still, then he finally managed to work it out.

'You need me to hack someone's phone?'

'Yes.'

'Ha! I mean, the fuck, man? If that's all it is, what separates you from this gang you say are so all-damned powerful?'

'I don't slit anyone's throat,' said Buchan. 'I give right of refusal. If you don't want to come with me, then don't. Stay here, see how you get on.'

'Why don't you arrest me, whether I agree to come or not? If you're so sure I'm a phone hacker?'

Buchan wasn't going to answer that. In a cell in the custody of Police Scotland did not seem too safe at the moment.

'I'm not going to arrest you,' he said, when Parkin seemed to be waiting for an answer. 'I don't have the time for the paperwork. Come with me, and we can do each other some good.'

'What good is it doing me?' said Parkin, though from his movement up onto the edge of the seat, the resigned tone of his voice, Buchan knew he had him.

'It'll probably let you live in relative freedom for a while longer,' said Buchan. 'Though I wouldn't go making too many plans…'

41

'Why Bridget?' Buchan had asked him.

'I like Bardot,' Parkin had answered, as though it was nineteen-fifty-seven. 'Thought it was a funny cover.'

'Does Mrs McLeod even know who you are?'

'She's my mum's cousin's sister-in-law, or something. We always called her auntie. But she didn't want any of the others knowing who I was, and she didn't want my mum knowing.'

'How d'you explain this flat to your mum?'

'She thinks I work for Google. She wouldn't be happy if she knew about Mrs McLeod.'

'Did they have an operation going before they brought you on board, or was the entire thing created as a way to make money out of your talents?'

'It's been going for years. Before I came, they used to ship the phones to China and India. Nothing cleared from them, all the owner's information and photographs and shit still on there.'

'So, why was Brian Ferguson murdered, then?'

Parkin hadn't wanted to answer that so quickly, but had finally forced himself, realising that Buchan had him now. His fate was to be in Buchan's hands.

'I got drunk one night, work's night out at the Betty Grable. I fucked it. Told Brian what was going on. Not much, but enough. He started badgering me, says he wanted in. Wanted a cut of what I was getting. When I says no, he moved on to extortion. Or bribery, whatever, you know, whatever the difference is. Basically, cut me in, or I'm landing you in it. Career down the pan, more than likely nicked.'

Suddenly the death of Brian Ferguson had made sense. His wife killing him had obviously always been a possibility, but there had never been a straight line from Baltazar's gang to Ferguson dying. This, though, fitted perfectly into the narrative.

The murder had been on the orders of Margaret McLeod.

'You told Mrs McLeod what Brian was doing?' Buchan had asked.

'Aye. And she says, don't worry, we'll take care of it.'

'How long after that was Brian murdered?'

'Couple of days.'

'Who d'you think murdered him?'

'I don't know.'

'Cam Leslie?'

Parkin had had a look about him to suggest that was exactly what he'd thought, but he'd stayed silent.

'Did you speak to the police?'

'You lot spoke to everyone in the section, but I just kept my mouth shut.' Another few moments, then he'd added, 'Some people say I'm on the spectrum, but I think they just say that because I'm really good at maths and computing. But I can play to it sometimes, easily enough.'

'You use it for your advantage.'

'Yeah. You though, you see through me. The other police officers, they didn't take the time.'

Buchan did not feel himself any more perspicacious than any of his team who had come before, he'd just known what he was looking for.

42

Another body. Another murder. Just like that, out of the blue, on a Sunday afternoon. Floating in the Clyde, some way up river. Way up beyond the garden centre at Rosebank. Tangled up in the bare branches of trees. Strangled, stabbed, the body dumped in the water.

'Ten, maybe twelve hours,' Donoghue had said.

Donoghue had had enough death. Donoghue had not wanted her Sunday afternoon, whatever she'd been doing with it, interrupted. She was snarky, barking at people. Agitated, like the waves on the river.

The body had been found by an eleven-year-old girl walking a dog. The dog, in fact, was the one to make the discovery.

'Such a bloody cliché,' someone had said within Buchan's earshot, though he wasn't sure who it had been.

He'd been about to come into the office to see the lay of the land, when the call had come through. Cam Leslie's disappearance was no longer a mystery.

Now, down by the river, Buchan and Kane side-by-side, watching the crime scene investigation unfold. The body had been brought from the water, and was lying in the undergrowth beneath the branches of a tall rowan tree. Donoghue had grumbled about there not being enough room. 'We're outside, and yet still cramped. Bloody pain in the arse,' she'd said.

Under other circumstances, Buchan and Kane might have shared a light-hearted line or two about the pathologist's irritability, but neither of them was in the mood. They didn't know what the other was doing, and they had their agreement not to share, yet neither was comfortable with the implied lack of trust.

Worse though was this, being here, at another murder scene. The Baltazar gang, or the Lansdowne gang acting on their behalf, had struck again. Another body, another investigation. That it was a criminal, and possibly Brian Ferguson's killer, who was dead, did not make it any easier. More than anything, it was what it represented. They had control. Baltazar or Lansdowne, it didn't matter. They had complete control. They killed when they felt like it, and when Buchan and his team had tried to fight back, they had casually sidestepped their attack, as though stepping out of the way of a stationary bus.

There was silence bar the sound of the river. Seven police officers present, plus the pathologist and six scenes of crime officers, and no one was talking. They all viewed the scene in the same way that Buchan and Kane viewed it.

'We're drowning,' said Kane. Her voice low, carrying no further than Buchan.

'Yes,' replied Buchan, finally.

'They kill at will. They've set Agnes up for Rose's murder. They brushed us off yesterday.'

Buchan didn't reply this time. She was doing no more than stating the obvious, but he had to let her get it off her chest.

'What have we got?' asked Kane.

Buchan only had the simplest of answers, but he wasn't going to share it. He had the most meagre of plans. A nothing plan, he thought it. Obvious. Transparent. Sitting there, waiting to fail. Nevertheless, all he could do was use the one piece of the pie which he had in his possession, and which, as far as he knew, no one else knew he had.

'We can hope,' he found himself saying, and Kane blurted out a rueful laugh and looked at him curiously.

'Hope?' she said. 'Were you replaced by a teenage American hippie while you were in Poland for two months?'

'Funny. We can hope, Sergeant, that's all. We have a murder. We have three murders, even if we can't investigate one of them. All we can do is look at the evidence and take it from there. Maybe we're relying on them making a mistake, but in that, at least, it's a bloody big operation, so you never know. This is Scotland, so let's not go pretending that anyone's capable of putting together a large operation where everyone's good at their job.'

Kane laughed ruefully again, for all it was worth, and she was saying, 'Thanks for the pep talk, boss,' when Donoghue approached, removing her gloves, pulling down the hood of her overalls. Buchan recognised she was, unusually, wearing a light touch of lipstick and eye liner.

That, he thought, explains her mood.

'Despite the marks at the throat, and the knife wound in the side, I think he died by drowning. Probably got into a fight, hands at his throat as part of that, he got stabbed. Impossible to know if his assailant received anything in return, and the body being dumped in the water means it's unlikely we'll find any alien matter, but you never know.'

'You think he was dumped, wounded and breathing in the water?' asked Kane. 'Or that the fight took place beside the river, his head was held under, and then… off you go, the body pushed away, after the fact?'

'Impossible to say at this stage. I'm not sure I'll get a definitive answer on that either, but I'll let you know. You might want to trawl the river, see if there's anything useful. And I guess you'll need to scour the bank from here on up if you want to identify the spot.' She turned, she looked at the river, perhaps aware she was telling the detectives how to do their jobs, things they more than likely had already set in motion. 'Apart from that,' she said, turning back.

'Look at it in the morning,' said Buchan, 'we don't need it before…'

He looked at his watch, he shook his head, he shrugged.

'I was going to say close of play, but it's Sunday. There is no close of play. Go home, do whatever you were doing, and –'

'I don't think he'll still be there,' she said caustically.

'Sorry.'

'It's not your fault, inspector. Nevertheless, it would be nice if you could make some inroads into this blasted case before the entire city gets murdered. It's getting very tiring being on this end of it.'

Buchan half-nodded, acknowledging her as she walked past them both, and then she was scrambling up the river bank, and heading towards the road, set further back behind another row of scrub and trees.

'You know if he was married?' asked Kane.

'He told me he hadn't seen his wife and kid in three years. Don't know if that was an exaggeration.'

'Are we telling anyone about this?'

'We have a couple of people to see,' said Buchan. 'You free to join me, or are you enmired –'

'Oh, I'm free to join you,' said Kane. 'Lead on.'

43

Margaret McLeod stood on the doorstep, arms folded, unimpressed to see Buchan back.

'What?'

'Can we come in, Margaret?'

'No,' she said. 'Just, no. I'm up to here with you. One of my people got murdered three days ago, and what have youse done? Bugger all. Not only that, one of you lot's actually been arrested for actual murder. I'm like that, really? So, you've been here already today, and if my memory serves me correct, you'd nothing to say then. So, no, you can't come in.'

'Cam Leslie's dead,' said Buchan. 'Strangled, stabbed, body dumped in the river.'

She held Buchan's gaze for a moment, then allowed herself a sneer.

'You sure he's dead? I mean, that sounds kind of like Rasputin levels of shit, does it no'? I mean, how many ways did they try to kill him? Sure he hadn't been shot and poisoned, 'n all?'

'Wasn't shot,' said Buchan, very matter of fact, 'but poison's not out of the question. We'll know more tomorrow morning.'

He liked the Rasputin analogy, even if he wasn't going to say. She barked out another laugh, and he forgot about Rasputin.

'I doubt it,' she said. 'So far you seem to know absolute diddly-squat.'

There was a redness about her cheeks, a distance in her eyes.

'When was the last time you talked to Cam?'

'We talked about this already. Whenever it was, it was before I talked to you, so what difference does it make? So, look at that. What will you do if it turns out that you, the great detective, were the last person to speak to Cam Leslie? Does that make you a suspect? You going to turn yourself in? Because that little tart of yours got herself arrested. Bad lot at SCU these days, the way I hear it. All on the take, only solving crimes on the rarest of occasions. Like the sighting of a red-tailed fanny warbler in summer.'

She laughed again, properly this time.

'What we talked about this morning hasn't changed,' said Buchan, persevering. 'They're coming for you. Baltazar, Lansdowne, whoever. They're coming for you, and Cam's death means they're one step closer.'

'I'll be just fine, inspector, don't you worry about me.'

There was a smugness about the smile, then she looked at Kane, turned back to Buchan.

'Now, bugger off.'

'How d'you know?' asked Kane.

'What?'

'How d'you know you'll be fine? Are you working with them?'

Another barked laugh.

'How can you possibly know you'll be fine, if you're not working with them?'

'Of course I'm not fucking working with them. They're killing my people. Jesus.'

'So, where does the misplaced confidence come from?'

'I don't know, call it what you will. Hubris, chutzpah, whatever. I'm gallus, me,' and she laughed again. 'Or maybe it's just three bottles of cheap plonk. What was that other thing I said? Right. Bugger off, that was it. So, bugger off.'

This time she didn't wait for anything further, slamming the door on the conversation.

They stood for a moment in position, as though something might happen, then Buchan half-shrugged at Kane, and together they turned away.

'She seems nice,' said Kane, as they were getting into the Facel.

44

‘We still don’t know – at least, *I* don’t know – why this is coming to a head,’ said Kane. ‘Why now?’

They were heading back into town, though not taking the route they would’ve done had Buchan been aiming to return to the SCU. Kane hadn’t asked where else they were going, not sure how much Buchan wanted matters to be discussed.

‘It’s not,’ said Buchan. ‘At least, I don’t think it is.’

‘No? Well, why now? Why all these deaths? Why Agnes’s arrest? Why are you back?’

Buchan tucked in behind a white Volkswagen as they approached a set of lights.

‘I read,’ he said, a random thought entering his head, ‘something about Volkswagen discontinuing manual transmissions soon. Obviously, they’re not the only ones. Last year in the UK, over sixty percent of new car sales were automatic. And, of course, with the phasing out of petrol cars, the days of the gearbox are almost done in any case.’

He stopped behind the VW. Glanced at Kane, looked back at the VW.

‘This depresses you?’ she asked.

‘I know it shouldn’t. It’s the passing of time, of technologies. Machines come and go, progress sweeps through. I’ll likely have the Facel until I don’t want to drive anymore, so it shouldn’t bother me.’

‘Maybe petrol cars will be completely banned before then. I mean, you could have another forty years behind the wheel.’

He nodded, his gaze distracted and vague.

‘I feel civilisation won’t last that long,’ he said. ‘Not in its current form.’

‘Seriously? What d’you think? War, climate, a great plague, or human stupidity?’

He smiled, and gave her a sideways glance.

‘The latter. It covers the first three, after all, and all sorts of other things besides.’

The lights changed, the car in front took its time, finally

they headed off.

'I genuinely don't think anything's coming to a head,' said Buchan, abruptly switching back. 'Why all these deaths now? Well, I'd say the two members of Margaret's little gang of soldiers were entirely because of what we've been saying. Lansdowne or Baltazar, or both, want to find out the identity of Bridget. Bridget, one might add, is probably the safest person in this story. Everyone wants her alive.'

He felt a pang of guilt at continuing the Bridget lie, but he had to stick to the agreement.

'So, why kill DI Savage?' asked Kane.

'They want to close down SCU. They've been screwing with us since last summer, now they're coming for the whole building. To be honest, I was half-expecting it to happen while I was away. This is just getting rid of what's left of a serious challenge.

'But look at them. They already control the streets. They control the drugs, and the cigarettes, and the extortion rackets, and the prostitution, and the whatever the hell else. They are not battling anyone for control. If they were actually in a turf war with McLeod, all her people would be dead by now. They need info, though, so they need to leave *someone* alive. They have dominion, and all that's left to challenge them is SCU. Once we get swallowed up, there'll be a fair shout that whoever has control over our operations will be in Baltazar's pocket, and that'll be that. Free reign. I mean, it looks like they have it already, but we can still cause them some difficulty.'

He drove on, the last line practically catching in his throat. Was it actually true, after all, or was this just Baltazar casting the final, crushing blow?

'So why bring you back?' she asked, though she did not sound sceptical of anything Buchan had said so far.

'I was wondering if maybe Baltazar had just wanted rid of me, because he was fed up with me trailing him around, but I don't think that's it. There was something Agnes said… It's personal, that's all. We got in his face last summer. Nearly managed to get him, but for all his smugness when he was able to walk away, we still got under his skin. Agnes and me. And this is him, coming back for us. Making his play. He'll crush SCU out of expediency, and he'll crush Agnes and me out of malice and a need for revenge. Even though, one might add, we've barely laid a finger on him in all this time. He doesn't actually have anything to avenge.'

Except, of course, that didn't entirely tie in with what Baltazar had said to him in Estonia, after what had happened in the south. When Roth had said the line to him the other night about something happening, and he didn't know what it was, it hadn't just applied to the fake text from Savage.

He cast a glance to the side. Unaware of his doubts, and thinking what he'd said sounded about right, Kane was nodding.

'Where are we going now?' she asked.

'Jimmy's Bistro,' said Buchan.

Kane gave him a furrowed brow, and a small head shake.

'Hope you're paying,' she said.

45

'You do most of the talking,' said Buchan, as they walked quickly along the road, having parked a couple of hundred yards away.

'What would you like me to say?'

'Wing it. We're interviewing a woman who's closely involved with virtually every organised crime activity in Glasgow.'

'OK,' said Kane, ruefully, 'is there anything you don't want me to say?'

'No. You have the floor.' A pause, then he added, 'When my phone rings, keep her talking.'

*

Kasia Adamczyk was sitting in the same seat, looking at her phone. Buchan elected not to bother with any artifice when greeted by the maitre'd, flashing his ID and walking past. The woman turned, looking worriedly over in Adamczyk's direction. The movement of Buchan and Kane was enough to have her glancing round, and she raised an eyebrow at them as they arrived at her table.

The restaurant was busy, the arrival of what seemed like two very obvious plain-clothed police officers drawing everyone's attention.

Buchan ushered Kane into the other seat at the table, then looked around, asked the question of three people at a table for four, lifted the chair, and sat down in between Kane and Adamczyk.

Adamczyk stared at Buchan, her face cold and grim, then she turned to Kane, expression unchanging. She had a glass of red wine, a glass of carbonated water, and seemed to be somewhere between the first and second course of her meal.

'Is two enough to call this a delegation?' she said. 'Or is it the start of an exponential curve? One of you yesterday, two today, four tomorrow, eight on Tuesday? What would that be…

two hundred and fifty-six by this time next week?' She looked around the restaurant, the faces of the crowd having largely looked away when no immediate drama had unfolded. 'Somehow, I do not think that will be enough. I am not sure how many of you it will take to arrest me, but I do not think you have the manpower over at that small building of yours. Nevertheless, if you are going to try, a word of advice. You had better get on with it, because it will not be long before your building gets closed down.' Another pause, and then, 'That is what I hear anyway. From my people on the inside.'

'What can you tell us about the murder of Cam Leslie?' asked Kane.

'I do not know who that is,' she said predictably.

'The inspector spoke to him on Friday morning. He was going to provide evidence linking the murder of Graham Mathieson to the organised crime activities of both William Lansdowne and Jan Baltazar.'

'Curious.'

She took a drink of wine, staring across the table at Kane, her narrow glasses reflecting the rich light of the restaurant.

'The organised crime activities of Jan Baltazar,' said Adamczyk. 'That is a bold statement about my employer, which I am not sure you ought to be making in public.'

'Didn't you tell me the other day you didn't know who he was?' Buchan couldn't stop himself saying.

'I must have misheard the question,' she said quickly. 'Mr Baltazar has never been found guilty of any crime, either here, or in our own country. You would not want to be facing a case of libel, along with everything else on your plate. And everything else seems to be getting to be rather a long list.'

'Slander,' said Kane, 'not libel.'

'As you say.'

'I'll keep it in mind.'

Buchan's phone rang. He stared at Adamczyk for a few moments, then said, 'Excuse me,' and took the phone from his pocket, checked the caller, and answered, without leaving the table.

'Buchan.'

Kane took out her phone, found the current case file, then the picture of the dead Cam Leslie, and turned her phone round for Adamczyk to see.

'You recognise this man?'

Adamczyk studied the picture for a few moments, then looked up at Kane. Her face almost showed pity.

'Why do you bother, sergeant? Where does any of this get you?'

'You recognise this man?'

Adamczyk held the look, contemptuous now, and this time did not bother with an answer.

'Sure,' said Buchan. 'I'll hang up, send it now.'

He ended the call, then looked at his phone, quickly typing, continuing to ignore the others.

A waitress arrived at the table, not reading the room, a smile on her face.

'Would you like to see a menu?' she asked, and then Buchan, laying his phone on the table, cut across Adamczyk's, 'They were just leaving,' to say, 'Can we have two still waters, not tap water. The sergeant would like the Caesar salad, and I'll take a cheeseburger with potato wedges and a green salad, thank you.'

'I'm sorry, we don't have Caesar salad. Perhaps I should get you a m –'

'You have a cheeseburger, though?'

'We have the house ostrich steak burger, which I'm sure the chef would be happy to garnish with chee –'

'Can we have two of those please,' said Buchan.

'Yes, of course. Fries and salad?'

'Like I said, wedges. I'm sure someone in the kitchen can cut the potatoes into the right shape.'

The waitress looked a little uncertain, more than likely because she recognised she was part of a small drama she didn't really understand, then she said to Adamczyk, 'Your main course is almost ready, ma'am. Would you like me to hold it until the ostrich steak burgers are ready?'

'Bring it now,' said Adamczyk, and the waitress nodded, and turned away.

'I like the sound of that,' said Buchan.

He stared at her, his voice and face as cold as she'd just been with the waitress. They stared grimly at each other, Kane suddenly relegated to the role of spectator.

'You like the sound of what?' said Adamczyk, and Buchan recognised she hated that she'd allowed herself to be drawn into asking the question.

'You getting pissed off,' said Buchan. 'That's good. So you

should be. You're getting busted, and this here, is part of you getting busted. Tell us about Cam Leslie.'

'Like I said, I do not know the name. If you are going to bust me, inspector, as you so boldly claim, then you have got me right here. Why not do it now? I presume you have handcuffs in your pockets, you all carry them around. The toys of the trade. Maybe I will make it more fun for you, and resist arrest.'

She did not smile along with the joke.

'We're still at the gathering evidence stage,' said Buchan. 'Putting a case together. Getting our ducks in a row. We're talking to you now, and we'll be back tomorrow morning to chat over breakfast. Maybe we'll come to your home in the middle of the night, but probably only if we can think of any other questions.'

'You have barely asked me any now,' she snarled, and again was obviously annoyed at herself for being drawn into it.

'Well, you continue to lie about Mr Leslie there,' said Buchan, indicating the photograph, 'so I feel we need to get past that before we can move on to all our other questions. If you still refuse to answer honestly, then I'm afraid we may have to trouble you at three a.m.'

'Interesting,' she said. 'I am sure my lawyers will be delighted at getting to flex their muscles in a police harassment suit. Let us see how much longer you are investigating Mr Leslie's death after that lands.'

Buchan's phone pinged, he took a quick glance, nodded to himself, didn't reply to the text, then said, 'You know, Ms Adamczyk, you're absolutely right.'

He pushed his chair back.

'We should get back to the office,' he said to Kane, and Kane nodded, face expressionless, also getting to her feet.

The waitress arrived, once again walking into a situation that was alien to her, Adamczyk's main course in her hand. Turbot, caramelised celeriac puree, tempura of cockles, red wine vinaigrette.

'Sorry,' said Buchan, 'we have to go. Apologies to the chef.'

'Would you like us to prepare the burgers to go?' she asked, apparently meaning the question seriously.

'We're good, thanks. If you could just put them on Ms Adamczyk's tab, thank you.'

Adamczyk was staring at them with undisguised contempt,

and Buchan could tell she was torn between letting them walk out, and venting her fury. He elected to force the latter by staring at her, knowing it wouldn't be long before she caved to her base instincts.

'You will not trouble me here again, inspector,' she said, unable to withstand Buchan's cold stare for very long. 'The money you were paid last night, I suggest you use quickly. You won't have much time to enjoy it.'

She glanced at the waitress now, and then lifted her knife and fork, paused for a moment to make a show of regaining her composure, and slowly cut into the fish.

'If I can show you to the door,' said the waitress.

Buchan afforded himself another few seconds staring down at the top of Adamczyk's head, and then turned away, acknowledging the waitress as he went.

*

'The money you were paid last night?' asked Kane, as they walked back to the car. 'Is that the money the Cunningham girl mentioned during yesterday's interview?'

'Envelope under the door as promised. I didn't count it.'

'You passed this information on to Liddell, right?'

'I left the envelope untouched for a while. Then I put on a pair of gloves, checked it contained money, though I never counted it, and sent a photograph to the boss to let her know what happened. The envelope was still lying on the floor this morning where I'd found it. Will be curious if it's there when I get home.'

'Why wouldn't it be?'

'Because they need the money back.'

'They don't seem like the kind of operation who are going to *need* fifty thousand because they're short.'

Buchan wondered about that, but didn't bother commenting. Appearances could be deceptive, after all. For every obvious gazillionaire with money to burn, there was a Trump, up to his eyes in debt, lies, hubris and self-aggrandisement.

'You going to explain what that was all about in there, by the way?' she asked.

'Nope,' said Buchan, as they got to the car.

Kane sat down, still smiling, as Buchan started up the

Facel.

'Who called?' she asked.

'Need to know basis,' said Buchan, and she glanced at him, expecting to share his smile. But he wasn't smiling.

Kane turned away, hoping at last her boss was on to something.

46

Buchan opened the door to the open-plan office on the fourth floor, and took a moment surveying the scene. The office was naturally the same shape as his office two floors above, but here the desks were laid out differently, packed in a little more tightly. Late Sunday afternoon, there were only four desks occupied, and a person standing on their own at the window, looking down on the quiet flow of the river on a lazy Sunday.

She turned at the movement at the door, and did not turn away again, Buchan's arrival grabbing her attention. Her face blank, a rigidness about her shoulders, she stood straight and humourless.

Here goes nothing, thought Buchan, with an unusual flippancy, even for the inside of his own head.

'Inspector Randall?' he said, approaching.

'You need no introduction, inspector,' she said in return. 'I was wondering how long it would take you to show your face down here. To step out of the ivory tower.'

Oh, for crying out loud.

'How's the investigation into Lansdowne coming along?' he asked.

There had been a few introductory lines running through his head, but getting straight into the meat of the case hadn't been one of them.

'Bold,' said Randall. 'I'm not sure I should be discussing that with you. Indeed, I'm entirely sure I shouldn't be.'

'You free to have a coffee?' he asked.

Not that he wanted another coffee, but he hardly wanted to ask her out for a drink.

'I don't think that would be appropriate either. It will be no surprise to you to know that the actions of you and your fellow department members, are under investigation by my unit. We will have a chat soon enough, but at a time of my choosing. I'll let you know when I expect that to take place.'

'My unit is under investigation by organised crime?'

'That's all I have to say on the matter.'

Buchan felt the anger rise inside him. He hadn't expected much from coming to talk to Randall, but to be pushed away and told there was yet another internal body looking into their actions came like another thunderbolt.

They stared at each other, Buchan trying to make sure his temper was under control before he said anything further. She lifted her eyebrows, a defensive look.

'Why?' he asked.

'Why what?'

'Why are you investigating us? We're already being investigated by an external inquiry. We're already being questioned by DCI Gilmour's team from Edinburgh with regards to Rose's murder. So why would you also be investigating us? And, more specifically, why *you*, when you were part of our unit less than a month ago?'

She swallowed. He made her nervous, and he wondered if part of it was because he was a man, standing tall, threateningly and accusingly before her. He took a step back, relaxing his posture as he did so.

'Like I said, inspector, this conversation isn't appropriate.'

'When was the last time you spoke to William Lansdowne?'

Another small, nervous movement of her head.

That's it, thought Buchan, that's who she looks like. Prime Minister Truss, walking head first into the death of a monarch on her first week in the job, looking terrified and hapless and completely out of her depth.

'Everything all right, ma'am?'

Buchan turned. Sergeant Hanahan, who'd previously worked up on Buchan's floor, but who'd never come directly under him in an investigation.

Randall looked a little wide-eyed.

'As you were, sergeant,' said Buchan, barely managing to suppress the sigh, then he was walking quickly out of the room, and taking the stairs two at a time.

*

Liddell's door was open, which meant she wasn't in the office. He hadn't expected her to be, but he'd come up in any case.

'Probably just as well,' he muttered, having stuck his head round the door, confirming her absence, and then he was trotting quickly back downstairs. He had a phone call to make, and the thought of the answer he was going to get made his stomach churn.

47

Buchan got back to his apartment at just after seven p.m. He entered quietly, and stood still. Door partway open, he hesitated for a moment, felt confident there was no one there, then he quietly closed the door, and took his phone from his pocket.

The envelope of cash was still on the floor, where it'd been since the previous evening, bar the moment when he'd lifted it to check its contents. Now he looked at the photograph he'd taken of the envelope just before he'd left the apartment – not the same one he'd sent to Liddell – and checked the alignment of the envelope with where he'd left it.

It had not been put back in exactly the same place.

It could have been the cat, obviously, but when you expected something to happen, and it had happened, it was usually for the reason you were anticipating. Someone had been in, and they'd checked the contents to see if he'd taken any of the money. Not that it really mattered, he thought, as they could easily manipulate images and bank accounts to make it look as though he had happily taken a bribe. But for him to have actually accepted the bribe, would obviously be even better for them.

'Every little helps,' he said darkly to himself, as he hung his coat, and walked through to the open-plan.

Everything in its place. Edelman was restless and waiting for him, which would also tie in with someone having been in the apartment.

'You scare 'em off, pal, did you?' he said, as Edelman approached for an ear scratching.

Buchan went through the rest of the house, a quick check in each room, a check on all the small markers he made so that he'd know if anyone had been through the apartment. And someone most definitely had.

Nevertheless, they would not, he thought, have found what they were looking for.

He came back into the open-plan, poured himself a glass of white wine, and then took it to his usual spot. At the window, looking down on the river in the soft evening light.

He had another call to make, but he was taking a moment before making it. What position was he in now? A Schrödinger moment. There could be nothing forthcoming, or there could be a massive breakthrough. Perhaps there was the third way, a crushing blow he hadn't foreseen, but he had to believe he'd managed to get ahead of the opposition on this one thing at least.

He wouldn't trust it, though, not until it had played out. Not until they'd won. Baltazar in prison, Lansdowne routed, Roth freed and exonerated. The other thing, the thing he felt he'd partway confirmed with his phone call just before leaving the office, he didn't need to think about now.

He took the second phone from his pocket, the one he'd used at Jimmy's Bistro when sitting beside Kasia Adamczyk. No messages had come through. That, nevertheless, was as it was supposed to be. His instruction had been for minimal contact.

Another drink of wine. A glance away from the river, to the ornamental chess set that had been on the table by the window since the previous summer. The pieces were set up for the start of a game, nothing moved. Obviously today's visit from the opposition had meant to be a secret. They were no strangers, of course, to the clichéd chess piece move to show an opponent their control over a situation.

'Come on,' he said to himself, 'let's see what we've got.'

He called the number, an unexpected nervousness in his stomach. He took another drink of wine.

One ring, the phone was answered.

'Did it work?' he asked.

'Of course.'

'You can send everything to this phone?'

'Of course.'

'Now,' said Buchan.

'Yes.'

The phone went dead.

Buchan laid the phone down on the table.

'Here we go,' he said to Edelman, who had jumped up into his usual spot on the seat by the window. 'Boom or bust.'

48

An hour later. Buchan still in position at the window. He hadn't drunk any more wine. Now, a cup of tea instead. Getting hungry, but he hadn't found his way to the freezer yet.

There were days when he could stand at the window watching the river, his mind in neutral, for hours on end. This was his quiet time. His down time. But this evening, his mind wasn't in neutral. Instead, it was buzzing, a great wave of information having been downloaded onto his phone.

Edelman was sitting in the chair, upright now, aware he was to be called to the party. The boss needed help.

The cat miaowed, Buchan glanced down at him, wondering if he was after something, but recognised instead his demeanour. He was offering assistance.

'First question is,' he said, 'can I trust it? Was it that straightforward to get all that information from Adamczyk's phone? She must have security procedures in place. I mean, everyone has procedures in place, and that's the point of Bridget – who isn't called Bridget, by the way. But that's the point of the guy. He has skills. The kid's like, I don't know, like that British guy in the *Mission Impossible* movies.'

The way he spoke to Edelman had changed since Roth had arrived. Now it was like he was speaking to her through the cat. Edelman had become the surrogate for when Roth wasn't there.

'But did Adamczyk know that was liable to happen, and have cover in place just in case? Or is this me doing that thing these people want me to do? Trust nothing. Trust no one. For me to think that they're seeing me coming from a mile away, so that they're completely on top of everything I do, always ahead of the game, playing me like an idiot.'

He looked at the cat, he indicated the phone.

'This… this is quite the information download. That would be one hell of a complex web to weave if all of it was fake.' He shook his head. 'Nope, I have to trust myself, trust the process I've set up. Bridget hasn't worked for Baltazar, we know this. Mathieson and Leslie wouldn't have died if he had. And thanks to the phone download, we know Baltazar's back in town tomorrow morning. We just need to go and get him. Straight off the damned plane, Polish diplomatic passport 'n all.'

He took another drink, he straightened his shoulders, he nodded to himself.

'Except, it turns out, it's maybe not Baltazar we need to be getting,' he said.

He lifted the mug again, this time he drained it, and then finally he walked away from the window, through the open-plan to the kitchen, setting the mug on the kitchen counter.

Then he went to the front door, lifted his car keys, threw on his coat, and walked back out of the apartment.

49

'Inspector?' said Liddell.

Buchan stood on the doorstep of the elegant, west end townhouse. Three floors, refurbished sandstone exterior, large bay windows.

The temperature had dipped with the coming of darkness, the evening now cold, the sky clear.

'You should come in,' said Liddell, finally finding herself, and taking a step back.

Buchan wiped his feet, and walked into the stylish downstairs hall.

A large rug, paintings of the Scottish Highlands on the walls, a wooden staircase with a maroon runner, leading up the left hand side of the property. In the air the smell of Asian cooking.

'Just finished eating,' said Liddell. 'Can I get you a drink?'

'I drove over,' he said. 'Just a quick word.'

'In here.'

She led him into a small sitting room off to the right. A warm room, and not one of those Buchan often imagined along this road, where the owners had decorated pompously, as though their home was a National Trust property. Nevertheless, there was a fire in the hearth, and Liddell had been sitting by it in a leather chair. There was a glass of brandy on the small table, and a book, spine creased, opened flat on the table.

'Take a seat,' she said. 'Let's talk.'

Buchan sat down, glancing at the cover of the book as he went. *The Rise And Fall of the Third Reich*, by William L. Shirer. Liddell saw him looking, and gave him a slightly rueful look.

'I like to reread it every few years. Give myself some ideas.'

Buchan reacted to the joke as best he could, but he wasn't in the mood, and she waved away the line as soon as she'd said it.

'Tell me,' she said.

'Tell me about DI Randall,' said Buchan. 'Where did she come from, why was she moved downstairs?'

'You've spoken to her?'

'Yes. And she said her unit was investigating my unit. I have *a lot* of questions about DI Randall.'

Liddell lifted the glass of brandy, took another drink, and stared into the fire.

'I think you're right to be wary,' she said. 'Denise is a particular personality type. And she has some skills, though they may not be immediately evident in a crime solving situation.' A deep breath, a glance at Buchan, signs of obvious discomfort talking about this, then the look back into the fire.

He did not read too much into the discomfort. He was asking his boss to talk about another detective inspector under her command. She had no reason to give him anything, and was obviously going to be careful about what she had to say.

'She's Glasgow-born, but went to university in Aberdeen, ended back up there when she joined detective branch. She was sent to us maybe five or six weeks after you'd gone. I'd been badgering Dalmarnock for someone, and Denise was who we got.'

'I take it you didn't get a choice.'

'If you can call take it or leave it a choice,' she said, giving him another quick glance. 'She started in early January, and straight off the bat it was apparent she wasn't a fit. We all have to take who and what we're given, of course, and this isn't a comment on your team at all. But it was obviously tough for them to adapt, and Denise made a lot of mistakes. And she's not one to admit to those mistakes. I haven't got to the bottom of who's been behind her somewhat rapid rise through the ranks, but… well, it's clear that she's got to where she is because of outside influence, rather than ability. In that, Police Scotland is no different than anywhere else.'

'Is it possible the outside influence is Jan Baltazar? Or at least officers higher up the chain who are beholden to Baltazar?'

Now she turned and didn't take her eyes off him.

'I can't think that about any of my people, inspector,' she said. 'Of course we're all wondering where these people are making their inroads, we're all looking over our shoulders, but I genuinely don't think so. If Denise isn't up to the job, if she has a fairy godmother greasing the wheels of her rise through the service, it needn't be due to malign outside interference. She'd hardly be the only one.'

'Why did you move her downstairs?'

She sat back a little, she folded her arms, though Buchan did not see defensiveness in it.

'I was asked to bring you back. You may think that was part of some grand plan, but at the time, and my opinion hasn't changed despite everything that's unfolded the last few days, I thought it was for the reasons I was given. The service is in dire straits. We're underfunded, and under attack from all sides. No one likes the police in Scotland, and no one wants to see us given any more resources. I'm not sure which way this is going, but everything else in this country, be it the UK or Scotland, feels like the government are keen to shed responsibility and hand everything over to the private sector. God knows how that'll look in relation to policing, but that's where we're going. Make the publicly funded option so bad the public end up welcoming private security. And then, wait and see where that gets us.'

'I got the phone call to come back five days ago. DI Randall was moved to the new department… what, four weeks ago now? Five?'

She held his look again. This appeared to be a conversation she had known was coming.

'There was infighting. Higher up, and don't ask me who was fighting who. I'm not entirely sure, and I don't want to speculate. But I understood you were about to be recalled, it was clear Denise wasn't working out with your team, Rose was getting the organised crime unit established, and I pulled the trigger. As Samantha will tell you herself, more than likely she and the others functioned better with Denise gone.'

Buchan didn't look particularly happy with any of that, but it was all believable at least.

'What else?' he said.

Another small sigh, another shake of her head, again she looked away at the fire.

'Denise came to me with information. She didn't want to reveal her sources, which I completely understand. We all do. After all, if any of us has an outside informant… these are the people we keep to ourselves. She's in organised crime unit, and that's her job. To play the gang members, get close to them, try to pick them off. To turn them against each other.'

'She's an idiot,' Buchan couldn't help himself saying.

'Like I said, inspector,' said Liddell, her voice with a little more edge, a little less forgiveness, 'she has some attributes.'

'What information did she bring you?' asked Buchan. 'And when? This woman literally headed up my section a few weeks ago. If there was something worth investigating, why on earth is she the one doing it?'

'Her suspicions dated from her time there,' said Liddell.

'Did they?'

Liddell had nothing to say to his scepticism.

'Had she voiced those suspicions at the time?'

A small shake of the head in reply.

'So…?' said Buchan, getting irritated that he was having to drag the information from the boss.

'So, inspector, at some point in the last week Inspector Randall came to me with information, some of it a few weeks old, some of it more recent, and said that she thought perhaps the mole in the service was on your floor. In what was, and has become again, your department. She asked that she run a shadow operation.' She held his gaze, but they were here now, she wasn't backing down, and it wasn't as though she was intimidated by him. 'I won't say I was entirely happy about that, but I consented.'

'Did she tell you who she thought the mole was?'

Cold calculation in her eyes, or perhaps Liddell was just getting as annoyed at Buchan as he was at her.

'No,' she said finally. 'I didn't want to know until she had proof. I communicated this to her, and now I will wait for that proof.'

Silence, bar the dull rumbling of the fire. From nowhere, as a fresh piece of wood started to burn, a loud spit, then a piece of wood slipping as the fire burned.

'What brings you here tonight?' asked Liddell.

Buchan had come for answers, albeit without particularly expecting to get any to his satisfaction, and was going to be as uncomfortable talking about what he knew, as Liddell was proving to be. It had to be done, nevertheless, to some level.

'I have information to suggest that DI Randall is the mole.'

Conversation, questions and revelations coming only with reticence, every word having to be forced. The fire crackled again, something small and fiery spat out onto the hearth.

'Where did you get that?' she asked.

'Information collected during my investigation into the

Baltazar collective.'

'You're not supposed to be running an investigation into the Baltazar collective, inspector.'

'Well, it's a bloody good thing I am,' he snapped, 'as the person currently in charge of organised crime division is likely on their payroll.'

'Mind your tone, inspector, and let me say again. You are not authorised to run that investigation.'

'Seriously? I should just let it go? Sit back while *she* investigates *us*?'

'You can protect your source if you have to, but you should pass what you've got on to Detective Chief Inspector Gilmour's team. Or do you think she might also be compromised? Do you suspect everyone who's not part of your close-knit gang of brave warriors?'

'Jesus,' he muttered, unable to keep his annoyance in check.

'Let me make myself absolutely clear, Inspector Buchan,' said Liddell, leaning into the conversation now, and speaking with more certainty than she had previously, 'your investigation into Baltazar, Lansdowne and any crimes, such as the murder of DI Savage, in which their involvement is suspected, is one hundred percent prohibited. You haven't been taken off the Mathieson case yet, though that may happen tomorrow. You still have a variety of cases the team were working on this time last week. The McGonigal insurance fraud, the serial rapist Harbin, the… God, I don't know. There's enough. This time last week your team was busy, and none of those cases have been closed. You have work to do, and I suggest you do it. Baltazar and Lansdowne are strictly off limits, and DI Randall is so far off your limits she might as well be on another continent.'

His teeth were clamped together, jaw working, fists clenched.

'You should leave, inspector. Go home, get some sleep, see what state this thing is in tomorrow. But make no mistake, the entire future of SCU, every damned department in my building, is under threat, and I will not have you *fucking* it up for everyone else.'

'I found Bridget,' said Buchan.

Liddell's demeanour changed, though there was nothing pleased about it. She looked curious, perhaps dubious.

'Bridget? The phone hacking genius?'

'Yes.'

'You found her in, what, two days? Two days after hearing of her existence, when Baltazar and Lansdowne must have been looking for months. What was your secret?'

'It was nothing special,' said Buchan. 'Followed my nose, I spoke to one person who those clowns hadn't thought to speak to. No secret, hardly brilliant detective work.'

Her face was relaxing, coming down from the adrenaline rush of genuine anger at her inspector. Already seeing the possibilities, wanting to believe they were real, and hadn't been contrived for the benefit of the opposition.

'That seems…'

'I know. I know what you're thinking. That makes it sound too easy, right? Like they wanted me to find her.'

'Yes.'

He took a moment, glanced into the fire. Once again thinking through the whole thing with Bridget, and whether he was being played.

'It feels real, that's all.'

'It?'

'The situation.'

'Who is she? Bridget?'

'He's not called Bridget for a start, so there's that.'

'Wait, what?'

'He uses a fake name of the wrong sex, that's all.'

'So, Bridget is a man?'

'Yes, Bridget is a man.'

'Good work, inspector. What's the plan?'

He hesitated, he nodded as they stared at each other in the light of the fire.

'Maybe I should take that drink,' said Buchan.

50

Driving home he took a chance. Sunday evening, the place would be quiet. There were still a hundred ways this could unravel, but he felt the sense of an ending, and there was something about it that made him slightly reckless. Nevertheless, this was barely stepping out of line, this was just doing something that someone somewhere would think inappropriate, and he didn't care.

Roth was being held unobtrusively at the local station in Dalmarnock. Nothing big made of it, no fuss, out of sight of anyone who might come looking for her, to take her photograph as she was led away to the High Court the following morning.

Buchan approached the front desk, producing his ID, holding it steady for the constable on duty to get a good look.

'Inspector,' said Constable Reins. 'What can we do for you this evening?'

Constable Reins looked like he was barely twenty-years-old.

'Would it be possible for me to speak to the prisoner, please?'

'We don't have any prisoners,' said Reins automatically, the lie told in his tone.

'I know Detective Constable Roth is being held here, constable, you don't have to pretend otherwise.'

Reins nodded, having been instantly seen through, and retreated instead to silence.

'Would it be possible for me to see Constable Roth?'

'I can't.'

'You can't let me see her?'

'That's correct.'

'Because you were told not to allow any visitors, unless accompanied by, or authorised by Detective Chief Inspector Gilmour?'

'That's correct.'

'Well, then, constable, you have a quandary.'

'Sir?'

'There's a detective from Edinburgh telling you not to authorise a visit, and you have a detective from Glasgow, asking for one.'

Reins did not look nervous about this. Instead, Buchan recognised his base annoyance at getting put in a difficult position. This would not be in Buchan's favour.

'Who are you going to choose, son,' he said. 'Glasgow or Edinburgh?'

'I can't let you see her, inspector.'

'This could play well for you,' said Buchan.

'How's that, sir?'

'You tell DCI Gilmour that I coerced you. Pulled rank. Started by offering you a helping hand up the ladder in your career, ended up with threats. Nasty, petty little shit, making sure you never get beyond constable while I'm on the force. You reluctantly relented. You let me see her. I told you to make sure you did not watch, and you did not turn on the microphones. You, of course, turn on the microphones, and listen to everything. You can report back. You did what you could. I look bad out of this, you not so much.'

'Really?'

It sounded thin. Buchan held his hands to the side. It was all he had.

'Was that actually a warning?' asked Reins. 'If I don't let you in, are you going to start threatening nasty, petty little shit, sir?'

Buchan quickly nodded an acceptance of defeat.

'Good man, constable. I apologise for putting you in the position. I shall leave you to your evening. I'd be grateful if you could mention to Agnes that I visited. How's she doing anyway?'

Buchan could tell that the instant backing away, and the fact that he'd had no tone about him since he'd arrived, was working. The softening of Reins' face was apparent.

'She's OK. She seems… I don't know, sir, I think if I was accused of murder, I'd be losing my shit, that's all.'

'She's a phlegmatic woman,' said Buchan. 'And innocent. So she has that on her side.'

He looked away, let out a sigh, double tapped the counter between them.

'Once again, my apologies.' He paused, he thought of something, then he added, 'Tell Agnes, Xander was here.'

He smiled, he started to turn away. He got a couple of paces towards the door.

'Inspector?' said Reins.

*

'You shouldn't be here,' said Roth.

'I know. The constable said I've got two minutes and he's calling the cops,' said Buchan, and Roth smiled. 'I think he was joking, but it was hard to tell. I can't be long.'

'I know. I love that you came.'

There was a bench down one side of the cell, a thin bed on the other. Roth was sitting on the bed, Buchan on the bench across from her. They were both aware of the camera positioned outside the cell, on the other side of the short corridor.

Silence for a few moments. An absurd situation, thought Buchan. Everything about it. But they were here now, and it was on his shoulders to get Roth out of it. There was nothing she could do.

'How's the food?' he asked, and she smiled in response, at the forced, almost comical ordinariness of the question.

'Surprisingly good,' she said. 'Duck breast, szechuan pepper, mandarin orange, and rainbow chard, with a side of truffled mash for dinner, perfectly matched with a lovely viognier. Then meyer lemon iced parfait, with kumquat marmalade for dessert, and an accompanying New Zealand Riesling.'

'Decent,' said Buchan.

A sad smile shared across the short divide. Buchan aware they could slide into silence, and just sit and stare at each other, and he didn't want that to happen.

'Your mum got in to see you?'

'She did. Poor mum. She's been desperate for me to leave the police since I joined, and here it is, just around the corner, and I go and do something stupid like get wrongly accused of murder.'

She tapped herself on the forehead.

'Are you all right?' he said.

'I'm fine.'

'This is a pretty lousy –'

'I'm fine, honestly. It's so… bullshit. I mean, I don't know, if they had me in here on something credible, for a reason based on something that I'd actually done, no matter how contrived, maybe I'd be worried. But you know I didn't kill Rose. Everyone who knows me knows I didn't do this. All they've got is me and Rose having some dumb argument, and some obviously planted hair beneath the nails.'

'You know that for a fact?'

'What else d'you think they might have?'

'Frankly, whatever they choose to make up. There are obviously people in authority who are lined up against us. There's no knowing what they'll be able to produce when the time comes. And it's clear that me trying to get anywhere near their investigation will be viewed as an act of war.'

'It's OK. You just need to do your thing over here, while they're doing theirs over there. You've got this.'

He smiled in response, choosing not to make a comment about her level of confidence in him. Rarely would he have such confidence in himself.

Silence threatened to return, sweeping through the cell, holding them there.

'You should go,' said Roth, perhaps just to release him from the awkwardness, an understanding tone in her voice.

'I've booked us a week in the Chedi Andermatt,' said Buchan. 'Week after next. Maybe we can bring it forward if we get this crap sorted out.'

She laughed curiously.

'Switzerland?'

'The room was three thousand a night, so, you know... you'd better be allowed to leave the country.'

She laughed again, her brow slightly creased.

'I can't tell if you're serious.'

Damn it, thought Buchan. Get out of here. Leave her like this, with a smile on her face. Go home, get your plans in order, sort this damned shit out, get the hell away from this damnable place.

He got to his feet.

'Yes, I'm serious. Something to look forward to.'

He smiled, he held out his hand.

The camera across the wall forgotten, Roth got to her feet, a moment, and then they were in each other's arms, her head on his shoulder, holding him tightly, wishing she never had to let him go.

51

On arrival at the SCU building the following morning, Buchan went straight to the first floor. To the armoury, to sign out a handgun. This was not something he'd done before, but he'd completed all the requisite training and testing to keep his arms certificate up to date. He might never have allowed himself to do so in the past, but he was at least in a position to withdraw a firearm. And at the rank of inspector, he did not have to get authorisation.

Sgt Fowler, the armorer, was a good man. Discreet, knowledgeable, knew the foibles and quirks of the weapons at their disposal, knew the weaponry that the police didn't have, but which criminals might possess.

There was a small sticker on the wall next to the reception counter in his one-man unit. The Nike symbol and *Do Your Job*. That was all. They all knew that *Do Your Job* summed up Fowler's approach. Don't worry about what everyone else was doing. Don't worry about whether the next guy is any good, or has been over-promoted, or won't be able to do his thing. Worry about yourself, and what's in front of you. That was it. *Do your job.*

'Inspector Buchan,' said Fowler. 'Interesting.'

'Alan,' said Buchan. 'How are things?'

'Seems to be picking up, sir. It must be getting ugly out there, if you're using our services.'

Buchan had nothing to say to that, and he responded with a small shrug, a *that's the way it goes* sort of a gesture.

'How can I help you today, inspector?'

'A handgun, please.'

'Glock 17 OK, or are you going to need –?'

'The Glock's fine, Alan, thanks.'

'Bear with me.'

He turned away, and Buchan retreated from the counter, looking around the sparse surroundings of the armoury. Then, for the fifth time that morning, he looked at his watch, and wondered what Roth was doing at that precise moment.

52

Twenty minutes later, not yet eight-thirty, Buchan in his familiar spot, standing at the office window, cup of coffee in hand, looking down on the river. A cold wind today, cloud having rolled in from the west, agitated waves on the water.

Cherry was in, already working. Buchan didn't even know what it was on, but understood it to be one of the cases Liddell had mentioned previously. There was, as she'd observed, plenty of work to go around.

Movement to his side, and then Kane was standing beside him, coffee in hand.

'Morning,' she said.

'Sam.'

They stood together looking out of the window, the city before them. After some time Buchan realised that Kane was more than likely waiting. He'd said they shouldn't discuss with each other the way forward, that they should work alone. Any change in direction needed to come from him.

'I saw Agnes last night,' he said, and she turned to him, concerned.

'Should you have done that?'

'I wanted to see her.'

'How's she doing?'

'She's OK.'

'Really?'

'Yeah, I think so. Something of the old spark about her. She's not fearful of how it plays out. She has a lot of faith in us clearing up this mess.' Now he turned to look at Kane, and added, 'So we'd better not let her down.'

Kane held his gaze for a moment, seeing something in him now that she was looking into his eyes.

'What are you thinking?'

'I'm thinking I'm fed up with this crap, and I'm fed up with getting walked over. And I woke up this morning, and I thought, fortune favours the bold. We need to go and face this head on.'

'Didn't we try that on Saturday?'

He held her look for a moment, then turned away, back to the river.

'I was eating breakfast, and I thought, where does that phrase come from? Fortune favours the bold. Who said that first?'

'It's usually Shakespeare.'

'That's what I thought. But no, it's from a variety of similarly worded old Latin phrases.'

'Not Shakespeare, then.'

'Interestingly, Pliny the Younger noted that his uncle said it, before sailing to investigate the eruption of Vesuvius.'

'Wasn't that how Pliny the Elder died?' she asked, and Buchan smiled, and she added, 'Great example.'

'To be fair,' said Buchan, 'the phrase is *fortune favours the bold*, not *fortune favours the idiot who sails towards the volcanic eruption*,' and Kane laughed. She was feeling strangely optimistic in the unexpected light of her boss's seemingly sanguine determination, but she wasn't about to let go of the obvious point she'd made.

'We tried being bold on Saturday,' she said. 'Look where it got us.'

'It was too broad an operation,' said Buchan. 'Too large, made with too little preparation, under the circumstances. This is you and me. We're going to get out there, and we're going to finish this today. And it may be as much of a cliché as the one about fortune, but we need to start at the top. We need to decapitate the monster.'

She looked at him appreciatively.

'So, what's the plan?' she asked.

He took another drink of coffee. He did not return the look.

'I don't have one yet,' he said.

'OK, that part needs work.'

'A little. Where did you get to yesterday?'

'I thought we were keeping this stuff to ourselves. I mean, I could've told you plenty last night.'

'It's time to share,' he said, his voice low, and Kane took a look over her shoulder.

Buchan had decided to make no exceptions on who he could trust. Not Liddell, not Kane, not even Roth. He himself was the only one in whom he could have confidence. And then the contents of Kasia Adamczyk's phone had fallen into his lap.

'Should we go elsewhere, then?' asked Kane.

'No, we're good. Tell me, broad spectrum, not too much detail, where you got to yesterday.'

She gave him another sideways glance, took another drink of coffee.

'I went to speak to William Lansdowne.'

'Plinyesque,' said Buchan approvingly, and she smiled.

'Guess I was feeling a bit like you are today. Of course, since he knew we weren't about to go arresting his entire gang of brigands, he was exactly where you'd expect him to be on a Sunday afternoon.'

'Did he treat you with amused contempt?'

'Of course. And I'd watched his place for ninety minutes before going in there, and there was heavy footfall. Malky Seymour, for one. Both of the sons. At least ten of his people. And, interestingly, Kasia Adamczyk. In fact, she arrived after everyone else, and left ten minutes later, before everyone else.'

'So, chances are it wasn't everyone getting together at Lansdowne's place in order for the boss to lay down the law, or update them on the state of play, it was for Adamczyk to do that.'

'Not according to Lansdowne,' said Kane.

'Where did you watch from?' asked Buchan, getting curious.

'The hill behind, across the street. Barely any view in between two houses. There are a lot of trees and shrubbery, undergrowth, that kind of thing, but enough, given there are no actual leaves on any of them. There's only a slender view through to the front of Lansdowne's place, so I was confident they wouldn't notice me. I did wonder, as I lay there in the dirt, whether they were just doing their thing with absolutely no shits to give about me learning anything. Kind of half-expected, when I went and knocked on his door, that he'd have some glib, smart-assed comment about wondering when I was going to show my face. But no, if he knew, he kept it to himself.'

'If he'd known, he'd have said. Nice job. So, what'd you learn?'

'I asked him about having Adamczyk to visit. He was a little… let's not pretend the man has any subtlety or artifice or anything about him. He's incapable. He talked around the margins, that's all. I feel like he's thinking it's time he separated from Baltazar. Or rather, that Baltazar withdrew from the city.'

'Hmm,' said Buchan. 'I kind of wondered if that's what he

was hinting at when I spoke to him the other day. Seems like remarkable hubris.'

'It does,' said Kane. 'Sounds as though he'd called Adamczyk there to tell her the way things were going to be, bravely surrounding himself with at least twelve of his lieutenants as he did so.'

Buchan looked at her with approval, gave a small nod.

'And you never said anything last night when we interrupted Adamczyk at dinner. Thank you.'

'Just following orders,' she said.

They drank coffee, a few moments, then Kane said the inevitable, 'How about you?'

Buchan took another look over his shoulder, the personnel in the office the same as they'd been the last time he'd looked, no more comings or goings.

'I found Bridget,' he said.

A moment, Kane's eyes widening.

'You found Bridget? Holy shit, look at you.'

'Don't sound so surprised,' he replied, drily.

'Just, you know, what did you do that Lansdowne and Baltazar didn't?'

Buchan, of course, did not really have an answer, other than the one he'd given Liddell the night before. So, he didn't answer, instead doing what everyone seemed to be doing these days, tapping the side of his head.

'Well, I'm impressed. You're sure it's not a set-up?'

He took another drink, the mug almost finished, and then he drained it. Licked the last of the coffee from his lips, lowered the mug, glanced around for somewhere to put it, though there never was when he stood here, and then he chose to hold on to it, as he continued to look down on the river.

'I completely believed it, pretty much from the off.'

'It being?'

'I got her to do something for me. Bridget is an exceptional talent.'

'What'd she do?'

'You know the share feature on iOS17? The one everyone gets told to turn off?'

She looked curiously at him, and then as awareness dawned on her, her expression changed, a silent 'wow' forming on her lips, before the expression of curiosity returned.

'I mean how did that even work?'

'How did it work?' asked Buchan, and he laughed lightly. 'You might as well ask me how light bulbs works, or why planes don't fall out of the sky. I don't know. But she gave me a phone with one helluva widget downloaded onto it. Get it into the proximity of another iPhone, it can disable the other phone's security settings, it can download information from it. Photographs, mail, messages.'

'Holy shit. I mean, *holy shit.* You got all that on Adamczyk?'

'I did.'

'The case is blown open?'

'Not as much as I'd want it to be,' he said. 'And let's be clear here, this is not admissible. We take this to the procurator, the woman is slamming the door on us. But you've just given me some confirmation of the veracity of the information on there, as there were messages from Adamczyk discussing the meeting, and that yes, she was extremely unimpressed with what Lansdowne had to say.'

'There must be more than that, though? Surely?'

'Tonnes,' said Buchan.

'You going to tell me?' asked Kane, once again taking a look over her shoulder.

'On the way,' said Buchan.

'Where are we going?'

'I'll tell you that on the way as well. You need to stop off at the first floor.'

There were several offices on the first floor, but Kane knew exactly what that meant. Suddenly, her curiosity having been piqued, she felt the same determination Buchan had had since he'd woken that morning.

'So, you do have a plan,' she said, and Buchan smiled darkly. 'Thank God someone has.'

They turned, Buchan stopping as they passed Cherry's desk.

'Danny,' he said, 'I've got a job for you.'

53

Tom Parkin was standing at the window of the small apartment overlooking the river. Eleven-nineteen in the morning. He'd been awake since just before five.

He wasn't sure what was coming next. He had no idea who he could trust, and he was nervous. His time at the company dealing with MoD records was over, that was for sure. From now on he was going to be working full-time on major security systems. Either to protect them, or to infiltrate them. More than likely, the latter.

Whose side he was going to be on remained open to discussion, although at that moment, he had to admit, Buchan held all the cards. The police already had him on phone fraud, which was a pretty big card for them to hold.

Nevertheless, he knew there was still a chapter or two to be written in the drama, and he was going to stay nervously on edge until it had played out.

He lifted the cup of tea, took a sip, his face screwed up, and he lowered the mug. It had gone cold. It had gone cold the last time he took a drink, about ten minutes earlier.

Buchan had thought of replacing the real Tom Parkin with a doppelgänger. It was such an obvious idea, since none of these people knew what he looked like. Find a non-Glasgow copper who he could (hopefully) trust, and insert him into the operation. It would be perfect. Right up to the point when someone handed him a phone, and asked him to crack the passcode. It might still have been possible to get valuable information in the initial period, before the obvious flaw in the plan kicked in. He'd even thought that perhaps Roth would have been perfect. She could've played Bridget just as people imagined her. She could've cut her hair, dyed it bright green, a nose pin and a fake tattoo, a new pair of glasses. She'd've been a different person.

Roth, however, was obviously not available, and Buchan knew he would never have asked her to put her neck on the line in any case. Not when she was just about to leave the force. That, he thought, would've been a classic movie situation. An end of career disaster waiting to happen.

For Buchan, there had been, at this short notice, no other option. Parkin had to be the bait, and Buchan was just going to have to trust in the process.

Parkin was turning away from the window when there was a knock at the door. An open-plan room, lounge, diner, kitchen, entrance hallway all rolled in to one. From his position at the window, he could see the door.

He did not move. He wondered about taking the tea to the microwave, blasting it, using it as a weapon.

'Don't do anything dumb,' Buchan had told him.

Scalding a guy who might well have a gun, would definitely fit into the category of dumb.

Another knock. He felt himself shudder at the sound, the hand encircling his stomach squeezing tightly.

A muttered, 'Crap,' escaped his lips.

A third knock, this time more forceful.

'Bridget,' said the voice outside, just loud enough for Parkin to hear. 'We know you're in there. Open up, man, everything's going to be cool. We just need to get you somewhere you're going to be safe.'

Parkin placed the tea on the small table to his right, and took a few steps nearer the door so he could hear better. The one thing about opening the door, he thought, was that at least they could all just get on with it. It was coming to a head, starting now, and if he opened the door and let them in, whoever they were, they might be more amenable towards him for having welcomed them in.

Another knock, louder this time, and now the words, 'Open the *fucking* door, Bridget,' had more of a strain to them.

A few steps short of the door, Parkin stopped. In the silence, he swallowed. The sound seemed to bounce off the walls.

Another, 'Crap,' the word having nowhere to go.

There was a scratching in the lock, as they started trying to pick it. Parkin took a step backwards. A moment, it did not take long, and the lock clicked. The door opened, immediately juddering loudly as it came up against the chain.

'Fuck's sake,' muttered from outside. Then, 'Give us the cutters, Billy.'

In the gap, the end of a pair of heavy-duty metal cutters being put in place around the chain. One squeeze, the chain was cut like scissors through Cellotape, and the door was opened.

Two men with whom Parkin was unfamiliar, walked into the room, quickly closing the door behind them. They stood still, assessing the situation, taking in the room, Parkin's position in it, and the likelihood of anyone else being in the apartment.

'You're Bridget, are you?'

Parkin had thought maybe he'd relax when the moment came, but now that it was here, he was terrified.

'Bridget?'

Parkin nodded.

'What's your name?'

'Tom,' said Parkin, one syllable being close to the limit of what he could manage.

'You alone, Tom?' asked Malky Seymour.

Parkin couldn't move, couldn't open his mouth.

Seymour reached into his back pocket and brought out an old Walther handgun, without aiming it directly at him.

'Just answer the question, Tom,' said Seymour. 'Are you alone?'

'Yes,' blurted Parkin, before Seymour had finished speaking.

In truth, Seymour hadn't needed the gun, Parkin finding the arrival of a hardened gang member genuinely intimidating.

Seymour, with a small wave of the gun, indicated for Billy Carntyne to search the apartment, and he too drew a gun, and headed for the bedroom door to his left.

'Wardrobes and under the beds, Billy,' said Seymour, and Carntyne grunted in reply.

'You wearing a wire, Tom?' asked Seymour, and Parkin shook his head.

'Let me see.'

Parkin didn't move, though it was obvious even to Seymour that this was because he was frozen with fear, rather than having no intention of complying.

'Let me see.'

Parkin lifted his T-shirt, revealing his bare chest.

'Get undressed,' said Seymour. 'Throw me your clothes, let me check them.'

Parkin swallowed again. Buchan hadn't mentioned this. As it was, Buchan had thought it not unlikely, but had decided to keep this kind of detail to himself.

Seymour made a gesture with the gun. Parkin lifted the T-shirt up over his head, getting a little entangled, then he tossed it at Seymour.

'Everything,' said Seymour.

'Everything?'

'You know the meaning of everything, don't you? The only reason we're here is because you're supposed to be a genius. Everything.'

Parkin unhappily removed his trousers, then stared down at himself. Black briefs, the kind that would look racy on a male model, but which just looked wrong on Parkin with his slight paunch and no muscle tone. Again, he muttered, 'Crap,' to himself, then bent down, removed his socks, quickly took off the briefs, and tossed them onto the floor in front of Seymour.

Hands in front of his genitals, Parkin shivered in the cold.

Seymour, stood on the clothing, then bent down, one eye and the gun still trained on Parkin, and examined them. Then he stood, and made another small gesture.

'Move your hands.'

'What?'

Carntyne emerged from the left-hand side of the apartment, shaking his head, said, 'Clear,' and then crossed to the other side.

'That there,' said Seymour, 'what you're doing, is pretty obvious. Natural. Whoever you're working with, the police, the God knows who else, they'd know that's what you'd do. They'll expect us to think it's natural. Move your hands.'

'You think I've got a microphone attached to my baws?'

'Move your hands, Tom!' barked Seymour, loud anger from nowhere, and Parkin quickly lifted his hands above his head. Seymour approached him, the bully enjoying the control, and stood unmoving, staring harshly at Parkin, then looked down at his vulnerable genitals, shrivelled with nerves and the cold. Then he moved Parkin's penis to the side with the end of the gun, inspected it for a moment, then let it back into place.

'You can get dressed,' he said.

A minute later, Carntyne having finished his quick, but thorough search of the property, Parkin was dressed, Seymour still standing in the middle of the room, gun in hand.

Seymour liked to call this kind of thing his Samuel L Jackson moment. Not, of course, that he had Samuel L's scriptwriter, and consequently, he wasn't half as much fun.

'We all good?' he asked the room, the question seemingly

directed at both of the others.

'Clear,' said Carntyne.

Of course, he'd only searched for people, and Seymour had only searched Parkin for a wire. Neither of them had bothered to check whether the apartment might be fitted with recording and filming equipment, so that when Seymour slipped the gun into his back pocket and said to Parkin, 'Come on,' and Parkin said, 'No,' and Seymour said, 'What?' and Parkin said, 'I'm not going,' just as Buchan had told him to say, so that Seymour brought his gun out again and said, 'Come on,' it meant that the coercion and attempted kidnap was being caught on film.

'He's not going to kill you,' Buchan had said, 'but I accept you'll want to stop short of him bringing the butt of the gun down across your face. Just make him work a little, that's all.'

'No,' said Parkin. 'I'm staying here.'

Seymour lifted the gun properly now, took another couple of steps closer, and held the end lightly up against Parkin's forehead.

'I'm sorry,' he said, 'I didn't hear you. Because I said, come on, meaning we're leaving, and you said something. I didn't catch it. What was it again?'

He gave Parkin's forehead a nudge.

Parkin might have been playing the situation a little, but he didn't have to pretend to be terrified. He'd never seen a gun this close before, and he didn't like it.

Finally he nodded, a constrained, partial nod, given the proximity of the weapon.

'Very good,' said Seymour. 'I like a sensible lad.'

He stood back, he made a gesture towards the door, Parkin started walking, and Seymour once again slipped the gun into his back pocket.

Carntyne went just in front, and opened the door.

The three men stopped.

A moment, and then Seymour said, 'Oh, fuck off,' his tone already dripping with defeat.

Kane stepped forward, putting her foot across the entrance, to make sure they couldn't slam the door. Buchan held his gun steady on Seymour.

'Don't let me see you reaching for the Walther, Malky,' he said, then he gestured for Seymour and Carntyne to put their hands on their heads.

'Oh, fuck off,' muttered Seymour again.

54

Seymour was behind the desk in the interrogation room, staring straight ahead. 'Not saying anything until I seen a lawyer,' he'd said.

So far Buchan hadn't let him make the call.

Buchan and Kane were on the other side of the two-way mirror. Not watching him as such, as there was nothing to watch. This was just where they were standing while they talked through what was going to happen next. For the most part, though, Buchan knew they were on the home stretch. From the minute he'd successfully identified Bridget's identity, they had been on the home stretch. He just had to make sure they were meticulous in their execution.

'We've got him,' said Kane, finding herself slightly discombobulated by her boss's silence.

Buchan didn't respond, and she gave him a small, sideways glance.

'Everything all right?' she asked.

'There's a problem,' said Buchan, and Kane asked the question with her eyebrows raised.

'How did Malky Seymour know where to find Bridget,' said Buchan. He wasn't asking the question.

Kane was nodding as he spoke. She hadn't asked too much, she'd just let it play out, doing what she was told, aware that Buchan was still trying to keep as much as possible to himself.

'So, who did you tell?' she asked. 'And how d'you know Bridget didn't just hand himself over to Lansdowne? Or, in fact, that Bridget didn't contact someone in Margaret McLeod's organisation, and they landed him in it?'

Buchan's demeanour had not changed. It was clear he'd thought it all through. In fact, it was clear the entire thing with Parkin had been a set-up, and it had played perfectly into Buchan's hands.

'I took him to that apartment myself, didn't use anyone else's assistance. He and I set up the cameras. I didn't leave him any means of outside communication. He was there until I, or someone else, turned up to get him.'

Kane was looking at Buchan, her brow furrowed. Still wondering what was coming, but getting the sense of its awfulness.

'It wasn't too long, and I had Danny keep a watch on the place.'

'Shit, Danny?' said Kane.

'No, don't worry about Danny. Danny had no idea who he was watching, or of the apartment's location. He was monitoring camera footage, that's all. Making sure Parkin didn't contact anyone, making sure Parkin didn't just up and leave, then he was ready to notify me when Seymour showed,' and he indicated the other side of the glass.

'Danny's in the clear,' he tagged on.

Kane swallowed. It was obvious Buchan knew more than he was saying, and his silence was disconcerting. There were only so many people it could be. Even fewer when one considered just how dark Buchan's mood had become.

'Tell me, boss,' she said. 'Who else knew he was there?'

Buchan kept his glare grimly on Seymour, and then slowly turned to look at Kane. Kane had never seen him look like this before. She'd seen him angry, certainly. Distraught. Determined. Gripped by grim fury. But this was something else, all of those combined, all multiplying each other, so that his eyes now betrayed the darkest depths of rage and betrayal.

55

'I told you I wasn't talking until the lawyer got here,' said Malky Seymour.

The two men stared angrily across the table at one another, Kane to the side, watching the scene with strange fascination, as though an outsider.

'We can do better than that, Mr Seymour,' said Buchan.

Malky Seymour scowled.

'Lawyer.'

Buchan leaned into the conversation.

'I don't give a damn about you,' he said, and Seymour scoffed.

'Amazing. I don't give a fuck about you either. Look at that, we're practically soul mates. You gonnae propose now? That wee slapper of yours'll be upset, mind.'

'We've got you. We've got a witness. Even if somehow something mysterious happened to the witness, we have video and we have audio. Attempted kidnap. Not the first time you've been nicked, but this is a serious crime, and with it not being your first offence, the maximum twelve-year sentence is not unlikely.'

'I'm quaking.'

'Don't care if you're peeing your pants with excitement, we all know you don't want to spend that long in jail, Mr Seymour.'

Seymour stared harshly across the table, a slight tic beneath his left eye. Face like stone, eyes blazing anger and hatred.

Kane had previously thought to herself that there was little better than this. The crook who knew he was busted, and was absolutely spitting mad about it. Malky Seymour, she now thought, sitting over there looking like his face was about to explode, might've been the best of the lot.

Silence from across the table. Silence around them. In here, virtually no sound from the rest of the building. A cocoon of nothingness.

Finally, Buchan sat back, straightened his shoulders, stretched his neck. Checked the clock behind the suspect.

Looked back at Seymour.

'We can do a deal, Mr Seymour. Like I say, I don't care about you. You weren't the leader of Davie Bancroft's gang, and you're never going to be the leader of William Lansdowne's gang, no matter how much William strings you along. It ain't happening. And maybe you think that one day, when he's gone, you'll be in a position to make a move. Reggie shouldn't be a problem, and while Michael's starting to earn his stripes, you'll be able to handle him. But it won't matter. Because William knows what you're thinking. He knows how it'll play out. So, when the time comes for William to step down… well that's going to be curtains for you, isn't it? And you know this. Which means, you likely have plans in place to get ahead of the game. To usurp William while he's still in power. Except, look…' Buchan snapped his fingers. 'Just like that, you're done. You've been sent off. You'll spend tonight in HMP Shotts on remand, you'll await trial in HMP Shotts, and then that'll be where you serve out your sentence. And you can't affect the game on the pitch, when you're sitting in the dressing room.'

'Fuck you, Buchan. I want to speak to my lawyer.'

'But like I said, Mr Seymour, I don't care about you. If we nail you…,' and he shrugged. 'Means pretty much nothing. You're not dictating anything. This is Lansdowne's show, and it's Kasia Adamczyk's show, and it's Jan Baltazar's show. But the Malky Seymour show? Nah, that's not a thing. Malky Seymour doesn't have his own show. Never got the spin-off series he'd been after. Never will either. You may be the most important person in the new landscape of Glasgow crime in your head, but not out there. Not where it matters. Not in anyone else's head, and certainly not on the streets.'

'Fuck me, Buchan, you don't half talk a lot when you get going. Fine, yadda, yadda, yadda, get to the point.'

Both Buchan and Kane recognised the change in tone. He was still trying to be cool, he was trying to act as though he had a measure of control, but Buchan had planted the seed, and there was every chance it would work.

'Tell me how you found out Bridget's location?' said Buchan, and Seymour barked out a loud laugh.

'Very nice, Buchan,' he said. 'Very funny. I think you might first have to tell me what's on the table, and you might have to persuade me that what you say's on the table, is actually on the table, because I don't know how much authority you have around here anymore.'

'I've got the authority of having William Lansdowne's third-in-command in custody, and absolutely bang to rights. And this, what we're doing now, doesn't amount to a hill of beans. I can't promise you anything, and since you've requested a lawyer and I've so far refused, I can't use anything you say. So this is where the real talking gets done, and then the lawyers and the procurator and the relocation scheme people get brought in and we see what we can do.'

'I don't want relocated,' said Seymour. 'Nae fucker in Glasgow's touching me with a stick.'

'Well, then,' said Kane, speaking for the first time, 'looks like a deal shouldn't be too difficult. You hand us your enemies, we see what we can do about mitigating your sentence. Everyone's a winner.'

Again, Seymour laughed, but his mood had completely shifted.

'Calamity Kane with the smarts there, eh? Good for you.'

'Oh, nice,' said Kane. 'Haven't heard that one since primary six,' and Seymour scowled again, though this time there was more humour in it.

They had him, and they knew it. Seymour was about to be turned.

*

An hour and a half later, Buchan and Kane were walking away, leaving Seymour in the cell, waiting for his lawyer. Calls to be made, but they were feeling confident now they would get the job done.

'Kids used to call you Calamity Kane?' said Buchan, giving her a curious sideways glance. 'Seems a bit of an arcane nickname for when you were in primary six,' and Kane laughed.

'Ha,' she said. 'Actually, I've never heard that before. Thought it was decent, to be fair, but I wasn't giving him the pleasure.'

Buchan nodded, allowing himself another grim smile.

56

Buchan had thought of bringing Cherry and Dawkins with them, a couple of back-up squad cars, using an enforcer on the door, making a show of the arrest. But there was no need for that now. And, despite feeling ahead of the game for the first time since the whole Baltazar thing had kicked off, he didn't want a repeat of what had happened two days previously.

They rang the bell, they stood back, they waited. The afternoon had darkened, the rain had started to fall. They ignored it, their coats getting wet where they stood.

Moira Lansdowne answered the door. Wearing an apron and a head scarf, a pair of kitchen gloves. Face like stone.

Often enough, of course, the woman was the power behind the throne. A little bit of a cliché, Buchan sometimes thought, nevertheless a cliché for a reason. This was not the case with Moira Lansdowne.

'What d'you two want?'

'We believe your son's here,' said Buchan.

She didn't answer.

'Is Michael in the house at the moment, Mrs Lansdowne?'

'No,' she said.

She did not lie well.

Buchan held her gaze, hoping she would capitulate before it, but she held firm.

'We need to speak to Michael,' said Buchan. 'We can do it here, or we can wait for him to leave. If it happens when he leaves, then the conversation, and everything that ensues, will be done out there, in the street. Ultimately, if he decides to hole up in your house to avoid us, we will get a warrant, and return mob-handed. Those are your options.'

'You can't bully me.'

'We believe your son committed murder, Mrs Lansdowne,' said Buchan, and she flinched, her head shook, a stilted move, an automatic reflex to information she just didn't want to know. 'Either you let us in, or his arrest will be a very public affair. He may like the sound of that, as might your husband, but they would be foolish to think it will end well. This time… this time it is not ending well for them.'

Her face was set hard, but they could see the fight leave her eyes. The glazing over, the acceptance there was nothing to be done. There was no escape.

She kept them standing there for a few moments, and then turned away, saying nothing, leaving the door open for them to follow.

They closed the front door behind them, and then followed her to the left, down the corridor into the back room that Lansdowne used as his office. The library, with shelves of books he'd never read, maps on the wall of places he'd never go. A large desk by the window, leather armchairs by the fire.

The fire was burning in the hearth. Lansdowne was sitting behind his desk, his back to the window. Reggie was seated on the other side of the desk, Michael standing with one hand in his pocket, the other holding a glass. Whisky, Buchan thought. Starting early. Possibly he'd started some time ago.

'They didn't give me any option,' Moira Lansdowne was saying, as Buchan and Kane entered the room a few paces behind her.

'Fuck me,' muttered Lansdowne.

Reggie, as was his way, looked disconcerted. He got to his feet, then did nothing when he got there. He wasn't cut out for this life. Everyone knew it, he knew everyone could see through him, and it made it worse.

Michael had a familiar look of disdain.

Moira Lansdowne stood to the side, intending to watch the drama, whatever it was going to be, play out. She did not last long. One look from her husband was all Lansdowne thought would be required, then when she hesitated, he flicked his hand in the direction of the door, and she turned and walked past Buchan and Kane, giving Buchan a look of hatred on the way.

'What?' said Lansdowne.

The room was warm, in the air the smell of cigarettes, as there always was in here, the one room in the house in which Lansdowne was allowed to smoke.

'Michael Lansdowne,' said Buchan, ignoring the father, 'you're under arrest for the murders of Graham Mathieson and Detective Inspector Rose Savage.'

There was always more that could be said, but he decided to leave it at that. He just wanted to get this done, and get

Lansdowne out of this smoky room and into custody.

The boy smirked.

The boy? What was he now? Twenty-eight maybe. Nevertheless, in terms of being an active and effective contributor to his father's crime network, he was a newbie. He'd seen the lay of the land with the arrival of Jan Baltazar, and the destruction of Davie Bancroft, and he'd stepped up to the plate, filling the shoes Reggie had never been going to fill.

'Really, Buchan,' said Lansdowne. 'I mean, are you actually doing this? We've been here before. You, frankly, have made an arse of yourself before. So, are you going to provide any evidence, or, I don't know, anything, any reason at all for this intrusion? The boy's giving you nothing. He's saying nothing. You're going to get him in there, he will tell you nothing, and within half an hour the place will be crawling with lawyers, and you will be fucked. Again. Why they keep bringing you back, I have no idea, but I wonder if maybe this'll be the last thing you ever do as an officer. That'd be sad, wouldn't it? I mean, maybe, I don't know. Would it be sad? Or would no one, anywhere on earth, have any fucks to give about it?'

'We don't, at this moment, have to provide any details,' said Buchan. 'The evidence will be put to both Michael and his lawyer, or his team of lawyers, in due course. He will be charged, and he will appear in court.'

'Get to fuck,' snapped Michael, an ugly snarl on his face, teeth bared.

Lansdowne got to his feet, a quick glance at the boy, then he leaned on the desk, pointing at Buchan.

'You're a cunt, Buchan. I don't know how you know, but you've found out Baltazar's coming into town, and this is what? Some sort of dumb power play? Is that it? You're like a little boy, running around after his big brother and his mates saying, can I play? I want to play! I'm good, honest. You're pathetic, Buchan, so why don't you just take your minion and leave? You're not welcome here. You and your shitty Serious Crime Unit are busted. It's over. You have no authority around here anymore.'

'Thanks for the input, William,' said Buchan, his voice as deadpan as ever. 'I'm sure you'll find out how it's going with Michael soon enough. Meanwhile, at some point, when it's all in order, we'll be coming back for you two, so don't be going anywhere.'

'Fuck you!' shouted Lansdowne, the anger spilling out. 'The second you're gone, I'm picking that phone up and your career'll be over by the time you get back to that shitty building of yours. And I'll tell you what else. We're going to be hearing from Malky shortly, and he's going to have something we've been after, and then see you, see all of you, and see that bastard Baltazar, youse can all get to fuck.'

Buchan held the gaze for a moment, contemplating the bursting of the balloon. Instead, he nodded in the direction of Michael.

'Cuff the suspect, please, sergeant.'

Kane produced a pair of handcuffs, and approached Michael, his face twisting further in response.

'Dammit,' muttered Lansdowne from behind his desk, suddenly looking resigned to the oncoming storm. When it came, it was a tornado, blowing in out of nowhere.

'Hands behind your back,' said Kane.

'Naw!'

'Hands behind your back!'

'Fuck off!'

She grabbed his left hand, and in a flash there was a blade in his right, and he slashed at her, catching her across the palm of her hand.

'Shit!' she said, whipping her hand away, blood flying, cuffs dropping in a clatter to the floor, as she pressed her hand against her chest.

'You heard my dad,' said Michael, spitting fury, knife held threateningly before him. 'Fuck off!'

Buchan took a quick glance at Lansdowne, sitting back behind the desk, face grim and dark. Reggie, a spectator, was a peculiar mix of thrill and fear, betraying just how far he was out of his depth.

'Damn it,' muttered Buchan, resigned to what he was going to have to do.

With a smooth movement he whipped the Glock out from the back of his trousers, and pointed it at Michael.

'Drop the damn knife,' he snapped, anger rising from nowhere, finding its way into his voice. 'Drop it!'

Michael's face was contorted, eyes filled with hate. He didn't want to drop the knife, having the kind of misplaced bravado that would allow him to think he could use the blade to win a gunfight. Then he couldn't help the glance at his father, who made the slightest of gestures to tell him to drop the weapon.

Another grimace, and then Michael held the knife forward and dropped it noisily on the wooden floor.

'You all right to cuff him, sergeant?'

'Might bleed on him,' said Kane, harshly.

Not taking her eyes from him, she kicked the knife away, then bent down and lifted the cuffs. Straightened up, then roughly grabbed his right arm and swung him round.

'Fuck off,' he spat, though this time he didn't resist.

She brought his left arm in, locked the cuffs, then span him round, holding on to his arm, blood still running from her wound.

'Everybody happy?' said Buchan, beginning to lower his gun, being greeted with scowls from the Lansdowne clan.

And then, something in the look on the father's face, and the inevitable, 'Drop your weapon,' from behind.

Buchan didn't immediately turn. A harsh laugh from Michael. A look from Lansdowne suggesting this had been inevitable. Buchan had always been going to lose, and what else could he have expected?

'I said, drop the weapon.'

Buchan turned. Tania, Lansdowne's bodyguard, was standing at the door, gun in hand, raised, aimed at Buchan, a watchful eye on Kane.

Buchan held the gun low, aimed at the ground for now. He wasn't dropping it.

'You're going to shoot a police officer?' he said.

'Doing my job,' said Tania. 'Drop the gun, inspector, and no one's getting hurt.'

'My sergeant's already been hurt,' said Buchan, and Tania's eyes flickered in her direction. A shadow across her face, a realisation she was on the wrong side, then she hardened her stance, a slight movement of the gun, and said, 'Last chance. Drop it.'

Buchan already had the angle. A small window, but he was going to take it. He relaxed, feinted to toss the gun to the floor, and then in a flash, lifted the Glock and fired.

The bullet struck Tania on the hand. She yelped unavoidably, her hand flying back. The gun fell to the side. The bullet, having passed through her third and fourth fingers, ricocheted off the gun handle and embedded in the wall to the side.

'Shit,' said Tania, pulling her hand close to her chest, in the same way that Kane had just done.

Kane moved quickly, picking up the gun, but Tania wasn't about to get into a fight. Not from a position of standing unarmed, her good hand shot through.

Buchan lowered the gun a little, looking harshly around the room.

'Anyone else want to do anything monumentally stupid, or can we all calm down now?'

He was greeted with anger and defiance and defeat in equal measure. Another movement at the door, this time Moira Lansdowne, bizarrely armed with a rolling pin.

'You're fine,' said Buchan, his voice still fizzing with annoyance, 'your boys are safe.'

She stared harshly at her husband, who once again dismissed her with a gruff nod. This time she didn't move.

'Sergeant, can you call it in, please? We need medics, and we need some back-up.'

'Boss,' said Kane.

She turned away to make the call, but did not leave the room.

Buchan looked at Tania, making a small gesture with the gun in the direction of the Lansdowne men.

Tania, hand still clutched to her chest, moved past Buchan, and stood beside Reggie. Buchan, a little warily, moved further back, and stood facing the four of them.

'That was all a bit unnecessary,' he said glibly, and Lansdowne grimaced.

'Didn't think you had that in you, Buchan,' he said. 'For all the good it'll do you.'

Buchan was done talking.

Kane came off the phone.

'On their way,' she said, and Buchan nodded.

57

Early afternoon, and suddenly, the rain was torrential. Buchan walked into Liddell's office, closing the door behind him, then stood in the middle of the room. The usual quiet of the top floor shattered by the sound of the storm.

Liddell hadn't turned on any lights, and there was an end of day darkness, as though it was several hours later than it actually was.

'How's it going?' asked Liddell. 'You should have come to see me earlier, I've been hearing stories, and I don't like just hearing stories.'

Buchan didn't immediately answer. There'd been a buoyancy about him, as he and Kane had gone about their business so far, but it had vanished as he'd walked up the stairs.

Now, in unnatural twilight, he stared grimly down at his chief inspector. They held each other there for a moment, and then Buchan turned away and walked to his usual position by the window. Outside the cacophony of nature, the waves on the river riotous, the heavy rain torn and tossed by the wind. On the far bank, traffic backed up along Clyde Street, a thousand lights blinking in the rainwater, the distant sound of a discordance of car horns, as anger bled into the elements.

'When this all started,' said Buchan, finally, and he turned to look at her. 'Way back, I mean, last summer, the first time we ever came across Jan Baltazar, it began with me standing here, and you asking me to investigate the disappearance of Claire Avercamp. You'd been at university with her father, and he'd called in a favour.' Liddell's face was impassive. 'You said not to speak to the guy, and I thought that was fair enough. I checked him out, made sure there was nothing funny about him, but it seemed above board.'

She continued to stare at him. She suspected what was coming, but she didn't know exactly what Buchan knew, so she was keeping her mouth shut.

'I called him yesterday. Just had a feeling. Well, I've had it for a while, but I thought, I'll just check up on a few things.'

'He couldn't have been very pleased to hear from the officer who failed to find his daughter alive,' said Liddell.

The cheap shot emboldened Buchan. This hadn't been going to be easy, but if she was going to push back, if she was going to start casting accusations at him and his team, like any of this had been their fault, it was going to be a lot easier.

'He's a decent man. More understanding than I thought I deserved for him to be. Still coming to terms with his daughter's death. Real life like that, the genuine face of pain…' He felt it, the man's torture, still fresh only nine or ten months later, and for a moment his voice drifted away. 'Turns out he had no idea who you are. I reminded him, and the name rang a bell, but only from last year's investigation, not from his time at university. Right enough, you both went to Edinburgh, and at round about the same time. Nevertheless, he didn't know you, and he never called you last summer. There was no favour.'

Liddell remained stoic and deadpan in the face of the unravelling. She had, after all, been expecting this to come for so long.

'At least, it wasn't Claire Avercamp's father who had the favour to call in, was it?'

Liddell took a deep breath. Buchan wondered if she would defend herself, go on the attack, try to turn this on Buchan. Justify her actions. Or whether she would retreat into silence, like so many trapped criminals.

'What's your history with William Lansdowne?' he asked.

She lowered her eyes, folded her arms. A look on her face like her gaze would be able to scorch its way through the top of the desk.

'You owed him a favour? Is that what this is?'

'We must pay our debts in this life, inspector,' said Liddell, coldly.

'That's a hell of a debt. What was it?'

Her chest was heaving. Deep breaths, trying to control her temper. Buchan, with far more right to be angry, was cold, calm and contemptuous. Ready for the boss to throw anything at him.

'It's none of your business,' she said. 'Now, you can take your leave.'

She made a dismissive gesture towards the door.

'Sgt Houston was killed,' said Buchan. 'Right in front of us. In front of you. He died saving you.'

'That was Baltazar, for God's sake!' she snapped, the

words whipping out. 'They may have ended up bedfellows – which is nothing whatsoever to do with me – but they weren't then. Not that night. Not at that point.'

'We have Malky Seymour in custody, and Malky Seymour is talking. With the help of Bridget, we managed to get access to Kasia Adamczyk's phone, downloading nearly a year's worth of messages and emails and photographs. We're getting the Polish translated, although there's plenty enough in English to keep us going. The picture is coming into focus.' He paused, recognising the change in her demeanour, as she realised for the first time that Buchan likely knew far more about what had been going on than she did.

'It was not Baltazar who ordered the hit on us,' said Buchan. 'It was your friend. William Lansdowne was responsible for Ian's death, and as soon as we get everything we need in place, he'll be getting arrested, for that and who knows what else besides. We've just arrested Michael Lansdowne for DI Savage's murder, and the murder of Graham Mathieson. Hopefully we'll also be able to get him for Cam Leslie. This nascent Lansdowne takeover of the streets of Glasgow is over. I don't know what you saw coming out of it for yourself, but when we know everything there is to know, and the Lansdowne family have started squealing for mercy, landing everyone and anyone in it to save themselves along the way, I don't think it's just your career that's going to be over.'

She leaned forward for the first time, the classic cornered prey coming out fighting. Elbow on the desk, finger pointing.

'Don't you dare, inspector. I've done nothing wrong. Nothing. Maybe I've had conversations with William I shouldn't have done, but I always put the force first. Your team, the other teams in this building. Now, I'll say it again, get out. Get out of my office, right this minute, I have heard enough.'

He didn't move. In the silence, the room still crackled with mutual contempt.

'I told you where we were hiding Tom Parkin,' said Buchan, his voice like cold, hard rock. 'You told Lansdowne, Lansdowne sent Malky Seymour. You compromised the biggest breakthrough we've had in this case in a year.'

'Don't blame me for that,' said Liddell, leaning into the fight. 'You told the team, so you need to find out whoever the hell –'

'I didn't.'

A beat, and then, 'What?'

'I didn't tell anyone else. I told you I had, but I lied. You and I were the only two people who knew Parkin's location. If Lansdowne knew, it had to be you who'd told him.'

She froze for a moment, and then sat back a little, retreating from the argument. Something different in her face now, impossible to read.

'You said you knew it was DI Randall,' she said, her mouth in an ugly curl.

'I also lied about that,' said Buchan. 'Far as I can tell, the inspector's usefulness to Lansdowne goes no further than her ineptitude. I *know* it was you who told Lansdowne where to find Tom Parkin. There's going to be a knock at that door in a minute. DCI Gilmour, here to escort you out of the building. Perhaps you'll be able to construct a defence where your actions can be made to seem reasonable and measured, but knowing what I know now – which is likely barely a tenth of it – I'm not sure how you're going to do that. You have impeded your own staff, you have aided our adversaries.'

'And what now, inspector?' she spat. 'You leave Baltazar in control? You clear out the Glasgow crime gangs, you bring disrepute to the SCU by losing me my job, and what does that leave? A singular power in Glasgow, that's all, free to do whatever the hell he pleases.'

Although there was no sound of footsteps from outside, Buchan got the sense of their imminent arrival. He was done. He'd said what he had to say, he had let the chief know what was coming. Her part in it was over.

He stared blankly at her with a familiar feeling of nothingness. The job was getting done, and this was just another part of it.

A knock at the door, then it opened, and DCI Gilmour entered, accompanied by a plain-clothed officer and two uniforms.

'Oh my God,' muttered Liddell. 'You have got to be kidding me.'

Buchan had had enough. He nodded at Gilmour, acknowledged her team, and then walked past and out of the office, heading back downstairs to get back on with what was only the beginning of the major operation to wrap up the Lansdowne gang.

58

He usually enjoyed the half-hour walk up High Street from his office to Glasgow Cathedral, in the lee of the Necropolis. The old buildings, the rise of the road, the murals, the cathedral beginning to raise its head in the distance.

Not today, the rain still incessant, the water running in the streets.

He took the Facel. He was thinking, as he started it up, that perhaps he and Roth could drive to Switzerland. He'd made the same trip the previous year, but this time, with Roth for company, everything about it would be different.

Originally he'd thought of booking the train, but he'd missed driving the old car, and he knew Roth liked it almost as much as he did. They could discuss it later.

He'd arranged with Kane for her to collect Roth from where she was being held in Dalmarnock. Meanwhile, unlike Malky Seymour, who remained in custody, with the best he could hope for in return for his cooperation being a lighter sentence, to be served in a more accommodating prison, Tom Parkin – known by most in the drama as Bridget – had been moved to a secure location. The deal that would be done with him, what he could do for the police in return for not facing any charges for his work for Margaret McLeod, would not be known to many. Ultimately, however, Police Scotland were going to have a job hanging on to him, once word reached MI5.

Roth's day had been a whirlwind. An early morning appearance at the High Court, hustled into the building under a blanket, beneath the urgent click of photographers, to make a plea of not guilty, before being returned to her cell shortly afterwards.

And now released, DCI Gilmour convinced by the sudden weight of evidence Buchan had been able to produce.

He'd known he could likely have headed Gilmour off at the pass, prior to the morning's court appearance, but hadn't wanted, at that stage, to reveal too much to Lansdowne, Kasia Adamczyk or, sadly, Chief Inspector Liddell. The court appearance had gone ahead, and the forces ranged against them had spent the first part of the morning believing they were still in control.

He parked on Castle Street, took a moment looking at the rain scudding off the windscreen in the dark of late afternoon, and then got out, closed the door, and walked quickly, without hurrying, towards the cathedral entrance.

In the door, he took a moment to shake the water from himself, and then he walked into the large open space of the nave. The sound of the squall was still loud in here. There weren't many people about. From the far end of the cathedral, in the quire, there was a choir singing, the beautiful sound carrying hauntingly throughout the building.

He listened for a moment, and then began walking through the nave. Someone nodded and he remembered to nod back. In one of the side chapels, there was a man sitting on his own, his head bowed. Not praying, thought Buchan, but despairing.

He walked on. Up the few steps to the quire, and he stopped for a moment in the entrance. The choir was small. He'd been expecting cassocks and regalia, instead, fifteen to twenty men and women in everyday clothes. A rehearsal, he presumed. There was a conductor, and eight people dotted around the pews listening.

He turned to his left, and then eased his way into the pew, sitting down beside the man in the grey overcoat.

Sitting there with his back straight, sombrely dressed, a hat placed on the pew next to him, Jan Baltazar looked like he'd stepped out of a le Carré novel.

For a moment the two men sat next to each other in silence, any two men at a concert, listening to the music.

When Baltazar finally spoke, his head moved almost imperceptibly, as he directed the comment towards Buchan.

'Looks like you won, inspector,' he said.

Buchan did not immediately reply.

Three Weeks Earlier

Southern Estonia, south of Võru, close to the border with Latvia and Russia. Buchan had been staying in a small hotel for three days, keeping an eye on an old villa on the outskirts of a small town, looking down along a narrow valley of larch and pine trees, ringed by low hills to the east and south. Snow in the cold air, but, this late in the season, not too thick on the ground.

Every day, after breakfast, Jan Baltazar would go out walking on his own. The first day, Buchan had presumed there had only been the appearance of solitude, but by the end of the second, he'd realised that Baltazar felt safe here. He'd travelled without protection. This wasn't home turf for him, but he obviously considered it so remote, he did not feel threatened.

Buchan had no idea if Baltazar knew he was there. Buchan himself was no threat, of course, so it hardly mattered. And the thing that had brought Buchan to Estonia – his search for incriminating evidence on Baltazar and his contacts – was not going to be found here. Baltazar was on his own, enjoying winter in a remote, eastern European forest. It made no difference to him whether Buchan was there or not.

Buchan noticed the change on the third day. Someone else was interested in Baltazar.

He spotted one of Baltazar's two house staff leave by the back door, a furtiveness about her that drew his attention. He followed, he saw her meet up with another women, passing something on to her.

Already jaded from a month and a half of not getting anywhere, and sure that Baltazar was doing little more than taking a break in the hills, he chose then instead to follow this new player in the drama. Aware that she might already have noticed Buchan's presence, he checked out of the hotel, and disappeared.

He wasn't sure what he was doing now, perhaps just playing at being something he wasn't, but he suddenly felt like he had a purpose, having immediately understood that this woman had come with malevolent intent.

Once he'd recognised that she was quite possibly an assassin, he'd wrestled with the idea of allowing Baltazar to die. Why not? He had no idea who would take over his empire in that event, and how chaotic it would turn out, but such was Baltazar's control, and seeming omnipotence in the pan-European crimescape, it was impossible to see how it wouldn't be to the benefit of law enforcement.

He'd cursed himself when he'd made the decision to intervene if he could, but he didn't want Baltazar to die in some distant land. He wanted him in court. He wanted him before a judge, answering for his crimes. Most of all, he wanted him tried and convicted for the murder of Detective Sergeant Ian Houston the previous summer. He'd promised himself, he'd promised the team, it would happen one day, and he wasn't going to let some random killer stand in the way.

*

It came on the second night. The assassin broke into the villa. Climbing a wall, gaining entry through a window on the ground floor. Lithe, fast, silent. There would be no gun. No loud explosion of sound in the night. Instead, a sheathed knife on a belt.

Into the sitting room, and then she crept silently through the house, her contact with the house staff allowing her to know exactly where to go. Up the stairs, a turn to the left. The poise, the relaxation, the taking time to come to one with the moment, listening to the house, and getting the sense that Baltazar was asleep on the other side of the door, and then she entered the room without a sound.

The shutters were open, a light breeze bothered the net curtain, the pale moonlight infiltrated the room.

Baltazar was asleep, alone, in the double bed. This was no set up, no heap of pillows beneath the sheets. Baltazar was topless, the sheet pushed off his chest. It was March and it was cold, but he was sleeping as though in the midst of a Mediterranean summer.

She stood above the bed, her approach so stealthy, so balletic, that Baltazar remained completely undisturbed. The assassin had set herself up for the clean kill. Knife silently drawn, she raised it just above Baltazar's neck.

The light went on. In an instant the rock unleashed from

Buchan's hand flew through the air.

The assassin moved with a speed that Buchan had never seen. A shift of the knife in the hand, a flick of the wrist, and the knife diverted the rock just wide of her head, as if she'd been aiming to do it by as narrow a margin as possible.

In the same instant, Baltazar was reaching beneath his pillow for a gun, and the killer had not come for that fight. Two steps and she was at the window, her escape already planned. Arms folded over her head, she leapt through the glass in the first cacophonous noise of the evening. Baltazar fired two quick rounds, then dashed to the window.

There was no sign of her, or of footsteps disappearing into the trees. She was gone.

A piece of glass fell, breaking on the path below.

Baltazar stood at the window for another couple of moments, wondering if he'd managed to at least wound his assailant, and then he stepped away, as if realising the vulnerability of his position.

He stared at Buchan, disconcerted by his presence, and then quickly walked to the doorway, and out into the hall.

He stopped, he turned.

'I have to make some calls.'

He moved off, then stopped again after another couple of paces.

'You saved my life. We will talk.'

Buchan watched him to the end of the hallway, and then Baltazar was down the stairs at a trot. Soon the distant sound of his voice on the telephone.

Buchan walked back downstairs, and left by the front door.

59

'DI Savage is dead. DS Houston died last summer. Chief Inspector Liddell will be gone, discredited, very possibly convicted. DC Roth had to go through more torture, as part of this preposterous game. God knows how many other casualties along the way. The bystanders and the people who wanted no part of the bloody game, who got drawn into it whether they liked it or not.' Buchan paused, his eyes straight ahead, the music of the choir swirling around them. 'It's no victory.'

'If there were no victims, there would be no police officers.'

A line about that not being a bad thing was in Buchan's head, but he wasn't here for gossip or chitchat. Somehow, for reasons unexplained, he trusted Baltazar. Trusted his word, at least. And he needed to know he was closing down his operation.

'How did you find her?' asked Baltazar.

'Bridget?'

'Of course.'

'Some fairly simple detective work,' said Buchan. 'I think you're well out of your association with William Lansdowne. They should have been able to find her easily enough. They're just not very good.'

Buchan felt the sideways glance. There was a lot left unsaid in that sentence, but that was how it would stay. Baltazar had had more than just Kasia Adamczyk on the ground in Glasgow, and they hadn't managed to work it out either. The inability of his team to carry out their jobs effectively was his problem.

'I need to know you're shutting down,' said Buchan.

'I already have. Most of my people have returned to Poland. We have broken all links with Mr Lansdowne, and closed off all funding streams. Our adventure in Scotland is over. Like I say, you win.'

'I don't believe you.'

'Really? Interesting.'

'You have a lot of money tied up here,' said Buchan. 'I

don't believe you're just going to walk away from it all.'

'Trick of the trade, inspector. When you are in my line of business, you have a broad portfolio. And, without giving too much of myself away, I would say that ninety percent of the portfolio is legal.' He paused. There was the hint of a smile on his lips that Buchan would love to have wiped off. 'Maybe eighty-five. The UK arm of my business will continue to operate our investments, the same as we run investments in sixty-two other countries around the world. The UK though… it is sad. A sad decline. I suspect that eventually those investments will be sold, and we will withdraw completely. Nevertheless, I leave that to others. My work here is done. My association with the petty criminals and gamblers of the streets of Glasgow is over.' He reached into his coat pocket, and produced a USB stick. 'I leave you with this.'

Buchan did not immediately take it out of his hand.

'What is it?'

'I am sure you will find it interesting.'

'What is it?'

Another smile from Baltazar, who seemed to be enjoying the engagement.

'A list of transactions between my organisation and officers in Police Scotland, and with members of the Scottish parliament. Eleven of the former, nine of the latter.'

'How can I trust it?'

'It is all there. I thought you might appreciate the help. If you need further proof… well, as they say, follow the money. You have it here, nevertheless, from the horse's mouth.'

Buchan took the memory stick out of his hand, and slipped it into his own pocket, then he thought to ask, 'Is there a Detective Chief Inspector Gilmour on there?'

Baltazar turned and looked at him a little curiously.

'Interesting,' he said. 'No, I do not know that name. I would, I must confess, struggle to name everyone included in this list. It has not, of course, been me who has been running the operation. But there is no Gilmour.'

Buchan nodded. He did not return the look, and Baltazar finally looked away.

'You saved my life, inspector,' said Baltazar, after another few moments. 'And now the debt is paid.'

'No, it's damn well not,' said Buchan, lowering his voice halfway through the sentence, as the choir's song came to an abrupt end. 'There is no debt. I stopped someone killing you, because that's what I do. The only reason I'm not arresting you now is because we haven't put a case together yet.'

Baltazar smiled again.

Was that true? Could they make a case if they wanted to? They had the contents of Kasia Adamczyk's phone, of course, although it had been illegally gained.

Nevertheless, with what they'd learned from that, and the interview with Malky Seymour, Buchan was convinced Baltazar had been little more than an outsider in most of these crimes of the past year. A myth had grown in the telling, and finally Lansdowne had tired of it. It had suited him for someone else to be the focus for the police. However, Lansdowne had come to be jealous, and had wanted credit for everything his family had been doing.

Regardless of the current situation, there was a pragmatism in Buchan not pursuing Baltazar any further. Let him go, let him take his organisation and his money back home. Give Buchan and the team, and the entire force in Glasgow, the opportunity to clean up the mess left behind by Lansdowne's collapse. A new order would take shape in Glasgow, and they would deal with that when it arose. At some point, perhaps, they could focus once more on Baltazar, and pass whatever they could find on to Europol.

He doubted, nevertheless, that anyone would touch it. Baltazar was one of those people. Too many connections. Too many people in his debt.

This meeting, Buchan and Baltazar, had never been going to be of much substance. Two men taking one last look at each other before going their separate ways. Buchan had wanted to look into Baltazar's eyes and believe him, that was all. Now he had done, and he did.

The choir began singing again, a low chorus of hallelujah, another tune unfamiliar to Buchan.

'I don't want to see you back in the city again,' said Buchan, starting to make his move.

'So soon?' said Baltazar. 'You do not find the choir's singing beautiful?' He checked his watch. 'We have another thirty minutes to go, then I need to head to the airport. You are more than welcome to stay.'

Another cold look passed between the two men, and then Buchan got to his feet and turned away.

60

'Thanks for stopping back in, inspector.'

Buchan had been intending to go back to the apartment after meeting Baltazar. He'd had enough of the day. He needed some of the feeling of lightness that he got just from being around Roth.

The whole business had made him feel grubby. Chief Inspector Liddell's part in it. Sitting next to someone like Jan Baltazar, and not feeling able to make an arrest. Just having to be in Baltazar's presence, as he played the part of the cultured business executive.

'That's OK,' he said.

'Got wild out there all of a sudden,' said DCI Gilmour, glancing over her shoulder at the weather.

'Yeah. It's one of those storms with a name,' said Buchan. 'I didn't catch it. Everything's got a name these days.'

'Back in our day things just happened,' said Gilmour, ruefully, and Buchan half-smiled along.

'How long have you worked with Chief Inspector Liddell?' asked Gilmour, abruptly deciding there'd been enough idle chatter. A look on her face to suggest she was aware of her own abruptness.

'Seven years,' said Buchan. 'There was another period of a couple of years a while ago. I've known her most of my career.'

Gilmour nodded along, as though she'd already known the answer. She looked tired. She rubbed her forehead, let out a sigh, seemed to be unsure how to put any of this to Buchan. She removed her glasses, rubbed the bridge of her nose, glasses went back on.

'You think this man, this Polish gangster, or whatever he is, Jan Baltazar, you think he has people on his payroll in Police Scotland?'

Buchan nodded.

'D'you think the chief inspector is one of them?'

'No,' he said. He really didn't. 'My sources,' he said, then he hesitated, the disingenuousness of it sticking in his throat, but he was here now, and he had to say it in any case. 'I have a source who says Baltazar is done here. I'm not sure how it played out in Glasgow for him, but he's not interested anymore. He wanted to get hold of Bridget, Tom Parkin, he didn't get him, and now he's pulling the plug. I can't say for sure, but I think if he has some of our officers on the payroll, they're going to find the money discontinued.'

'Who's your source?'

Buchan looked her in the eye and shook his head. She nodded.

'You don't have names of any officers?'

Buchan hesitated, but he'd made the decision back in the cathedral, sitting next to Baltazar. This particular fight was above his pay grade.

He reached into his pocket, took out the small memory stick and placed it on Gilmour's desk.

'Receipts,' he said.

'Go on.'

'Payments from the Baltazar group, or their associates, into the accounts of various officers, and politicians in Scotland.'

Gilmour's face showed genuine surprise, her lips parting a little, her eyes widening.

'You're serious? Where did you get this?'

'I haven't looked at it. You might want to have a tech guy put it through a standalone in the first instance in case it's corrupted.'

'This is a hell of a source you've got.'

Buchan didn't reply.

Gilmour lifted the stick, toyed with it for a moment, and then slipped it into her pocket.

'How d'you know it's not going to incriminate you?' she said. 'Or Constable Roth? Perhaps your entire team?'

'Why give it to me, then? The person I got it from… they would assume I'd use it for personal gain, because that's what they'd do. But I don't want anything from it. It should be used to root out the corrupt.'

She held his look, thinking it over.

'You don't know me,' she said. 'Yet you're giving this to me.'

'I trust you,' said Buchan.

'I arrested your girlfriend two days ago.'

'You acted properly on the information in front of you.'

Gilmour nodded.

'Thank you, inspector,' she said. 'If it contains what your source claims it to, it will be used appropriately.'

'You've spoken to Chief Liddell?' asked Buchan.

'We had a short interview. She's been placed on leave without pay, pending a full investigation. She appears to have let the situation spiral out of control, but she believed the principal bad actor in all of this was Jan Baltazar. I'm not sure why she was blinded by William Lansdowne. Would you have any idea?'

'They know each other from university,' said Buchan. 'I understand, I think, that he saved her in some way back then. She's always felt she owed him. I don't know the story. I'm not sure, however, why she didn't think the debt repaid some time ago.'

'I believe she genuinely thought this a battle between small-time Glasgow gangsters and this European behemoth. That in helping the little guy, she was helping Police Scotland. Getting Lansdowne to do the dirty work for us.'

Buchan realised he'd had enough of the conversation. He didn't want to be here anymore. At some stage he needed to talk to Liddell about it. Maybe he'd learn something, though he doubted it. He doubted she would ever be forthcoming.

'I may be getting played, but I don't think so,' he said. 'Baltazar's involvement started last summer in a dispute with Davie Bancroft. It was Baltazar's people that wiped them out. You can tell, because of its efficiency and cold-bloodedness. Meanwhile, he'd already enlisted Lansdowne's help. After that, Baltazar was little more than an investor in the project, with the occasional player leant out on loan. Where we saw Baltazar, more than likely it was Lansdowne. That definitely includes the murder of DI Savage, and goes all the way back to the murder of Detective Sergeant Houston last summer. And, I might add, the attempted murder of me the same day.'

'I didn't realise,' she said, concerned.

'The chief likely didn't know, and there was no way Lansdowne was ever telling her. Nevertheless…'

He let the sentence go, tired of talking about it.

Gilmour recognised his irritation, and nodded her acceptance.

'You play with fire…,' she said. 'Right, inspector, I shall let you go. My team and I will be here for another few days, I think. Maybe longer. I'm sure we'll chat again.'

Buchan pushed his chair back, got to his feet.
Nothing else to say, he turned away and walked to the door.

61

Roth was at the apartment when he arrived home, his coat still wet from the few minutes he'd been outside.

The rain still thundering down, the lights of the buildings across the river bright in the grim light of early afternoon.

Roth and Edelman were in place, on chairs by the window. Roth, her legs tucked beneath her, the MacBook open on her lap.

'It's OK,' said Buchan, as she started to get up, and he walked over to the window. He'd let her know he was coming, and there were two glasses of wine on the table. Edelman, comfortable with the new domestic arrangement, did not stir.

Buchan hesitated, then leaned down and kissed Roth. Her lips tasted of wine.

He lifted the other glass, made a small cheers gesture, then looked out at the river. There was a woman in a single scull, rowing against the wind and the tide and the flow of the river, her back lashed with rain. Roth got to her feet, and stood beside Buchan, and together they looked down at her.

'She's got balls,' said Roth, after a while.

'You all right?' asked Buchan, finding himself, having immediately got lost in the mire of the day.

'Sure. Sarge picked me up. I had to fight off my mum. Said I'd see her –'

'Sorry I couldn't be there.'

She squeezed his arm.

'Don't be daft,' she said.

'Really,' said Buchan, 'are you OK? It's been a shitty couple of days.'

'Don't worry. As you know, I've had far shittier than this. I knew I hadn't done anything wrong, so did you, and I knew you'd sort it out.'

Buchan nodded, and as so often happened, could think of nothing to say to show the appreciation he felt for her belief in him.

'Sarge told me about the chief,' she said. 'Holy shit, that is… it's just horrible.'

'Yes,' said Buchan. 'I don't know yet how deep it goes. But she's already been removed from duty. The sections have been told to run themselves the rest of this week, Dalmarnock will try and have someone in place by next Monday.'

'Is she the only one? I mean, often enough it's felt like it goes much higher, much further than just her office.'

'She won't be,' said Buchan, 'but too early to say how that plays out. DCI Gilmour can handle that side of it. I like her, what she did to you notwithstanding.'

'She did what she had to, given the information available to her,' said Roth, and Buchan nodded.

'She'll do a good job,' he said. 'As for those officers on Baltazar's payroll, they're about to find the carpet pulled out from beneath their feet.'

'How d'you mean?'

'He's gone.'

'He was in Glasgow?'

'Until a short time ago.'

'Seriously? Why didn't you get him?'

'Because he still has his diplomatic passport, and we still don't have concrete grounds on which to make an arrest.'

'Surely we have something by now? Sarge said you managed to get the contents of Kasia Adamczyk's phone.'

'He's gone,' said Buchan, 'taking his team and his illegal backhanders with him. Closing down his operations. They won't be back.'

'How d'you know? That kind of man doesn't just walk away.'

Buchan gave her a glance, and then looked back out onto the river. He wanted to tell Roth everything. Maybe some day he would. But just because it looked like they were getting on top of the situation, finally ahead of the game after nine or ten months, it didn't mean there weren't twists and turns left to come. If they were to be dragged back into the swamp, it would be better for Roth not to know anything about Buchan's dealings with Baltazar.

'One day,' said Buchan.

Roth gave him a slightly worried glance.

'You're going to have to do better than that when Gilmour, or whoever, says they want to throw the book at Baltazar. You'll not just be able to say, it's fine, he's not going to be any more trouble.'

'Yes,' said Buchan.

He took a drink, he let out a long sigh.

'You didn't secretly kill him, did you?'

He smiled, he thought of the mild irony in that.

'Quite the reverse. Anyway, d'you want to take your last four days off. Given what's –'

'Oh, no,' she said. 'Like I said, sarge was filling me in. There's plenty of work to do, and it'll be a while before we get to be fully staffed again.'

'I'm not letting you stay on after Friday, so don't be getting ideas.'

'Don't worry,' she said, laughing.

They drank wine, they looked out on the day, its sepulchral darkness deepening while they watched.

He realised she was smiling, and he turned to look at her.

'What?'

'You still going to be able to come to the Alps, or are you going to blow me off now?'

'Hotel's not booked until two weeks today. Think we should be good. We can leave on the Saturday. Stop overnight on the south coast, get to somewhere south of Paris on the Sunday, Andermatt on the Monday.'

'I looked at that place. Holy shit, are you sure? That's like a year's salary for two nights.'

She was laughing again.

'I had to book a basement room,' he said. 'No view, outside toilet, breakfast not included.'

They looked at each other. For a while the smiles endured, then slowly died away.

For the first time, Buchan noticed the silence. Usually there'd be Oscar Peterson, or Duke, or Hoagy. This evening, nothing bar the low hum of the building, and the sound of the rain sweeping down the river from their left.

Roth slipped her hand into Buchan's, their fingers entwining.

DI Buchan will return

in

I WANTED TO MURDER

FOR MY OWN SATISFACTION

Printed in Great Britain
by Amazon